'What are you doing?' I gasped when at last I managed to disengage my lips.

'Loving you, sweetest girl,' he said, his voice heavy with desire. Then I could say no more, for he was kissing me again. His hands were everywhere; all my resistance melted. My arms went around him and I started to respond to his kisses with an ardour equal to his own. In no time at all my bra and panties were lying on the floor and I was naked but for a suspender-belt, nylons and my high-heeled shoes: a combination which always seems to me to add a delightful touch of indecency to a woman's nakedness . . .

SENSUAL LIAISONS
Anonymous

Translated from the French
by
Alan Shipway

NEXUS

A NEXUS BOOK
published by
the Paperback Division of
W. H. Allen & Co. plc

A Nexus Book
Published in 1990
by the Paperback Division of
W H Allen & Co plc
338 Ladbroke Grove, London W10 5AH

Copyright © Alan Shipway 1990

Typeset by Medcalf Type Ltd, Bicester
Printed and bound in Great Britain by
Cox & Wyman Ltd, Reading

ISBN 0 352 32605 0

Contents

Translator's Introduction

'. . . je me plaisais à le considérer comme un sultan au milieu de son serail, dont j'étais tour à tours les favorites différentes. En effet, ses hommages réitérés, quoique toujours recus par la même femme, le furent toujours par une maîtresse nouvelle.'

. . . it pleased me to think of him as a sultan in his seraglio, of whom I was successively his various favourites. Indeed, although it was always the same woman who received his reiterated tributes, it seemed to him each time to be a different mistress.

Les Liaisons dangereuses, Laclos

It seems to me that the Marquise de Merteuil's words in the above quotation express a masculine ideal which is just as applicable to an anthology of erotic stories as it is to a woman! Such a book should be a kind of literary harem assembled by the compiler for the delectation of the reader considered as a sultan. Although it is just one book, as the marquise was just one woman, it should have the protean ability to appear in many different forms in order to satisfy the desires of the reader/sultan. Considered in this way, each of the stories must be a seductive beauty, each one offering an enticingly different approach to eroticism from the one which preceded it.

The title-story of the present collection, obviously inspired by *Les Liaisons dangereuses*, has voyeurism as its principal theme, and mirrors play an important part in it. The piece is written in the form of a miniature epistolary novel and, while it is perfectly explicit, has something of the elegance of Laclos' famous book.

Estelle deals in a very voluptuous way with the subject of fellatio and and also contains an extremely tongue-in-cheek warning to those husbands who want to persuade their wives to gratify them in this manner.

Troilism is the theme of *One Marvellous Night*, and it contains a vividly erotic description of two men making love to the same woman at the same time! There is something about this story which makes one feel that it may well be based on a real-life incident.

In *The Dangers Of Reading Erotica* you can read about Charlie, an ordinary young man who is transformed into a kind of sexual superhero for a few memorable hours one Sunday when he reads an erotic novel for the first time.

Degradation, the shortest but by no means the least entertaining story in the book, graphically depicts the perverse relationship between a pretty young prostitute and the client who likes to degrade women, but who is degrading whom?

However, to enumerate the stories in this way is as misleading as it would be to try to categorise the women in a harem simply by stating each one's particular sexual skill. There is so much more to them than just that! When I was making my selection I tried to choose stories which were not only erotic but which also displayed at least some literary merit and some degree of originality.

As regards these two latter qualities, I should particularly like to draw the reader's attention to *Pages From A Young Man's Secret Diary*, which ingeniously combines the erotic tale with science-fiction while, at the same time, vividly evoking the atmosphere of the Cold War in the nineteen-fifties; of course, like all the other pieces in this volume, it was actually written and published during the fifties.

Another thing which all of these tales have in common is the fact that they have all been selected from my personal collection of erotic books, the fruit of more than a quarter of a century of browsing in secondhand bookshops in various corners of England, Belgium and France. The books were published anonymously and clandestinely at a time when censorship, both in France and England, was much stricter than it is now and, if I had the time and the space, I could tell some interesting tales about my acquisition of some of them. However, all I can say now is that translating this selection has been a labour of love, and if the stories in it give as a much pleasure to my readers as they have to me, then the task will have been well worthwhile!

Alan Shipway, Berkshire, 1990

Degradation

Hélène Belavoine

Eyes closed, face flushed, mouth hanging slackly open, the naked man leaned the back of his head against the settee and moaned with pleasure. 'Yes! Oh, yes!' he gasped. 'That's right. . . rub it. . . oh, you little darling!'

These words were addressed to the young woman sitting on the settee beside him, skilfully manipulating his erect member with her slender, well-shaped fingers. She was naked too, except for the frilly black suspender belt, sheer stockings and red high-heeled shoes she always wore when engaged in 'professional' activities. The young woman's name was Catherine, but everyone called her Cat. The man had told her to call him Edouard, but she continued to think of him simply as 'the man', or even 'a man'.

She gazed down at her energetically moving hand, feeling neither disgust nor even distaste. Edouard's left hand cupped and caressed one of Cat's breasts, his right arm, short and hairy, encircled the young woman's smooth shoulders. His moans intensified and his face flushed an even deeper shade of red as she speeded up her rubbing in the hope of bringing this business to an end, for her hand was beginning to ache.

He suddenly pushed his partner's hand away. 'No,' he said, 'not that way!'

'I told you, I'm not willing to . . .'

'I know, I know,' he said, looking up at her with a blue-eyed smile. She thought he looked quite boyish with those eyes and that charming smile, in spite of his flabby middle-

11

aged body, in spite of the thinning grey hair. 'I want you to suck me.'

'I can't do that,' Cat replied.

Edouard stopped smiling and sat up. 'Say, what kind of a whore are you?' he demanded indignantly.

Cat jumped to her feet. 'You haven't got the right to talk to me like that!' she said, eyes flashing with anger.

Edouard gazed at her with admiration: she looked really desirable standing there naked in high heels, suspenders and very sheer nylons. His member was still erect: he couldn't remember the last time he had been so stiff for such a long time!

'I'm sorry,' he said in a soft, conciliatory tone. 'I didn't mean to be rude, but you must admit that it's a bit unreasonable to expect me to fork out sixty francs, just for a . . .!' and he used a crude term signifying masturbation. 'I mean to say,' he went on, 'you won't get very far in your, er, profession if you won't do anything but hand jobs, will you?' He used the familiar '*tu*' form of 'you'.

Cat's anger had subsided; she looked thoughtful. She sat back down beside Edouard, cuddling up to him, stroking his erection. He put his arm round her again. 'You're right,' she said, 'but, you see, I've never done *that* before . . . it would be the first time,' the young woman added in a small voice.

Edouard felt himself becoming even more excited by this revelation. He pushed a troublesome doubt about its veracity to the back of his mind, for what man can resist the ego-boosting idea of triumphing over virginity, in whatever orifice it may be?

He took the bait: 'I'll give you another ten francs if you'll do it,' he said.

'Make it twenty and I will,' replied Cat in a business-like tone.

'Alright,' said Edouard, 'but only on condition that you won't mind me calling you names while you're doing it . . . it excites me,' he added rather needlessly.

'Very well,' the young woman sighed. Then she bent down

and without any more ado took the rigid member into her mouth. Edouard sighed with contentment and leaned back against the settee again, closing his eyes, savouring the exquisite sensations which that warm, wet, sucking mouth was giving him.

Cat sucked with an expertise which belied her claim about this being the first time, but Edouard didn't care: what man would with a pretty young creature like Cat fellating him? He opened his eyes and gazed at the girl's head with its short fair curls bobbing up and down. He stroked the warm flesh of her back with his stubby fingers, moving down to explore her generous bottom.

'Ooh! That's lovely!' Edouard gasped, eyes glazing. 'What a dear little prostitute you are!' And he said several even more indelicate things while Cat's head continued to bob up and down. She didn't really mind him calling her 'whore' or 'prostitute'. In fact she had a slightly masochistic streak which made her enjoy being called such names during sex: she had only objected earlier for the sake of appearances, and perhaps to enhance her value, in the most literal sense.

But although he was making a lot of noise, Edouard seemed to be taking a long time to reach climax; Cat's jaws were aching, so she withdrew her mouth and said rather breathlessly, 'I must have a rest!'

The man's stiff member, wet and glistening with saliva rested against his hairy belly. Edouard looked at Cat, at her soft, slack mouth thinking how vulnerable she looked: women always look particularly vulnerable at such moments, he told himself complacently.

Cat broke in on his thoughts: 'Shall I finish you off with my hand?' she asked softly. Edouard nodded his head, so the young woman encircled his member with the thumb and first two fingers of her right hand, then she rapidly jerked the foreskin back and forth over the swollen, mauvish head. It didn't take long: within seconds the man was writhing and grunting as he spurted forth his seed. 'Oh! Oh! . . . Ooh!' he gasped as the liquid splashed on to his flabby belly.

13

Then it was all over: Edouard slumped into an exhausted heap. Cat disengaged herself and went over to the chair where her things were.

She had put her panties back on and was reaching back to fasten her brassiere when suddenly 'the man', as she thought of him, said, 'There's one other thing I'd like you to do for me before you go, Cat.' The young woman looked across the room to the settee where he still sprawled, naked and inelegant. The fact that he had retained his socks and shoes added a touch of the comical to the unlovely. She sighed audibly, then consulted her watch. 'It won't take you a minute,' he said.

Cat walked across to him, hips swinging, looking enticingly sensual in her black lacy lingerie. 'What is it?' she demanded.

Edouard pointed at the blobs of whitish fluid on his belly. He said, 'I'll give you another twenty francs to lick this stuff off and swallow it.' He looked up at the girl, a pleading expression on his face.

Cat wasn't particularly shocked by this request: nothing to do with sex or bodies had ever disgusted her, but she instinctively realised that Edouard, 'the man', wanted some resistance. So she said, 'Well, I don't know if I could do *that*!' But after a little more cajoling and wheedling on her client's part, plus the incentive of another twenty francs, the young woman obediently knelt down by the settee, bent forward and used her small, pink, agile tongue to lick all the stuff off Edouard's hairy belly. He sighed with satisfaction; his member, which had lost its rigidity after the orgasm, twitched appreciatively. He was one of those men who can only really enjoy sex if they think they are degrading their partner.

'There's a good girl!' he said when she had lapped it all up and swallowed every drop.

A few moments later, when Cat had put her dress back on, it was time to settle up. Edouard, who now looked much more civilised in a white shirt and a pair of blue trousers,

14

counted notes to the value of a hundred francs into the girl's elegantly manicured hand. This was a moment Cat always enjoyed, when a client paid her. She couldn't have said why, but at such times the tips of her breasts hardened while a sensual wet warmth grew between her thighs.

Edouard said, 'You're very trusting. Most, er, professional ladies insist on having the money first.'

'Well, I only go with men who seem to me to be gentlemen,' Cat replied with a charming smile.

Edouard smiled too, with self-satisfaction. 'You're a most unusual girl,' he said. 'Surely with your looks and your obvious intelligence you could find something better to do?'

'You mean like a good job?' said Cat.

'Well, yes,' he replied.

Cat picked her handbag up off the dressing-table and stuffed the money inside. 'I've had several so-called 'good' jobs,' she said sadly. 'I found them stressful, exhausting and, above all, boring. My colleagues, both male and female, were petty, vindictive little people with no sense of humour. I was always too tired to do anything worthwhile when I got home at night . . . !

'Such as?' Edouard enquired.

'Well, I love reading . . . and listening to serious music . . . But I found my pleasure in both seriously diminished after a day in an office or in a classroom trying to instill the elements of French grammar into twenty or thirty little donkeys. I felt diminished.'

'And you don't feel diminished by what you do now?'

Cat smiled at Edouard's question. 'On the contrary. I only have a few clients, regulars. I make enough money to live comfortably - I'm not greedy. It doesn't take up too much of my time, so I have a lot more time as well as energy to do the things which interest me.'

'Well, you certainly give excellent value for money,' Edouard said. 'I'd like to see you again. I shall be here again two weeks from today. My surname is Jouy; you can ask for me at reception.'

'Right,' said the young woman. 'It's a date, Monsieur

15

Edouard Jouy. I'll see you here in the hotel two weeks from today at the same time.' She consulted her watch. 'Goodness, I must fly!' She gave the fat little man a kiss on his cheek, started for the door but suddenly caught sight of herself in a mirror hanging on the wall. 'Good grief!' she exclaimed, 'I look a mess!' Cat took a comb from her handbag, moved in close to the mirror and pulled the comb quickly through fluffy honey-blonde curls as she peered at the reflected image of herself.

'*I* don't think you look a mess,' said Edouard, who had moved up close behind the girl. He stretched out a hand and caressed the full round cheeks of her bottom through the thin material of the dress.

She took no notice of that groping hand but concentrated on swiftly applying some lipstick; then she turned round, smiled sweetly at him and said, 'See you in two weeks then.'

'I'll look forward to it,' he replied sincerely.

The young woman walked quickly to the door, opened it and disappeared into the corridor softly closing the door behind her, leaving Edouard standing by the mirror.

After Cat's departure he thought how small and dingy the hotel room seemed without her presence. There was no doubt about it, she was a really nice girl with a lively personality.

'All the same,' he told himself, 'she's on a downward path.' His member twitched appreciatively at the idea and he sat down on the edge of the bed to savour it. 'A few more years on the game and she'll have lost all her freshness and sparkle,' the fat little fellow reflected. He unfastened his fly, liberating his now fully resurrected organ, gently stroking it with short stubby fingers, an unpleasantly lustful expression on his face. Delightful images of those pert white breasts with the prominent nipples being fondled by dozens of greedy male hands filled Edouard's mind. His prurient imagination conjured up pictures of the young woman's mouth being profaned by an endless procession of male members of every shape and size. By this time he was

16

energetically rubbing himself, swept along on a rising tide of lechery. 'She'll end up in total degradation!' he gasped aloud as his clenched hand moved rapidly up and down the rigid shaft. Although she wouldn't permit sexual intercourse at present, sooner or later she would start opening those plump white thighs to her clients' needs: titillating visions of different men having sex with Cat, their bare behinds pumping up and down between her widely spread thighs, filled Edouard's mind . . . Then the ringing of the telephone on the bedside table brought him back to reality. He picked up the receiver.

'Is that you, Ed?' He cringed inwardly, recognising the voice of his boss, Pierre Connard. He hated to be called Ed, and he hated him!

'Yes, it's me here, Pierre,' he replied, his respectful tone concealing his true feelings.

'Everything fixed up for tomorrow?'

'Yes. Ten-thirty tomorrow morning . . .'

'Good . . .' There was a brief silence, then Pierre's heavy voice with its hateful, affected American twang said, 'Ed, don't screw up on this one whatever you do, will you?'

'Everything's going to be alright, Pierre. Trust me!'

There was an unpleasant laugh from the other end of the line: 'I trusted you with the Coulé business! Remember, Ed?'

Edouard squirmed uncomfortably, his face flushed with embarrassment. 'Anyone can make a mistake . . . ' he stammered.

'But I don't pay you to make mistakes! . . . ' There was another brief, pregnant silence, then: 'Ed, if you screw up on this one, so help me I'll bust you down to filing-clerk, even if you are my son-in-law! Bear it in mind tomorrow . . . ' There was a click as the man at the other end hung up.

When Edouard put the receiver down his hands were trembling. 'The bastard!' he said. 'God, how I hate him!' Whenever he had an interview with his father-in-law he always emerged from it feeling somehow diminished, but today he was so angry, so humiliated that he felt like throwing himself over a cliff!

17

The poor wretch sat on the bed by the phone, brooding over his misfortunes. Pierre had never liked him, never accepted, never forgiven him for marrying his darling little girl, Marthe! And Edouard had no doubt that if things went wrong tomorrow Pierre would not hesitate to demote him — the bastard would take a sadistic pleasure in doing it! He slumped back on the bed and lay staring at the grey plaster of the ceiling, eventually drifting off into an uneasy sleep . . .

At about the same time, in her comfortable little apartment on the other side of town, Cat put aside Georges Simenon's latest novel which she had been reading, switched off the bedside lamp and snuggled down under the sheets. She adored Simenon's psychological crime stories but, for some reason, could never really get into his Maigrets.

As she lay there savouring the warm comfort of the bed, she thought how much more rewarding life was, in every sense, as a lady of pleasure than as a wage slave. With Edouard she now had six 'regulars', and with a few 'casuals' from time to time Cat could easily make enough money not only to pay her way but also to be able to buy a few luxuries too: luxuries such as good books, records, nice clothes, meals in excellent restaurants and days out in Paris (only an hour's drive from the little town where she lived).

She stretched luxuriously, 'like a cat,' she thought and chuckled . . . Life had never been better!

The Dangers of Reading Erotica

'Une gorge blanche . . . une jambe bien faite, montrée jusqu'au genou . . . une croupe charnue, voluptueuse, lubriquement agitée . . .

'*A white bosom . . . a well-turned leg, displayed as far as the knee . . . a well-rounded voluptuous behind swaying lubriciously.*' Nicolas-Edme Restif de la Bretonne (1734-1806) was the author of '*Monsieur Nicolas*, or *The Human Heart Unveiled*.' The most recent English translation was by Robert Baldick, published in 1966 by Barrie & Rockliff.

In *Monsieur Nicolas*, Restif de la Bretonne's voluminous autobiographical novel, there is an extremely amusing passage in which the author, presumably very much tongue-in-cheek, recounts how one morning he ravished several attractive young women who had come to visit him, this outrageous behaviour being the direct result of reading an erotic novel which a friend had lent him. Nearly two centuries later, in 1959, I had a very similar experience which I should like to tell you about now.

As in Restif's case, a book was the cause of the trouble, but it wasn't lent to me by a friend: I found it discarded in an otherwise empty cupboard in the house my wife and I had just moved into on the outskirts of Rheims. Presumably it had been left there by the previous occupier.

The book was a rather tatty paperback, a translation of an American crime-story, which contained many nearly-explicit descriptions of fucking. Now, incredible though it might seem, although I was twenty-eight years of age that was the first time I had ever read a book containing such passages. Yes, it's true! Consequently you can easily imagine how it set me going.

I found the book one Sunday morning when, of course, I didn't have to go to work. The title was *Les Nanas sont faites pour ça! (That's What Broads Are For!)* by a writer called Jim Tomlinson. I took it to our bedroom, which I used as a study during the day, sat down in an armchair by the window and started to read . . . It was incredibly badly written, but the sheer crudity of the sex scenes started a kind of forest fire in my senses! My dick stiffened and I gently caressed it through my trousers as I was reading to intensify my pleasure.

After I had been reading for about twenty minutes or so, Marianne came upstairs to get dressed. I heard her splashing about in the bathroom as she performed her morning ablutions. Then she came into the bedroom. Quite unconcerned by my presence, my wife took her dressing-gown off, then her nightdress: the former she hung up behind the door, the latter she folded neatly and put under the pillow on her side of the bed. After that she put a pink suspender belt on, pulled on some sheer nylons and eased her feet into a pair of black leather shoes with quite high heels.

As Marianne moved about performing these tasks her tits quivered and bounced. I should explain that she was in the early stages of pregnancy, expecting our first baby, and although her belly was still quite flat, her breasts were swollen, their smooth whiteness etched with faint blue veins: she'd always had big provocative nipples.

My wife was about to step into a pair of pale pink knickers when I threw my book down, jumped to my feet and said, 'Hold it right there, baby!'

She looked at me with an expression of astonishment in her wide blue eyes. 'Why are you speaking with that ridiculous American accent?' she demanded.

'Never mind that, my little honey-twat,' I drawled. 'Just

look what big daddy has got for you!' And I unzipped my fly, letting my upstanding tool spring out. Then I went round to where my wife was standing, on the other side of the bed, and took her in my arms. I kissed her full soft lips, fondled and fingered the pretty creature a bit but was too worked up to spend much time on preliminaries. So I pushed Marianne up against the wall, drew up a chair, made her put her left, high-heeled foot upon it and said in a leering tone, 'Open your twat for me, baby,' which she did, using her long, sensitive, scarlet-tipped fingers. Then, breathing hard with anticipation, I guided my knob into that pink, wet, open love-hole . . .

A really earth-shaking fuck ensued! Delightfully obscene it was, with me, a fully-clothed guy shafting a near-naked broad (to express myself in the language of the novel I was reading). Marianne's stockings and high-heeled shoes added greatly to the piquancy of the situation. If some voyeur had been able to see us, it would have looked to him like a scene in a brothel.

Unfortunately, however, my pleasure was very short-lived, for I was much too worked up to make it last. In a matter of seconds I attained the moment of ecstasy and felt the spunk rushing out through my jerking organ . . . then it was all over. I pulled away from Marianne and flopped down on the bed to recuperate for a few moments while she went back to the bathroom to splash some soapy water up her snatch. Shortly afterwards when she'd dressed and gone downstairs, I went back to the armchair by the window, and my book.

In less than half an hour that wretched book had got me to a fever pitch of desire again. There were things in it I'd never even thought of, such as fucking one's partner over the kitchen − table, for example. That idea really appealed to me! In fact it appealed to me so much that I threw the book aside and rushed off downstairs, determined to try it out immediately.

Marianne was in the middle of preparing lunch and protested when she realised what I wanted to do, but I

21

brushed aside the poor girl's objections, persuaded her to turn the gases down under the saucepans, then in next to no time I got her tight little knickers off, pulled her skirt up to the waist and eased my wife down so that she was lying flat on her back across the kitchen-table.

'The lunch will be spoilt!' she said in a plaintive voice.

But at that moment I couldn't have cared less about lunch. I was much more interested in Marianne's blatantly exposed charms: the long nylon-clad legs, so well-turned and pleasing to the eye, the suspendered thighs, so white in contrast with the dark stocking-tops and, of course, above all, the hairy treasure which nestled between those thighs.

'Oh, baby, what a lovely cunt you've got!' I croaked, my voice made hoarse by emotion.

Then I fell upon her, eagerly opening the moist pink slit with my fingers and easing my engorged knob inside . . . It took me longer to come this time because less than an hour had elapsed since my last orgasm but, nevertheless, it was a most enjoyable fuck.

As I worked my bottom back and forth, I undid the buttons of the pretty white peasant-style blouse my wife was wearing and got her big swollen titties out so that I could fondle them, squeeze them and tweak their raspberry tips. I should have liked to rip it open as Eddie, the hero of the novel, would have done, but didn't fancy the row which would inevitably have ensued.

'T-Toinette w-will b-be h-here s-soon,' Marianne gasped, her whole body shaken by my energetic thrusts.

'I'm nearly there, honey,' I panted and, indeed, a few seconds later I groaned with an almost uncomfortable pleasure as I disgorged the contents of my wildly swinging bollocks into Marianne's soft, wet, clinging love-flesh . . .

Then, just as I was finishing, the front doorbell rang. Toinette had arrived, just as my wife had predicted. There was a flurry of activity in the kitchen: Marianne got up off the table and made herself decent as quickly as possible, while I tucked my rapidly dwindling penis away and zipped myself up. Then as my wife was stepping back into her knickers I went, glazed of eye and unsteady of step, to open the front door.

Toinette is my wife's younger sister. At that time she was a pretty eighteen-year-old, fair of hair and face, whose affectation of girlish naivety was belied, both by the knowing expression in her eyes and by her reputation. There was gossip about her in the locality; malicious tongues attributed a wealth of sexual experience to her. In those days, when she was young and still single, she used to come to our house and have lunch with us most Sundays. She's married now, of course, with three kids and we don't see her very often.

'Hello, Charlie,' she said, giving me a hug and a sisterly kiss on the cheek as she came in. 'You look tired.'

I felt my face flushing with embarrassment. 'Marianne's in the kitchen,' I said awkwardly, ignoring her remark. 'Go on through.' Then as she disappeared into the kitchen, I went back upstairs to have a wash and shave and generally try to make myself look presentable before lunch.

Sunday lunches were always pleasant, leisurely affairs which were considerably enlivened by the presence of Toinette. She was the only member of my wife's family in whose company I felt really at ease: I never felt that she disapproved of me like the rest of them did and, in fact, she always seemed sympathetic and well-disposed towards me. Besides, she was an extremely attractive young woman, with her long fair hair, her experienced eyes and her air of perverse naivety.

That particular Sunday, as Marianne was dishing up the pudding, I told them about *Les Nanas sont faites pour ça!* expressing my astonishment that a book could be so badly-written yet so sexually exciting. My wife looked disgusted and said she didn't know how I could read such rubbish, but her sister seemed quite interested and asked me some questions about it.

After lunch my wife went upstairs to have a nap — a habit she'd got into since the start of her pregnancy — leaving me to keep Toinette company. We sat in the lounge and

23

chatted about this and that for a while, then suddenly the young woman said, 'Show me that book you were talking about, Charlie.' Her blue eyes sparkled.

'Sure thing, Toinette,' I replied and went off upstairs to get it. Marianne was already asleep, breathing regularly, the bedclothes pulled up to her chin. I picked the book up off the arm of the chair where I'd left it, then ran lightly back down the stairs.

When I'd left Toinette she'd been sitting on the settee; when I came back she was reclining upon it on her right side, facing the armchair where I had been sitting. She'd kicked her sandals off, tucked her long slender legs up and put a cushion under her pretty head: she had both arms around the cushion, cuddling it as a child cuddles its teddy-bear. She presented a charming sight!

'Nothing like being comfortable,' I remarked.

She smiled up at me languidly. 'It's the wine: it's made me feel quite sleepy.'

'I've got the book,' I said, holding it out to her. She didn't take it but looked interestedly at the luridly sexy picture on the cover, then the pretty creature looked up at me again, gave me another of her charming smiles and said, 'Why don't you read some of it to me, Charlie?'

'All right,' I said, somewhat surprised by her request, and went over and sat down in the armchair facing Toinette. As I turned the pages, trying to make up my mind which would be the best bits to read to her, the equivocal nature of the situation was beginning to make me feel sexually excited, or, to put it more crudely, I was beginning to get a hard-on!

'Read me a really sexy bit!' my companion said, and the tone of voice in which she said that brought me to full erection.

'Right,' I said, in my American-style French, 'get a load of this, baby!'

Then I read her a passage where Eddie, the private-eye hero, went into his girlfriend's bedroom and gave her a good juicy fucking while she was still half asleep. The author did not use obscene words, nor did he describe in very graphic detail what was going on, the censorship laws wouldn't have permitted that, but nevertheless he succeeded extremely well in *suggesting* an atmosphere of crude fornication; of panting, sweating lust.

But although it all seemed pretty exciting to me, apparently it did not have that effect on Toinette, for when I paused and looked in her direction after I'd been reading for a while, it was to see that my dear little sister-in-law had fallen fast asleep! I felt somewhat taken aback because she'd appeared to be so interested at first, but I quickly came to the conclusion that the wine we'd had with our lunch, plus the fact that the weather was quite warm were the reasons for Toinette's lapse into unconsciousness rather than lack of interest in the book.

I sat and gazed at the sleeping girl for a few moments. She really was a charming sight! Her lips were slightly parted; her bosom rose and fell gently. The short skirt of the white cotton dress she was wearing had ridden up, revealing two round knees and an expanse of smooth bare thigh.

I put my book down, got up from the armchair then went across to the settee where I stood gazing down at Toinette, not so much with desire at first, although that was by no means absent, as with the feeling one has when one watches the soaring flight of a swallow or a cat stretching: a sense of the miraculous, for a lovely girl is just that, a miracle!

The material of her dress was very thin and unequivocally revealed the soft enticing curves of Toinette's body: the deep valley between her breasts was displayed provocatively in the v-neck of the bodice. As I continued to gaze down at the lovely sight, I felt my penis beginning to show signs of interest again after a short period of repose.

I knelt down beside the settee then, obeying a sudden impulse, bent forward and gently, oh so gently, so as not to wake the sleeping beauty, I gave her a fleeting kiss upon the lips. Oh, how soft and warm they were, those lips! Miraculously soft and warm!

Toinette sighed and murmured something unintelligible

and for a moment it seemed she was going to wake up, but she didn't: instead she suddenly turned over on to her back, at the same time stretching her right foot out so that the heel was resting on the floor, but raising her left leg, bending it at the knee, drawing her foot up to her buttock. This new position caused the skirt to fall right back, completely exposing the young woman's thighs and the lower part of her belly, and then I could see that my naughty little sister-in-law wasn't wearing any knickers! Still on my knees, I moved down a bit in order to get a better view: yes, her cunt was blatantly exposed to my gaze, and how I gazed at that dear hairy little treasure! Oh, how delightfully indecent, how invitingly wanton Toinette appeared in that abandoned pose!

I looked at her face. Her eyes were still closed, she was breathing regularly, but something about the way one of her eyelids flickered reinforced an already-growing suspicion in my mind that the little hussy was only pretending to be asleep. Well, if she wanted to play games that was all right with me!

I placed my hands on the warm bare flesh of her hips then ever so gently, so as not to 'awaken' her, shifted the lower part of her body towards me and got myself between her thighs. While this was going on Toinette mumbled something incoherent but didn't 'wake up'. I gazed down at the young woman's vagina, which was now but a few centimetres away from my face. Its delicate lips were pouting slightly, the clitoris seemed very prominent. A pungent womanly odour came to my nostrils. I put my hand down between us and gently inserted a finger into the slit. It was very wet! I had no doubt at all now that Toinette was only feigning sleep, but who cared? I didn't mind fucking a sleeping beauty!

I continued to frig and finger-fuck her for a few moments while she moaned softly and wriggled her arse responsively then, unable to restrain myself any longer, I unzipped my trousers, got my penis out and inserted the swollen shiny glans into the girl's more-than-ready sex-hole. I slid all the way in with the ease of the proverbial knife going through butter . . . Oh, it was so lovely up there! What could be more exquisite than the feel of a woman's love-sheath round one's cock when she's aroused and ripe for a vigorous shagging? It's so warm, so clinging, yet so gentle! I looked at Toinette's face again: her eyes were still closed but a telltale flush had come to her cheeks. She knew she had a nice stiff prick up her, no doubt about that!

Then, placing my hands on the soft warm flesh at the tops of the girl's thighs, I began to fuck her, gently at first, savouring the sweetness of that gaping cunt, but my movements rapidly speeded up as my desire intensified. Toinette started to move her buttocks in response to my poking; she sighed and gasped while I panted and jabbed away inside her, but all the time she kept her eyes closed. Then suddenly the moment of crisis arrived: I gave a cry and jetted my stuff deep into my sister-in-law's receptive depths. My third come in less than four hours!

No sooner was it finished than remorse came too, demanding payment for my all-too-brief moments of pleasure. I felt terrible! Not only had I been unfaithful to my wife, but to make matters worse I'd done it with her sister! But that was not all: I had also behaved with criminal irresponsibility by taking the risk of making the girl pregnant!

I quickly disengaged myself from Toinette and got to my feet. I stood there looking down at her as I put my now diminished organ back into my trousers and zipped myself up. What a charming picture she made lying there on the settee, apparently still asleep, skirt up around her waist, bare thighs spread indecently apart, her hairy slit clearly visible: its lips gaping slightly apart and some of the gooey white stuff I'd so recently spurted into it beginning to ooze out and form a little puddle on the cushion underneath.

How I regret now that at the time it didn't occur to me to take a photograph of her like that! It would have made a wonderful erotic study, as well as being a memento of a really enjoyable fuck. I would have entitled it 'Just Poked!'

But that Sunday afternoon as I stood there in our lounge

looking at Toinette, guilt had dampened my ardour to such an extent that taking an erotic photograph wouldn't have seemed like a good idea, even if it had occurred to me.

Then all of a sudden I felt an urgent desire to get out of that room; out of the house in fact: so I left my sister-in-law to come back to the land of the living in her own good time and cleared off out for a walk, feeling like a criminal fleeing from the scene of his crime.

A few years later, while browsing in a second-hand bookshop in Rheims, I came across an astonishing little book of erotic memoirs by an author called Jean-Jacques Bouchard, who lived in the first half of the seventeenth century. His first mistress was Angélique, a chambermaid in his parents' house.

He says: 'The girl was unapproachable when she was awake, but provided that she thought that you believed her to be sleeping, she would let you do what you liked, thus Orestes penetrated her every night, as far as the posture of a sleeping girl permitted, and sometimes he would do it in the daytime as well; for when her mistress went out, she would feign sleep in the most propitious of attitudes. She would adopt a kneeling posture, her head resting on the pillow and her derrière raised high, so that Orestes could easily do it to her from behind, in her fig.'

When I read this passage I immediately thought of Toinette and that Sunday afternoon when I'd fucked her on the settee. It would be interesting to know how many women have used such a ploy, and precisely what the point of it is.

I went for quite a long walk: I was away for more than an hour and when I returned Toinette was nowhere to be seen. Marianne had got up; I found her sitting in a deck-chair in the garden reading the Sunday paper. She told me that her sister had gone home earlier than usual because she was going out later and wanted to wash her hair. From the amiable way in which my wife spoke to me it was plain to see that she had not the slightest inkling of what had taken place during her nap . . . I felt relieved. Perhaps everything would be alright after all . . . as long as I hadn't made Toinette pregnant — but we'd cross that bridge if and when we came to it!

Feeling decidedly lighter-hearted now (such is the inconsequentiality of human nature) I went back to the house to get my book. I found it on the coffee-table in the lounge where I'd put it at the beginning of my session with Toinette. I looked at the now vacant settee. What had taken place on it such a short time previously now seemed remote, dreamlike, an impossible fantasy. The only trace of our lovemaking was a barely visible stain on one of the cushions.

I picked the book up and carried it out into the garden where I spent the rest of the afternoon comfortably ensconced in a deck-chair reading . . . By tea-time I was beginning to feel horny *again*! I should have liked nothing so much as to grab Marianne by the hand and take her upstairs to the bedroom to try out some of the lewd ideas which the novel had put into my head; but fear for my health restrained me. How many times a day can a man, even a young man such as I was then, come without harming himself, I wondered.

We had our tea in the lounge. We sat on the settee (the famous settee!) with the tea things on the low coffee-table in front of us and while we ate, watched a crime film on the television.

The heroine was a pretty brunette who wore very low-cut blouses and short skirts which showed off her long shapely legs advantageously. In one scene she appeared in a nearly-transparent white slip and fastened her dark stocking-tops to her suspenders, which I always think is one of the most erotic things a woman can do. One can easily imagine the effect that watching that scene had upon my already exacerbated senses! In fact the young woman reminded me very much of the heroine of *Les Nanas sont faites pour ça*! and she gave me a terrific hard-on as we sat there having our tea!

As soon as we'd finished, I got up, pushed the coffee-table to one side, then took my trousers and pants off.

'What on earth are you doing, Charlie?' my wife demanded, her eyes going to my prick which stuck out truculently from between my shirt-tails.

'I want you to suck me off, darling,' I replied in that peculiarly insinuating tone in which men sometimes express themselves when they are in the grip of intense sexual desire.

'But that's not nice!' Marianne protested. 'Besides, you've already done it twice today.'

'Three times', I rectified mentally, but I said aloud, 'Come on, baby, take your dress off, there's a good girl!'

Marianne got to her feet and none-too-willingly took off the flowered summer dress she was wearing, then she stood there looking at me reproachfully, clad in nothing but a flimsy apricot-coloured brassiere and matching panties. Her ripe white tits filled the bra cups to the point of bursting. My prick was a solid steel bar of lust!

I took my wife in my arms and kissed her on her soft unlipsticked mouth. I felt her relax against me then begin to respond . . . Within a couple of minutes I'd coaxed the little darling out of the bra and panties, then I was sitting on the settee — what a lot of action it was seeing that day! — with Marianne kneeling on it beside me, completely naked. My right hand caressed the warm white flesh of her bottom.

'Suck it for me then, honey,' I said.

With a plaintive sigh she took hold of my stalk with her sensitive fingers, lowered her head, then I felt my knob enveloped in a sweet warm wetness which was more exquisitely delightful than anything I had previously experienced.

'Ooh,' I gasped, 'it's better than a cunt!'

It was by no means the first time that my wife had sucked my cock, but for some reason it felt nicer that evening than ever before.

The television was still on. The film had ended and a TV personality was making an appeal on behalf of some charity, but Marianne and I were both too preoccupied to pay any attention to it.

As my wife's head bobbed up and down I fondled her big swelling tits with one hand, while with the other one I fingered her damp love-hole. Then I moved my hand up a bit and played with the tiny puckered aperture between her buttocks. She wriggled uncomfortably but went on sucking; however, when I tried to ease my finger into her anus she stopped, raised her head and protested:

'No, Charlie, don't do that!'

So I had to be content with just fingering that dear little arsehole while Marianne resumed her indelicate task. She sucked and sucked and sucked and sucked, but all to no avail: she just couldn't bring me off . . .

At length, she withdrew her mouth, sat up and said, 'It's no use! I can't do any more, my jaws are aching!' Her mouth looked pathetically soft and vulnerable; there was a dazed expression in her wide blue eyes.

I looked down at my cock, which was still as stiff as ever and glistening with Marianne's saliva. I wouldn't feel comfortable until I'd had an orgasm, there was no doubt about that, but what could I do?

Suddenly an idea occurred to me. I got my wife to kneel down on the carpet between my thighs then, with loving words, persuaded the little darling to kiss and lick my balls while I picked up my book and read one of the most arousing passages in it . . . it worked like a charm — with a little help from my right hand! In less than a minute I was gasping as my cock convulsed, jetting gobs of semen on to my hairy belly. What a relief! Marianne must have been relieved too, poor thing! I kissed her and cuddled her with the greatest tenderness, and thanked her sincerely for being so patient with me.

We spent the rest of the evening on the settee with our arms round each other watching television, frequently exchanging tender words and kisses. Marianne loved that, for she has always been a sentimental rather than a sensual woman.

The next morning Nemesis caught up with me and exacted a cruel retribution for my excesses of the previous day. When I got out of bed my back ached unbearably; my neck was so stiff that it was impossible for me to turn my head at all. It was an effort for me to stand up, let alone walk, so I went straight back to bed while Marianne, looking very concerned, phoned the doctor's surgery. I felt sure I was going to die!

Doctor Coudrier, a tall, thin, balding man with rather humourless features, arrived shortly after ten: we must have been his first call after morning surgery. When I had told him what my symptoms were, he subjected me to a thorough examination. He made me sit up in bed, felt my neck, my back, then made me lie down again on my back and raise first the right then the left leg straight up in the air, something which I was able to do without too much difficulty. The doctor asked me if I played sports or went in for athletics, to which I replied truthfully in the negative . . . he seemed frankly puzzled. I got the distinct impression that he didn't really quite know what was wrong with me; but, of course, I had a pretty good idea what was the matter, although I could never have brought myself to confess the truth to such a stern authority figure as Doctor Coudrier! Anyway he wrote out a prescription and a medical certificate which he gave to Marianne and told her to make sure that I stayed in bed for at least a couple of days. He told me to go and see him at his surgery on Friday morning, which relieved me for it seemed to show that he thought I was going to get better. Then the doctor bade me a rather curt *au revoir*, and was about to leave the room when he changed his mind, came back over to the bed and made me roll over on to my stomach. He pushed my pyjama jacket up then examined my back again, pressing his fingers firmly but gently into the spine. But apparently he still couldn't find a satisfactory solution to the mystery, for he left still looking puzzled.

I was away from work for three weeks altogether: it took all that time for my neck and back to return to normal!

However, it took another three *months* for me to finally overcome my anxiety and remorse about what had happened with Marianne's sister that Sunday afternoon. She didn't come to lunch with us any more, but on the few occasions when we met she always behaved in a friendly relaxed manner towards me and no mention was ever made by either of us to what had taken place. Then in November Toinette announced her engagement to a young lawyer called Gérard, and my guilt-feelings began to disappear.

Marianne never did find out about my infidelity, and I was more relieved than words can tell about that, for the last thing in the world I wanted to do was to hurt her or run the risk of losing her! She was very precious to me; come to that, she still is! All's well that ends well, as a great English poet said.

At the end of his little story about the dangers of reading erotic fiction Restif de la Bretonne tells of the antipathy towards such books which he felt thereafter – strange words for a man who spent most of his life writing novels ranging from the mildly allusive to the frankly pornographic, but which nearly all dealt with sexual relationships in one way or another!

Anyway, my first encounter with an erotic novel affected me quite differently: far from inspiring me with aversion, it aroused my interest in such books, and in the years which have elapsed since my adventure with Toinette I have built up quite a collection of them, both classics and more modern works.

Reading them has not turned me into some kind of sex-monster with uncontrollable urges. In fact, if anything, they have proved to be beneficial because they have made me into a more inventive lover and frequently intensified my pleasure in my relations with Marianne. To be honest, it seems to me that the only real danger in reading erotic novels lies in the possibility that they might make one discontented with real life, but isn't that true of any kind of fiction?

At all events, ever since that memorable Sunday, so many

years ago, I have always been careful never to let the excitement engendered by reading such books lead me into doing anything which might impair my health or jeopardise my marriage.

Translator's Postscript

I thought that readers might be interested to know the title of the book which Restif de la Bretonne alleged depraved and corrupted him: it was *Le Portier des Chartreux* (*The Doorkeeper of the Chartreux Monks*) better know perhaps by its more obscene title of *Dom Bougre*.

This novel, which was first published in 1741, had a tremendous clandestine success and was republished many times. It was widely read by people in all classes of society. Madame de Pompadour, the most influential of Louis XV's mistresses, possessed a beautifully bound copy of the book.

It deserved its success, and deserves to be better-known amongst today's reading public, for there is no doubt that it is a masterpiece of the genre, comparable to works such as John Cleland's *Memoirs of a Woman of Pleasure*, or Andréa de Nerciat's *Félicia*. I would urge anyone who is interested in the development of the erotic novel, or just interested in reading a well-written, well-constructed erotic tale, to acquire a copy of *Dom Bougre*.

To my knowledge there are two English translations: one published in the fifties by the Olympia Press in Paris under the title, *The Adventures of Father Silas*, and the other published in 1988 by Nexus Books with the title *The Lascivious Monk*. The Olympia Press edition would be difficult to find now and would undoubtedly cost quite a lot of money, being a collector's item, but the Nexus Books translation is still readily available, and at an extremely moderate price.

If you do decide to buy it I can only hope you will have as much fun corrupting and depraving yourself with it as Restif did two hundred and fifty years ago.

Rear View

Revenge is sweet, the proverb tells us: what it doesn't say is that it is only sweet in the short term; in the course of time the sweetness has a strong tendency to become bitter.

Of course, the desire for revenge is only natural when a husband finds out that his wife has been opening her box of tricks for another man's delight, but my advice to such a husband would be, have a good long think before you do anything. Do you really want to end up in a magistrate's court, or lose your fair lady?

The following little story will show what I mean. It is not only amusing and instructive, but it also has the merit of being quite true. All I have done is to change the names of the people involved and a few other details, for obvious reasons.

After three years and five months of marriage, Jerry Potts had become convinced that his wife was being unfaithful to him. Jerry was an Englishman living in the beautiful old town of Poitiers with his French wife, Agnès. He worked in the local *lycée*, where he taught English; she had a part-time job as a secretary in the civil service.

Let me say straight away that by no stretch of the imagination could Jerry be considered a credit to his nation. He combined an extremely small stature with a very over-inflated opinion of himself, although he was not a bad-looking young man, it is true, with his fair hair and moustache and the well-cut suits he always wore, but his incessant bragging got on everyone's nerves: according to him, no-one had ever conducted themselves more heroically during their military service, no-one understood the political situation better than he did and, of course, no knight of love ever wielded his lance of flesh more effectively in the battle of the sexes. Casanova was a mere amateur by comparison; Don Juan a fumbling schoolboy.

In fact, the truth that lay behind all this bragging was dismal in the extreme: Jerry had spent the whole two years of his military service (or national service, as the English call it) sitting behind a desk in an office while many less fortunate young men of the same age were dying in Korea; his assessment of any given political situation was invariably banal, trite to the point of childishness, while as to his performance in the bedroom, in all truthfulness it must be admitted that he rarely rose to the occasion.

Jerry's wife was a slender girl with rather elfin features, a Louise Brooks hair style, and an extremely ardent temperament: Agnès loved the feel of a man inside her, but that was a sensation she'd not been experiencing much with Jerry lately. He seemed to have become insensible to the young woman's charms, so perhaps she may be forgiven for looking elsewhere in order to find the satisfaction she craved.

In fact, she found it in the person of Jacques Bertrand, a young man who worked in her office. Jacques was not a great improvement on Jerry, in physical appearance at any rate, being a prematurely bald little runt of a man who peered short-sightedly through horn-rimmed spectacles and who expressed himself practically exclusively in trendy clichés . . . However, Nature had endowed this little fellow with a tool fit for digging deeply in the garden of love, a weapon any woman would be delighted to polish, a veritable broadsword of delight, a gun which never seemed to run out of ammunition! So it is easy to understand why Agnès was so attracted to him. In fact, she fell in lust with him quite some time before she became acquainted with his magic wand; some deep feminine instinct must have told her how well-endowed he was . . . Women instinctively know these things!

Anyway, Agnès made up her mind to have him and during the next week or two instituted a campaign of intensive seduction which even a eunuch would have found hard to

resist! She started wearing very low-cut blouses,or dresses
with short skirts which showed off her long legs to perfection
and also sprayed herself with a musky perfume guaranteed
to raise lewd thoughts in the male mind. At every moment
of the day she would find pretexts to bend down in front
of Jacques, giving him a lust-raising view of the deep valley
between her breasts; or she would sit near him, one nylon-
clad thigh crossed over the other, skirt hitched so high that
he could glimpse the young woman's suspenders and soft
white thighs.

What red-blooded male could long resist such
provocation? By the end of the first week of the campaign
poor Jacques literally ached with longing: that is to say, he
was afflicted with acutely aching acorns! Every man knows
how uncomfortable that can be. Even so, the young civil
servant might never have found the courage to make
advances to Agnès if that young lady had not herself taken
the initiative . . .

It came about this way: one evening, when everyone else
had either gone home or was about to leave the office, Agnès
found a pretext — something about some files she needed
for the next day — to get Jacques down to the basement,
where there was nothing much except a lot of filing cabinets,
dust and cobwebs and where hardly anyone ever went.

There in the dim light cast by a solitary bulb, they
consummated their illicit passion for the first time: that is
to say, for the first time they became acquainted with each
other's private parts. Agnès pulled down her panties and
let Jacques explore her dear little hairy treasure with eager
fingers, then Jacques undid his trousers and placed his staff
of life in the young woman's hand. Oh, how that excited her!

Their love-play was of very short duration, for these
young people were too eager to satisfy their lust to spend
much time on preliminaries. Agnès bent over and supported
herself by gripping her ankles with her hands; Jacques
flipped her skirt back, revealing the twin milky moons of
her buttocks and then, after the briefest of pauses, during
which he appreciatively fondled those warm hillocks, he

37

guided the rubicund head of his serpent into an eager, wet open mouth which avidly gobbled it up. Agnès gave a loud hissing gasp of sheer delight. Never had her fruit-pie been so well-filled! Never, never had she been so stretched!

Jacques was well-pleased too: he loved the feel of that warm, liquid-velvet sheath and for the next sixty-five seconds showed his appreciation by pounding away at it with his piston-rod. At the end of that time the too-long-contained tide of his desire burst forth and he paid a copious tribute of liquid lust to his mistress's charms.

Of course, there was no stopping them after that! Agnès, as we know, had for some time been but ill-served by her husband, and now that she'd found a man capable of giving her what she so longed for, she simply couldn't get enough of him. As for Jacques – well, he was married, it is true, but his wife was of a rather chilly disposition and quite incapable of really satisfying a man as generously endowed as her husband.

So our two lovers did it anywhere and everywhere, whenever an opportunity presented itself: sometimes Agnès bounced up and down, panting and dishevelled, astride Jacques in his car; sometimes he gave her the piston-rod treatment against a filing-cabinet at work, after everyone else had gone home; it happened in motel rooms, seedy hotel rooms, in fields with the blue sky above, and they did it in every conceivable position . . . They were insatiable!

Of course, with the indiscreet way these two young people were carrying on, it wasn't long before her husband began to suspect that he might be growing horns! Perhaps he took a little longer than another man might have done to tumble to the fact because of his egotistical self-absorption, but soon even he began to notice things calculated to arouse the suspicions of the most stupid of husbands: frequent and unsatisfactorily explained lateness in arriving home, strange marks on her neck and arms (love-bites?) and, above all, that expression of self-satisfied contentment on his wife's face: the look of a cat who's had the cream! Then, one of his colleagues at the *lycée*, delighted to have the chance of deflating the little Englishman's ego, made some very equivocal remarks which could be taken as implying that Agnès had a lover and *that* made him decide to try and find out whether his suspicions were justified.

Jerry's mind was naturally disposed towards deviousness, so it didn't take him long to come up with a plan: he told Agnès that he had to go back to England for a few days to visit an old aunt who was seriously ill. He told the same story to his principal at the *lycée* and got a week's leave of absence.

Then one morning, after kissing his wife goodbye with a display of tenderness he was far from feeling in reality, the little Englishman left home and went to a small hotel across the other side of the town where he booked in under an assumed name.

Of course, Jerry's absence was far from being a hardship for Agnès. The prospect of being free to spend several nights in her lover's arms filled the young woman with joy! So great was her contempt for Jerry's intellect that it never even occurred to her that he had become suspicious.

On the evening of the very first day when the little man was supposedly in England, she committed the imprudence of taking Jacques home and into the conjugal bedroom in the first floor apartment where she lived. As the young woman lay there on the bed completely naked, eyes closed in ecstasy, while Jacques puffed and panted between her widely-spread thighs, she had no idea that Jerry had seen her come into the house, accompanied by her lover! The little Englishman was standing in a doorway on the other side of the street, wearing dark glasses and an unfamiliar tweed hat.

In spite of his previous suspicions, the sight of Agnès entering their house on the arm of a strange man came as an unpleasant revelation to Jerry. He just couldn't believe that his wife could be unfaithful to such a wonderful husband as himself . . . and with such a little runt into the bargain! He was nearly bursting with indignation . . . what an ungrateful bitch!

Without being fully aware of what he was doing, Jerry wandered off down the street away from the building in which the adulterous couple were frolicking — to put it politely! He wandered around for a while submerged in alternate waves of self-pity and righteous indignation. Eventually he found himself back in the place from which he'd started. The young Englishman looked up at the windows of his apartment. The bedroom curtains were drawn . . . the bitch!

Suddenly, Jerry knew just what he was going to do: he was going to go in there and catch them red-handed! He'd go up there, get that little bastard and throw him out on his ear! That's what he'd do!

Fired by this commendably manly zeal, he crossed the road and entered the building. As he went up the stairs to the second floor the expression *in flagrante delicto* kept running insistently through his mind.

By that time Agnès and Jacques had finished their first bout of lovemaking and were lying on the bed, both stark naked, playing one of those post-coital games which are the delight of lovers everywhere. Fortunately for their peace of mind, they were quite unaware that Jerry had entered the apartment and was watching them from the adjoining room through a gap in the door.

'Who do these belong to?' Jacques was saying, fondling his companion's lovely breasts.

'Why, to you of course, you naughty boy,' she replied with a coy giggle.

'And these?' he demanded, tweaking the raspberry tips.

'Ouch!' she gasped . . . 'To you, to you?'

'And who does this little thingumyjig belong to?' he enquired in a lewdly suggestive tone, placing his hand on her dear little pussy and stroking it with gentle fingers.

'Oh, to you, my love,' Agnès purred ecstatically, opening her thighs wide.

Then Jacques rolled the young woman over on to her stomach and, placing his hand proprietorially upon the snowy hillocks of her behind, asked, 'Who does *this* belong to, dearest heart?'

But Agnès did not reply as he supposed she would: instead she answered, 'All the rest is yours, my love, but *that* belongs to my husband . . .' Whereupon she let forth a loud and extremely unladylike fart, adding with a malicious laugh, 'That's all he's worth!'

Jerry, who had heard all of this from behind the door, was near to bursting with outraged, scandalized indignation . . . How could she? . . . How dare she? But the little Englishman had already shelved his plan to burst in on the lovers: he was really much too big a coward for that. Instead he continued to stand there, peering through the gap in the bedroom door, waiting to see what the adulterous pair would do next, rooted to the spot by an unpleasantly prurient curiosity.

Jerry watched pop-eyed as his wife rolled her lover over on to his back on the bed, then leaned over him, took hold of the pet snake slumbering between his hairy thighs, and slipped its head into her mouth. The young woman sucked it with the eager enthusiasm of a schoolgirl sucking a lollipop while Jacques lay back, eyes closed, savouring the feel of that loving mouth at work.

Soon Agnès had restored the beast to its former rampant glory but could no longer contain it in her mouth, so the naughty girl rubbed it vigorously with her hand until the great thing was sick all over her face. Then Jacques rolled Agnès over and, sticking his head between the young woman's milky thighs, did his best to bring contentment to her bearded lady with his tongue. He succeeded too, judging by the cries of sheer joy which came to Jerry's ears.

That unfortunate young man's feelings were in a state of indescribable disarray: anger, desire, envy, humiliation all battled for supremacy in his mind as he watched the indecent antics of the couple on the bed. Then as his wife attained the moment of supreme fulfilment, locking her smooth white thighs around her lover's head, wailing a song of sated lust, he judged it prudent to withdraw.

Late one night about a week later, Jerry stayed up for some time after Agnès had gone to bed because he had quite a lot of marking to catch up on . . . When he closed the last exercise book he looked at his watch and saw that it was getting on towards midnight. The little man stretched, yawned, then got up and went into the kitchen where he drank a glass of water. Then he turned out the lights in the kitchen and living-room and entered the bedroom.

It was quite a warm night; the window was open and Agnès lay face down, the bedclothes thrown back, eyes closed in sleep. The young woman's flimsy blue nightdress was rucked up round her waist, revealing the white half-moons of her bottom. As she lay there, bathed in the tranquil glow of the bedside lamp, she looked enchanting. And Jerry was enchanted, for as he looked at his wife's behind, an idea came to him: a way to avenge himself for the insult she had inflicted upon him.

Treading softly so as not to wake the sleeping beauty, he went across to a large wardrobe on the other side of the room, opened the door as quietly as possible, groped about on the top shelf inside and found what he was looking for: a camera. With equal stealth the little Englishman went back to the bed then, raising the camera, took a photograph of that charming naked posterior.

The sudden glare of the flash disturbed Agnès. She stirred, gave a plaintive sigh, then rolled over on to her back; however, she did not wake up, but just lay there, dark head resting on the pillow, arms flung wide, thighs slightly parted. Her nightdress was still rucked up and as Jerry stared down at his wife's smooth belly and the dark tangle of pubic hair between those parted thighs, he felt his manhood stiffen. He'd forgotten just how desirable she was; it had taken another man's desire for her to remind him.

Jerry went to the wardrobe, put the camera away, then quickly removed all his clothes. When he was naked, he got on to the bed between his wife's thighs and quickly pushed his unimpressive little drumstick into her. Agnès sighed, put her arms around him and, still half asleep, murmured

'Jacques, darling!' in a languorous voice. But even this untimely remark didn't make Jerry angry: for the moment he was enjoying the feel of his wife's wet love-grotto too much to care — besides, he'd already worked out an extremely satisfactory plan of revenge.

It is one of life's strange little ironies that braggarts often boast about qualities they do not possess, but hide their real light under a bushel! Jerry spent so much time boasting about his sexual prowess, but never, ever talked about his very real talent as a photographer! He really was very good and the picture he had taken of Agnès was a miniature masterpiece of erotic art.

The photo showed the young woman's bare bottom in close-up. Its soft swelling whiteness formed a pleasing contrast with the blue nightdress and the darker blue of the satin sheet. The deep furrow between those buttocks seemed to invite an exploring finger, or perhaps something rather more substantial! The vertical slit of the sex, with its fleece of pubic hair was clearly visible between the parted thighs. No man with red blood in his veins could have looked at that bottom for long without wanting to make love to it. Jerry had every reason to be pleased with his work. The moment of revenge was fast approaching.

In fact it came one Tuesday evening, a few days after Jerry had developed the photograph. On that particular evening two of his male colleagues at the *lycée* had come round for coffee and a chat, as they frequently did on Tuesdays, not because either of them liked the Englishman, any more than any of the other teachers at the *lycée* did, but both men wanted to practise their English, which they spoke rather well and, besides, Agnès made excellent coffee; truth to tell, perhaps they were both a little in love with Jerry's pretty wife!

Anyway, the four of them — Jerry, Agnès, and their two visitors — had been sitting there in the comfortable living-room of the young couple's apartment chatting for about an hour when the little man decided to drop his bombshell.

The conversation had come round to what constituted the difference between erotic art and pornography.

'Pornography is always so coarse!' the younger of the two men was saying.

'I hate coarseness!' said Agnès emphatically.

'I think that would be most women's reaction,' the older teacher remarked.

'Oh, I don't know . . .' said Jerry, with a sly smile. 'I'd like to show you something,' he went on, reaching into the inside pocket of his tweed sports jacket and drawing forth the photograph of his wife's bare bottom. He looked at it appreciatively for a few seconds, then passed it over to the two men who were sitting on the settee. They gazed at the picture, fascinated by what they saw.

Agnès got up from her armchair and went across and stood behind the settee, peering over the visitor's shoulders at the photograph. Then she bent forward to get a closer look. An expression of mingled incredulity and anger came to her face; her cheeks flushed bright crimson.

'It's beautiful!' exclaimed the younger man with considerable fervour.

'Maybe,' Jerry replied nonchalantly. 'Nevertheless, the owner of that lovely bum is an extremely coarse woman. Do you know,' he continued, his eyes fixed on Agnès, who was staring at him in deathly silent pallor, 'she's so coarse that she thinks nothing of letting off when she's with a man and, what's more, the slut told her *fancy man*' (he literally spat those two words out) 'that her arse is the only part of her body she allows her husband to make use of . . .'

As he said that Agnès gave a cry – whether of rage or of wounded pride it is difficult to say – then ran from the room, slamming the door behind her.

Jerry suddenly felt embarrassed. He grinned stupidly at his two guests and made some clumsy remark about the unpredictable nature of women.

The older man rose to his feet and gave the little Englishman a look of withering contempt. 'What on earth did a nice girl like Agnès do to deserve a husband like you?'

he said coldly. Then he turned to his companion and said, 'Shall we go?'

'Yes,' the latter replied, jumping to his feet. 'Let's go. There's a bad smell in here!'

'Now wait a minute,' Jerry expostulated. 'You don't know the whole story —'

'We know enough to know you're a rat!' the older man growled and made for the door, closely followed by his friend. Jerry watched them go, his cheeks hot with rage and humiliation; then he went into the bedroom. Another unpleasant shock awaited him there: Agnès was packed and ready to leave. She wore the cherry coat with the dark fur collar which suited her so well. Her face was drawn and very pale but she wasn't crying.

'What are you doing?' the young man demanded, somewhat pointlessly.

'I'm leaving you, Jerry,' Agnès replied tonelessly.

'B-but where will you go?' he said, his voice growing squeaky with emotion.

'That's my business,' she said.

Then the door bell rang.

'That'll be my taxi,' the young woman said, picking up her case and heading for the door.

Jerry ran after his wife, begging and pleading with her to reconsider. He followed her, still pleading, downstairs and into the street, but all to no avail. The taxi-driver put Agnès' case into the boot, then held the door open while she got in; then he got into the front seat, slammed his door and drove away leaving Jerry standing there alone on the pavement in the jaundiced light cast by a street lamp.

'All right then,' he yelled in English after the departing taxi, 'bugger off! See if I care!'

But as the car disappeared from sight at the end of the street, a sense of desolation overcame him, a terrible realisation of what he'd lost through his own stupidity, and as he went back into the house to face the now formidably empty apartment, he carried that knowledge with him, like a ball and chain . . .

The Secret Life of a Poet

La Vie secrète d'un poète, from which the following extracts have been taken, appeared anonymously in Paris in 1963. Some experts believe it to be the work of Marc Vallon, an extremely original surrealist poet who died in 1965 at the regrettably early age of thirty-three.

If Marc Vallon is indeed the author, and there seem to be good reasons for thinking that he is, then this book may throw some light upon an otherwise obscure life, for although his poems have earned him an honourable place in the history of twentieth century European literature, little is known of his private life.

The Secret Life of a Poet is really a series of mainly erotic reminiscences covering the period from 1949 (when the poet was seventeen) to 1963 (shortly before his death). It could be described as a sort of autobiographical novel in which the author has improvised upon some incidents which really happened to him.

It is a book of strange contrasts where beautiful, sensitive passages are followed by almost brutally explicit description of erotic encounters. But this element of contrast is also present in Vallon's poetry, where exquisite lines are sometimes juxtaposed with shocking or disturbing imagery.

The book is an excellent one of its kind and deserves to be republished in today's more liberal climate. Copies of the original edition have become extremely hard to find.

The Secret Life of a Poet

'Ses yeux me parlaient de son sexe
Ses seins etaient lourds de mon désir.'

*'Her eyes spoke to me of her sex
Her breasts were heavy with my desire.'*

Marc Vallon

I reached my seventeenth birthday in the spring of 1949 without having lost my virginity. I had not even had the pleasure of fingering a girl's sex or of fondling a pair of soft swelling breasts under a blouse or jumper.

What made matters worse was that all my comrades at the *lycée* appeared to have had carnal experience and often boasted of their amorous adventures with waitresses, shop-assistants or their mothers' maids, and one even claimed that he regularly possessed his mother's best friend, a charming woman of forty or thereabouts. It never seemed to occur to me that these young men weren't telling the truth or, at best, were exaggerating wildly. But it was noticeable that not one of them ever claimed to have done anything with the young women at the *lycée*, either pupils or teachers! All of that gave me a terrible inferiority complex and increased my shyness and awkwardness with members of the opposite sex, especially when they were attractive.

In the summer of 1949 I was on holiday with my parents at Saint-Tropez but I did not see all that much of them, for even after twenty years of marriage, they were still very attached to each other and liked to go off alone together to do their own thing. We would have breakfast together,

48

then off they would go, leaving me to my own devices until we met back at the hotel for the evening meal at about seven o'clock. So I spent most of the day alone, not that I was unhappy most of the time, for I loved reading and walking and going to the cinema, and thus managed to occupy myself quite agreeably.

The only trouble was my member which often stiffened into erection at the most inopportune moments, stimulated by the proximity of some passing girl with swaying hips and quivering breasts. I had always had a very active virility: even when I was a small boy my pencil-thin little thingumyjig would stand up stiff and straight when my mother gave me a bath.

'Why does it do that?' I asked her on one occasion. Her face flushed; she looked uncomfortable.

'It's because you want to go wee-wee,' she said in a tone which brooked no argument.

I knew perfectly well that I didn't want to go to wee-wee, but my mother was not the sort of lady one argued with! So it all remained a mystery to me for some years after that incident . . . a half frightening, half exciting mystery.

Of course, with the onset of puberty it didn't remain a mystery for long. I had my first orgasm, an involuntary one, during a maths lesson at my *lycée* when I was thirteen. It was like a bomb going off in my trousers! I was quite unprepared for it. As far as I can recollect, I hadn't been thinking about anything particularly voluptuous that afternoon — it just suddenly happened: some form of erotic spontaneous combustion, I suppose.

Then a short time after that I had my first wet dream: I can't remember any details of the dream itself, but I can still recall the delirious pleasure of the orgasm, and waking up wondering why my pyjama trousers were wet and sticky.

No-one taught me to masturbate: that happened quite spontaneously. One summer evening in that year, 1945, when I'd had my first orgasm, my parents took me to see an American film in the centre of Annecy, where we then lived. I can't remember the name of the film, but the star was Alice Faye. Wearing a low-cut sequined evening gown she sang a hauntingly beautiful song called 'No Love, No Nothing.'

That night as I lay in bed in the dark, I thought about Alice Faye, her blue eyes, blonde hair, and the exposed cleavage between her breasts. My member grew stiff. I thought how nice it would be to pull that dress down and fondle those ripe fruits, then my right hand – guided by instinct – found its way under the bed-clothes, my fingers encircled the rigid shaft and started to work the foreskin back and forth over the glans. In a matter of seconds I was gasping as I ejaculated violently.

But I have wandered a long way from Saint-Tropez, that artists' paradise, and the summer holidays of 1949. As I have said, I kept myself occupied most of the time and was reasonably happy, apart from intermittent sexual frustration, which was invariably sparked off by a sudden half revelation of the naked charms of some pretty female. Of course, in a place like Saint-Tropez at the height of the season one is surrounded by delectable, half-naked girls all day long, so I often found myself with a good solid erection!

One afternoon in that hot August of 1949, I was sitting on the beach in the sunshine reading a copy of *La Liberté ou l'amour* (Love or Liberty), that marvellous novel by Robert Desnos, the great surrealist poet. I was more than two thirds of the way through the book and wanted to get it finished before dinner-time; however, it was not to be. I hadn't been there for more than a few minutes when two girls came and sat down on the shingle a few metres away from me. One was tall, rather thin, with her dark hair caught up behind her head in a chignon. She didn't appeal to me, but the other girl did! She was not so tall as her companion, and plumper, with fair hair cut quite short. She wore one of those bathing costumes with a halter top, which leave the back completely bare. Hers was a lovely back, smooth and unblemished; it's delicate whiteness indicated that this young lady had only just arrived at the popular holiday resort. The dark-haired girl seemed rather taciturn, but Blondie chattered away frequently punctuating her words with merry laughter . . . what a vivacious little thing! I felt my member stiffen in my bathing trunks. How I should have loved to kiss that warm, bare back, to caress those expressive shoulders, to fondle those plump buttocks! My virility throbbed rigidly between my thighs!

However, the girls took no notice of me: they were too absorbed in their conversation, and their backs were turned to me. I became annoyed with myself for wasting time on such trivialities and returned to my novel. But it was no good: my eyes travelled across the page without registering what they were seeing. I found the pretty little blonde so attractive that I couldn't stop looking at her.

Then suddenly she leaned forward to say something to the dark girl and the top of her halter sagged open, almost completely exposing her left breast. It was one of those excitingly full round breasts, very white and delicate, like her back, and crowned with a prominent reddish-brown nipple. Oh, how the sight of it affected me! I became quite breathless with lust, my member stood up like a steel bar, and it wouldn't have taken much to make me ejaculate into my trunks . . .

Then the pretty blonde straightened up and that beautiful breast was concealed again by the halter-top. A few moments later she lay on her back, eyes closed, soaking in the sunshine while her companion sat and stared out to sea where some yachts were sailing and the seagulls soared and wheeled.

I could see the blonde's slender legs, her smooth thighs and her flat stomach now. I should have liked nothing better than to go down to her, lie down on top of her, spread those thighs and give the lovely girl a vigorous shafting! But, as I have said, at that period of my life my shyness with members of the opposite sex was a painfully inhibiting factor: there was no question of my accosting the girls.

It was all too frustrating for words, so I closed the book, got up and walked away, with not too much difficulty as my member had by then subsided to a condition of semi-rigidity.

It would have been all too easy for me to go back to the hotel room, lock the door, take my trousers down then rub myself until I ejaculated into the air but, like most Catholic boys, I had a sense of guilt about doing it which remained dormant most of the time but tended to persecute me if I masturbated too often, and I had done it rather a lot that week. So I wandered around the quays of the port, looking at the boats and trying to put Blondie's nubile flesh out of my mind.

Eventually I found myself in a narrow little street where my favourite café was situated. I went in, sat down inside (there were no tables outside), and ordered a cup of coffee with cream. The establishment was almost empty. A ceiling fan whirred, keeping a current of warm air circulating. The waitress, a plain, uninspiring woman, brought my coffee and I opened the Desnos novel again and started to read. My sexual delirium had died down somewhat, my member had returned to its normal state of uneasy slumber, so I was able to concentrate on literature once more.

Then a woman came in and sat down at a table facing mine. She was by no means a pretty woman but, unfortunately for my peace of mind, she positively exuded what I believe the Americans call *sex-appeal**. She must have been considerably older than the girl on the beach — about thirty, or even thirty-five — and much more sophisticated. She had fluffy shoulder-length black hair, her rather angular face was carefully made up, and she wore gold pendant earrings. A young man of about the same age accompanied her and sat at the same table. I didn't like the look of him at all: he was quite good-looking, in spite of a receding hairline, but his air of self-satisfied smugness immediately irritated me.

When the lady sat down she had pulled the skirt of the pretty yellow and white summer dress she was wearing right up to the tops of her thighs in an effort to keep cool — it really was a hot afternoon! She wasn't wearing stockings

* In English in the original text.

and her long bare legs were very smooth, very shapely. My
member rapidly stiffened into full erection again!

The dreary waitress had already taken their order and now
brought them their drinks — a pastis for the man and a
coffee for the lady. They sat and talked in low tones,
seemingly oblivious of my presence. The young man put an
arm around his companion's shoulders and with his free
hand gently caressed one of her bare thighs. Then he glanced
across to where I was sitting and I quickly averted my gaze.
I pretended to be reading my book, but within seconds my
eyes were drawn back to where the couple was sitting. The
man's hand had now left the young woman's thigh and was
fondling one of her breasts through the thin fabric of the
dress.

'The animal!' I thought. 'To do such a thing in public!'

But I continued to stare, fascinated by that hand
massaging the woman's breast, my virility throbbing stiffly
at my crotch. She didn't seem to mind what he was doing,
but just sat there smiling fondly at him, eyes half closed.

Then the young man leaned forward, nuzzled his
companion's neck with his lips and whispered something in
her delicate shell-like ear. She laughed a low throaty laugh
of acquiescence then, placing one of her small feet in its
bright red high-heeled shoe on one of the cross-bars of the
chair he was sitting on, she opened her thighs wide giving
me an excellent view of her most intimate secrets, veiled only
by the flimsy covering of a pair of tiny blue silk panties!
My member was so stiff that it positively ached! I had at
that time never seen a woman's sex in the flesh, as it were,
but I knew what it looked like because a friend of mine at
the *lycée* had let me borrow an illustrated sex manual a few
months previously . . . Now here was this lovely lady
showing me her all (her 'ole) . . . or almost ('olemost)!

Then her companion looked across at me and smiled . . .
a friendly smile, and I realised that, far from being angry
at my voyeurism, he was enjoying it! Perhaps he wasn't such
a bad fellow after all!

Suddenly concerned about the presence of the waitress

he glanced towards the counter; so did I, but we needn't have worried, for she was absorbed in reading a sentimental photo-novel and had eyes for nothing else. Then he leaned forward again and kissed his sweetheart passionately. I could see that she was responding ardently. Then his hand moved between her parted thighs, he inserted his finger under the elastic of the blue knickers and began to frig the young woman. She gasped and pulled away from him, at the same time closing her thighs on his hand, but he pulled her back to him, kissed her again and persisted with his frigging until she relaxed and opened her thighs once more. He must have been titillating her dear little clitoris, making it go rigid with his wiggling forefinger. A woman can rarely resist a finger skilfully applied to the little thorn of flesh at the heart of her carnal rose − that was something subsequent experience taught me!

They were paying no attention to me now: the man had become absorbed in his indelicate task, the lady was well on the way to the seventh heaven. The waitress was still absorbed in her photo-novel; so I eased my rigidity out of my trunks and, keeping my eyes on the loving couple, rapidly masturbated under the table. The young man's fingers rubbed furiously, then the woman disengaged herself from his lips, threw her head back, eyes closed, moaning softly as she flooded her lover's hand with her warm female secretions, and at that moment I came too, as one does at the age of seventeen, ejaculating copiously . . . the underside of that table must have been covered with the viscous evidence of my pleasure. Some drops fell on the floor at my feet.

Then, of course, it was all over. The really nice things in this life almost aways are, as I'm sure you've noticed. Some people came into the café; the woman quickly adjusted her skirt and I rapidly got myself decent again. Then I paid for the coffee and left, hoping that no-one would notice the damp patch on the front of my swimming trunks and trying to conceal it by holding my book in front of it.

I never saw the dark-haired woman or her companion

again, which was a pity for, looking back at that afternoon in Saint-Tropez with the wisdom of hindsight, I feel pretty certain that I could have had my first experience of sexual intercourse with them if I had hung around and really got acquainted with the couple. I feel quite certain now that they were Parisians and old hands at the game of perverse eroticism. They were probably habitués of the Bois de Boulogne, cruising around at night in their car, looking for unusual erotic delights. However, it was not to be; my shyness and inexperience were against me and I was not destined to lose my virginity then . . .

During my first six weeks in the army I had had neither the time nor the energy to think about sex or women, but now that my life was beginning to acquire some semblance of normality again sexual desire began to torment me once more. My fellow recruits must have been in the same situation too, judging by the compulsive obsessive way in which they continually spoke about sex. Think of it − three hundred healthy young males who had all been deprived of female company for more than six weeks, all brought together in that training centre! The atmosphere was quite electric with sexual desire! It would have been impossible for me to forget about sex for long: it was the topic on everyone's lips, at every moment of the day or night.

The man who had the bed next to mine (there were thirty of us to each barrack-room) was a thick-set fellow with a very sallow complexion who came from Paris; his name was Vantard. He used to show me photos of all the young women he'd possessed; they were all extremely pretty. What Vantard loved to do was to display his pictures one after the other while giving a running commentary the purpose of which was to demonstrate how lucky the girls had been to be possessed by him and how grateful they were for the privilege. It wasn't at all erotic, just nauseatingly vulgar, and I came to detest him.

I had an infinitely more rewarding relationship with Jean-Luc, a young man from Amiens. He was in a different barrack-room from me, but we got talking one day in the mess. He was a slightly built youth with a fair complexion and a passion for jazz and poetry. We immediately became firm friends. We lent each other books, spent many delightful hours discussing literature, philosophy and politics, and he initiated me into the joys of listening to Duke Ellington, Charlie Parker and Count Basie. We sometimes discussed women, but always in an idealistic way: there was never any crude sex-talk between us. He was a dear man and I loved him like a brother; his death a few years later came as one of the worst setbacks of my life . . .

What a contrast to my friendship with Guillaume! Although I don't know whether 'friendship' is quite the right word . . . perhaps it would be more correct to describe him as my erotic mentor. Guillaume was a fair-haired young man with very flushed cheeks and a deep cultured voice. He was the only son of a well-to-do bourgeois family and had all the advantages of a good education and plenty of money. He later obtained a commission and had a very distinguished career in the army, eventually attaining the rank of colonel! When I made his acquaintance in that summer of 1950, he was an enthusiastic erotomaniac. I don't think I have ever met *anyone* who was so obsessed with sex! He hardly ever talked about anything else . . . I never really liked him: my Catholic upbringing made me feel that to be so interested in sex was wrong — besides, he tended to treat me in a rather condescending way. Nevertheless he fascinated me; he knew so much about the subject!

It was Guillaume who introduced me to pornographic photographs. I have no idea where he got them from, but he seemed to have an inexhaustible supply of the things. They were all in sets of five, and all in black and white. One can easily imagine the sort of effect that those pictures of naked male and female bodies engaged in every form of copulation had upon such a young, inexperienced man as I was!

My friend, or mentor, was very generous, for he would often pass those photos on to me and would ask for nothing in return. They taught me a great deal about all the ways in which men and women can give each other satisfaction but, unfortunately, they also taught me some of the more perverse aspects of eroticism, thus arousing deviant longings in me before I had even experienced straightforward sexual intercourse!

There was one set which made a particularly strong impression upon me: it featured one man and one woman (many of the other sets featured two men and a woman, or two men and two women, etc.) They were both quite naked, except that the woman wore big pendant earrings as well as very high-heeled shoes. She was dark-haired, pretty in a rather vulgar way, with a plump well-rounded body. The first photograph showed the woman reclining on a bed, lying on her right side, half sitting up, the right elbow supporting the weight of her body. It was taken from behind and one could see the lady's white, curving back and the big soft bottom cheeks. She was smiling up at the man who was standing beside the bed, bending over her. One of his hands caressed that lovely bottom; the other was out of sight but undoubtedly employed in fondling one of her breasts. His penis stood up, obscenely erect, and the young woman's left hand was stretched out to cradle his hairy testicles.

The second photograph featured a close-up of the lady licking the penis; it was a very long, very stiff penis with a large swollen glans. You couldn't see anything of the man himself, except for his genitals and part of his curving hairy belly. The woman's tongue was delicately titillating the underside of the glans.

In the next picture the woman had taken the penis into her full, well-shaped mouth and was sucking it. Her cheeks were hollowed with the effort of sucking. I could not look at that picture without getting a tremendous erection myself. I wondered what it must feel like to have a warm wet mouth sucking one's member like that, taking it right in. I could picture her head bobbing up and down . . .

The fourth photo was taken from a different angle: the woman lay on her side again in a similar position to that of the first picture, but this time the photo had been taken from the foot of the bed so that you had a good view of her breasts, which were quite large and well-shaped, and of her sex, for she had spread her thighs. The man knelt on the bed beside the young woman and she was sucking him again. His right hand was between her thighs, fingering that delicate pink slit . . .

The final picture of the set featured another close-up. You could see nothing but the girl's face and the man's organ, which had now lost some of its rigidity, and his hand grasping it near the base. I have since found out that that type of photo was what the Americans call a *cum shot.** In fact the guy obviously had just come — all over the lower part of his companion's face: she had blobs of semen all over her cheeks, lips and chin, but she didn't look unhappy about it: quite the contrary! She was smiling up at her partner (and probably thinking about the money she'd be getting!)

Those were the kinds of pictures my friend, Guillaume, introduced me to, and you can see what I mean when I say that they aroused deviant longings in me, for I found myself desiring to be fellated by a woman before I'd even had the experience of possessing one in the normal way!

One evening I was strolling down a narrow street not far from the Place d'Armes when I noticed a girl standing in front of an antique shop looking at an oil painting which was on display in the window. The little street was deserted apart from us.

Emboldened by sexual desire, I went over and stood beside her. She didn't move away but continued to gaze at the painting, a rather striking one which represented a calm sea in the rays of the setting sun. She was slightly taller than me, with abundant red shoulder-length hair. I could smell her perfume . . .

Making a herculean effort to overcome my shyness I said, 'The sea looks calm tonight.'

* In English in the original text.

'Yes, it does, doesn't it,' she laughed. The soft womanly tones of her voice appealed to me.

'You don't fancy going in for a dip?' I went on, pursuing the same bantering style.

She laughed again, sweet feminine music — 'No, it's too cold at this time of night.' She had now turned towards me and I saw her face for the first time. It was not a beautiful face, but its expression of open honesty immediately put me at my ease. Anyway, after we had discussed the picture for a few more minutes, I invited her to have a cup of coffee with me at a nearby café, she accepted and off we went.

The young woman told me her name was Laurette. She was eighteen, lived with her parents in the new town and worked as an auxiliary helper at the General Hospital. I quite liked the girl, she put me at my ease, as I have said, but to say that we got on well together would not really be true. We had nothing in common but sexual desire and conversation between us did not flow easily. Moreover things were not helped by the fact that Laurette was devastatingly honest — some people might say completely tactless! If she thought you were talking rubbish she told you so in no uncertain terms and several times that first evening she ruffled my self-esteem with her forthright comments; but the fact remained that she was a reasonably attractive girl, I wanted to have sex with her and she seemed to be willing, so I persevered. I asked her if she would like to go to the pictures with me, she said she would, so I took her to a little cinema called 'The Rex', which was not far from the café.

When we entered the foyer of the cinema she took off the light fawn jacket she had been wearing: underneath it she wore a dark green and black woollen dress which looked rather threadbare and unfashionable, but I noticed with satisfaction how her breasts thrust against the thin fabric of the bodice! She was what the English would call *a fine figure of a woman** sturdily built but attractive, with the robust seductiveness of an eighteenth century serving wench

* In English in the original text.

and, like an eighteenth century gentleman, I was hoping to tumble her soon!

At my request the usherette showed us to two seats in the back row. There weren't many other people in the cinema, just a few young servicemen like myself with their girlfriends and most of these couples were paying more attention to each other than to the film — a crude science-fiction tale about an evil carrot from outer space — so the circumstances were propitious for what we had in mind.

We started necking almost immediately . . . We kissed and cuddled and she responded ardently to my advances, readily opening her lips to mine and thrusting a warm agile tongue into my mouth. It was the first time I had ever experienced such kissing; it both repelled and excited me; my member strained uncomfortably against the fabric of my underpants. On the screen a U.S. colonel shouted orders unheeded by most of the couples in the audience.

We continued to penetrate each other's mouths with our tongues. My left arm was around Laurette's shoulders. Emboldened by her facility, I dared to put my right hand on her thigh under her skirt! She offered not the slightest resistance. I could feel the warmth of her flesh through the sheer nylon stocking. My virility had never been so stiff! We continued to kiss, her hand caressed my cheek and I moved my hand up even higher under Laurette's skirt to caress the sweet warm flesh above the stocking-top. But when I tried to put my hand between her thighs she closed them tightly together whispering, 'No, darling, not here!'

Undeterred by that, her first resistance, I went on kissing Laurette, thrusting my tongue into her warm wet open mouth . . . by now we were both breathing heavily and the young woman's resistance began to crumble; her thighs were no longer closed so tightly. Soon my fingers found the very centre of her femininity, pushed aside the silken panty-crotch and started to explore that other warm wet open mouth. Laurette moaned softly as I frigged her; her head fell back, eyes shut, mouth open, thighs now widely parted. My fingers were wet and sticky. There was a heady odour of sex and perfume in that stuffy cinema.

Then suddenly I became aware that a soldier two or three rows down had turned his head and was staring at us. I became embarrassed, withdrew my hand, pulled my companion's skirt down and whispered to her that we must leave. The poor girl, who must have been teetering on the edge of an orgasm, seemed to have difficulty in coming back down to earth. But, driven by a growing conviction that everyone there knew what we had been up to and was sniggering at us, I managed to get her to her feet and out of that claustrophobic place.

It felt so good to breathe the fresh evening air when we were in the street! It would have been about nine o'clock, I suppose, and night was falling. Laurette seemed upset, so I apologised for the brusque way in which I had ushered her from the cinema and explained briefly why it had been necessary.

She flushed up, hung her head and said, 'I feel so ashamed!'

I did my best to reassure her, but without much conviction: my holy Catholic bourgeois upbringing had taught me that girls who gave in too easily to sexual advances *ought* to feel ashamed of themselves! When we were embracing in the Rex the uncomplimentary thought had been passing through my mind: 'My goodness, this little hussy has been around!'

But, as I have said, I did my best to reassure the poor girl and in order to try to cheer her up, took her to a rather chic little restaurant I was in the habit of frequenting at that time. It turned out to be not such a good idea, for Laurette came from an indigent working-class family and was ill at ease in such a place. She kept blushing and stammering and thanked the supercilious waiter humbly and profusely every time he served her. As for me, the young woman's discomfort did not diminish my enjoyment of the meal; quite the contrary, it was an added condiment: I savoured her embarrassment!

61

Re-reading the above lines now makes me wish that such a thing as time-travel were possible so that I could go back to the year 1951 and give the little prig that was me then a good kick up the backside! Fortunately though Laurette's embarrassment did not last very long, for I ordered a bottle of wine and a glass or two soon restored some of her self-confidence; in fact, she became rather too talkative but, nevertheless, the rest of the meal passed off pleasantly enough.

When we left the little restaurant we walked along lamplit back streets towards the new town where Laurette lived. There weren't many people about and the click-clack of the young woman's high heels was very audible. We kept stopping to embrace and exchange increasingly passionate kisses. My member had stiffened again; my testicles ached uncomfortably with unfulfilled desire. I was simply going to have to have her soon!

After we had stopped for the third time in this way, she pulled away from me and said rather breathlessly, 'We're never going to get home at this rate!' It was at that moment that I noticed a dark alleyway between two tall warehouses. I took hold of Laurette's hand and, in spite of her feeble objections, pulled her into it.

What happened next? Well, we got straight down to business, that's what happened . . . No more groping or fumbling — just straightforward shagging, as a certain NCO of my acquaintance would have said. My companion was an experienced young woman who knew that we hadn't gone into that dark alley to whisper sweet nothings! Laurette knew all about erections . . . in fact, her own little fleshy thorn must have been stiff and peeking out between her sex-lips.

Once we were in that dark corner she lost all sense of shame: I went to embrace her but she stopped me, saying in a low voice, 'Just a minute, *chéri*.' Then the little slut (that, alas, is how I thought of her at the time) raised her skirt, then quickly pulled her panties down, stepped daintily out of them, teetering precariously on those high heels, and stuffed the fragile garment into a pocket of her coat.

Then I got the young woman up against the wall and, as we resumed our passionate kissing, boldly thrust my hand up under her skirt and put it between her thighs to feel the first vagina I had ever encountered! My exploring fingers came into contact first of all with a thick fleece of pubic hair, then a very warm, very wet, very open orifice. My goodness, what depths that girl had! I soon had three fingers up it frigging away, and there was room for more! I wondered how many times she'd been possessed before, and by how many men. But that thought did not diminish my ardour . . . quite the contrary!

Laurette had flung her arms around my neck, gasping and moaning as I vigorously masturbated her . . . But now it was impossible for me to wait any longer: I undid my trousers, liberated my quivering rigidity, then inserted it into Laurette's silken-smooth love-passage. Oh! How lovely it felt up there! . . . The young woman sighed in ecstasy as she felt my manhood sliding right up into her belly . . . she clasped me in her arms again, drawing me as close as possible as I began to thrust in and out . . . in and out . . . in and out. I put my hands on her generously proportioned buttocks, which she wriggled in response to my vigorous shafting . . . in and out . . . in and out . . . in and out . . . faster and faster! A mingled odour of perfume, sweat and female filled the air . . . Then suddenly Laurette cried out, clasped me even tighter and her sex contracted, bathing my pistoning ramrod in hot liquid as she came. No more was needed to set me going too! With a groan I attained the moment of supreme release, the delightful spasms of fulfilled lust! I shot and shot my seed into that palpitating love-grotto as if I should never stop . . . I nearly died of ecstasy!

Then at last it was over. We stood there pressed together, trembling, weak at the knees, clasped in each other's arms like two frightened kids lost in the woods, my subsiding virility still buried inside her. I don't know how long we stayed there like that: one loses all sense of time at such moments. I was just aware of my penis returning to its normal state and slipping out of its lodgement . . . Then

63

I became conscious of the fact that Laurette was crying: her face buried in my chest, arms still clasped around my neck, the young woman's body shook as she wept silently against me.

'Darling! Whatever is the matter?' I asked, affecting a concern which I was a hundred thousand light years from feeling.

'I-I'm no good!' she said, her voice choked with tears.

'What a silly thing to say! Why aren't you good?'

'Because I make myself cheap!' she wept.

'Nonsense!' I said in a voice as comforting as I could make it. 'Your're an extremely nice girl! . . .'

We went on like that for some time, with me vainly trying to convince the poor creature that she was not totally worthless; but I had no words of real comfort to offer, only conventionally reassuring sounds of the 'there there, it'll be all right' variety. I was too inexperienced, too much of a victim of the prejudices of my class to be able to understand her wretchedness. Eventually, however, I prevailed upon Laurette to dry her tears: I gave her a handkerchief, she blew her nose vigorously and then I took the poor downcast young woman home.

Poor, unfortunate Laurette! She is one of the great regrets of my life: one of my missed opportunities. How I wish I could go back in time and comfort the dear girl as she needed to be comforted!

I never did find out exactly what was making her so unhappy — and that in itself is an indictment of my callous indifference — but it is not hard to guess what was wrong: she had undoubtedly sacrificed her virginity to some young man who had persuaded the naive girl that he loved her, then when inevitably he let her down she'd drifted into a series of brief liaisons, driven by the sensual longings that first lover had so irresponsibly awakened . . . Laurette judged herself according to the stupid, unfair code of sexual morality with which the Catholic Church poisoned all our minds: she was a fallen woman, a shameless hussy, a woman of easy virtue, little better than a prostitute! That's how she judged herself and, to my shame, that's how I judged her too.

We went out together a few more times but we never had full sexual relations again: first of all she had her period, so I had to be content with fondling her breasts and having her masturbate me; then she was on night duty at the hospital for a week and we weren't able to meet; then when we did get together again Laurette suddenly got scared about becoming pregnant and would not permit full penetration. I became very frustrated . . . I was impatient with her fears about pregnancy: it seemed to me that having once let me make love to her she had an *obligation* to let me do it again . . . how arrogant young men can be! How immature!

I bought a packet of condoms, but even that did not make her relent: she was willing to allow a great deal of intimacy, but no more penetration. Perhaps that was Laurette's clumsy way of trying to make me respect her, a belated attempt to make our relationship respectable: she desperately wanted to recover her lost 'decency'! But, of course, at the time I didn't realise that.

In the end I told the poor girl that it would be best if we didn't see each other any more. She didn't cry, not in front of me anyway, but she looked so very sad, so cast down! Laurette made no attempt to play upon my feelings, no attempt to manipulate me into changing my mind. She just thanked me, without a hint of irony, for having been so kind to her. Then we parted. I never saw her again and left Toulon shortly afterwards.

One Marvellous Night

Je ne pensais point à dormir; je faisais mieux, je jouissais, et cette nuit fut la plus douce que j'aie passe((ac) de ma vie.

I did not think of sleeping; I did better, I enjoyed myself, and that night was the most delightful night of my life.

Pigault-Lebrun

As soon as I set eyes on her I knew that something marvellous was going to happen between us.

She came and sat down opposite me just as the train was pulling out of the station. Her rather plain features were offset by abundant rich auburn hair which she wore quite long, to shoulder length. We had the compartment to ourselves.

I was returning home to the small market town of R— where I lived, after spending the day in the lovely old university town of Poitiers, browsing in the second-hand bookshops, strolling around the narrow streets, and admiring the picturesque buildings.

The woman was quite plump but well-proportioned. When she sat down she crossed one leg over the other and her skirt rode up, revealing smooth nylon-clad knees. She gave me a rather melancholy smile and said, 'Would you mind if we opened the window a little, monsieur?'

'Not at all, madame,' I said, jumping to my feet. I lowered the window a few centimetres, then sat down again. 'It is quite warm for the time of year, isn't it?' I said.

'Yes indeed,' she smiled again.

'Have you been on a shopping expedition?' I asked,

encouraged by her relaxed, friendly manner and looking at the fancily-wrapped packages on the seat beside her.

'Yes, and I've spent too much money,' she sighed.

I laughed. 'Well, you're entitled to spoil yourself sometimes.'

The woman smiled but said nothing. She rested her chin on her hand and stared out of the window at the passing landscape: we were out of the town now; dusk was beginning to settle on the fields and trees. *Clickety-clack, clickety-clack*, went the wheels. I found myself looking at the woman's legs again: they were slender, well-shaped and sheathed in the finest nylon: her dainty feet were encased in black shoes with stiletto heels.

'Do you think I have nice legs?' her voice broke in on my thoughts.

I started guiltily. 'I'm sorry; I didn't mean to be rude.'

She gave me one of those rather sad smiles of hers: 'I don't think you're being rude. But you haven't answered my question . . .'

'They're very nice, very elegant,' I said. My certainty that something wonderful was going to happen between myself and this woman was growing stronger by the minute.

The train pulled up at a little country station. Three people got off, doors were slammed, a whistle blew, the train jerked, then we were off again. We still had the compartment to ourselves.

'What were *you* doing in Poitiers?' she asked.

'Oh, just wandering around mostly, and looking in the bookshops, the second-hand ones.'

'Oh,' she said, 'you're a book collector?'

'In a rather modest way,' I replied.

'Did you see that programme on TV last week about Marcel Proust?' she said.

Some instinct told me that this lady was not a book lover, that she was simply trying to talk about something which would interest me, but I didn't think of her as a hypocrite: I was rather touched by her efforts to please me.

68

But the topic was soon exhausted. I said, 'Did you buy something nice in Poitiers, madame?'

'Oh, please call me Lucille,' she said.

'What a pretty name!' I exclaimed. 'My name is Paul.'

'Well, Paul, I did buy some rather nice things today.' She delved into one of the bags beside her and showed me an extremely fetching blouse; then from another one she produced a pretty dark blue hat with a little veil; then there was a pair of red open-work shoes with semi-high heels.

'Very nice!' I said. 'Very tasteful, but what's in that one?' I pointed my finger at a small gift-wrapped package. She blushed prettily.

'It's indiscreet of you to ask and it would be even more indiscreet of me to satisfy your curiosity!' But her tone was sad rather than reproachful.

'Forgive me, Lucille,' I said, feeling acutely embarrassed. 'I didn't mean to offend you.'

Her only reply was a gentle smile and a barely perceptible nod of the head. At that point the train again ground to a halt at another little station. No-one got off or on and within a few seconds we were on our way again.

Lucille had fallen silent for a few minutes; now, with the air of a woman who has suddenly come to a difficult decision, she said, 'My husband always says I'm a prude! . . . Would you really like to see what's in here?' She held up the little gift-wrapped package with its pretty paper and bows.

'Only if you don't mind letting me see,' I replied.

The young woman quickly undid the bows, unwrapped the paper and produced a pair of white lace-edged camiknickers in fragile nylon.

'There,' she said, blushing with a very becoming modesty, holding them up so that I could get a good look. 'What do you think?'

What I thought would not have been repeatable! I was thinking that that dainty garment would soon contain Lucille's soft white breasts and that the dear hairy little treasure which nestled between her thighs would be pressed tightly against the crotch as she walked or sat down and, in response to those lustful imaginings, my virility awoke and stood up.

But all I said was, 'They're lovely!' I don't think I could have articulated another word just then.

'My husband likes me to wear such things,' she said, rewrapping the camiknickers and retying the bow.

It was quite dark outside now. we should be arriving at R— in about ten minutes.

'Where do you live, Lucille?' I said.

'We've got a little place at P—,' she said. P— was the next stop down the line, about fifteen minutes after R—

'Well,' I said regretfully, 'I'll be having to say goodbye to you in a few moments.' The lights of the town could be seen now and the train was beginning to slow down as it approached the station. I began to get my things together.

'Look,' said Lucille earnestly, 'are you doing anything this evening? I mean, are you in a great hurry to get home?'

'No,' I said. 'Why?'

'Well, I know Gérard, that's my husband, would like to meet you: he's very keen on books. You could have dinner with us, if you like . . .'

I felt somewhat deflated: I didn't want to meet her husband — I wanted to make love to Lucille! The train was drawing into the station. She leaned towards me, took one of my hands in hers and said, in the same earnest tone, '*Please* say you'll come!' The element of distress in the young woman's voice helped me to make up my mind.

'All right,' I said, 'but I'll have to make a quick phone call when we get to P—'

'Oh, good!' She gave a sigh, one would almost have said of relief, then gently withdrew her hands and leaned the back of her head against the seat.

Half way between R— and P— the train was halted by signals. It stood there in the silent countryside, the engine sighing like a tired old woman.

'There's something magical about the countryside at

70

night,' said Lucille. She stood up, let the window down and leaned out. 'Oh, there's such a lovely fresh smell to the air,' she said. 'Come and smell it.'

I too stood up and leaned out of the window with her. She was right — there was a magical quality to the scene: the fields and hedgerows were bathed in the gentle radiance of the stars and a crescent moon. It was a fine October evening: not a cloud in the sky! We stood there together enjoying the fragrant night air and the serene peace of the countryside. I became conscious of the warmth of her body pressing against me.

Suddenly the signal turned from red to green, the train whistled and jerked forward and I was forced to put my arms around Lucille in order to keep my balance; then I don't know how it happened exactly, but I found myself kissing her eyes, her cheeks and her full lips.

She let me go on for a few moments, without responding, then pushed me away and sat down. I too sat down again, very conscious of the throbbing stiffness between my thighs.

'You don't waste any time, do you?' she said. Her face was flushed and she seemed quite annoyed. 'I hope you're not going to make me regret having invited you!' She pulled the hem of her skirt down so that her knees were covered.

I was beginning to feel annoyed myself. What the hell was this woman playing at?

'Well, perhaps we'd better forget the whole thing,' I said coldly. 'I can get the next train back to R—'

'Yes, perhaps you'd better do just that!' she replied.

By this time the train was slowing down as it approached the little station at P— We prepared to leave the compartment. Lucille stood up and put the coat back on which she'd taken off at the beginning of the journey: it was a very elegant, well-cut cherry coloured coat with a black fur collar.

A few moments later we were standing on the platform at P— looking rather uncertainly at each other.

'Look,' I said, squeezing her arm gently, 'I really am

terribly sorry if I offended you . . . you're a very nice person.'

She smiled that charmingly melancholy smile of hers and said, 'I'm not offended . . . Are you going to come and have something to eat?' She looked so appealing, gazing up at me with her pale features framed by her auburn hair and the dark fur collar of the coat she was wearing.

'If you're sure it will be no trouble,' I said.

'No trouble at all,' she replied. 'Come on, young man,' and I followed her docilely out of the station.

'There's never a taxi to be had,' said Lucille as we emerged into the little space in front of the station. She slipped her arm through mine. 'Never mind, it's a lovely night and it's not far to walk.'

We walked along the village street. There weren't many people about and all the little shops were closed. The big clock on the grey stone tower of the church of Saint Benoît indicated that the time was seven o'clock.

'Let me carry those for you,' I said, relieving her of the packages. I slipped my arm unobtrusively round her shoulders; she didn't object and we went on our way chatting in friendly tones about this and that. My main preoccupation now was how to persuade Lucille to let me kiss her again: the memory of those warm, yielding lips was haunting me, goading me on. But how to do it without making her angry again?

Then I suddenly remembered a scene in an eighteenth century erotic novel I had been reading not long before where the young hero had been faced with exactly the same problem . . .

I said, 'I'm sorry about what happened on the train.'

'Don't give it another thought!'

'You're not angry any more?'

'No, I'm not.

'You're sure?'

'Absolutely.'

I stopped, so did she and we stood there facing each other

72

under the stars and the crescent moon. We were almost out of the village now . . . there was no-one in the street but us.

'There is a way you could show me that you really have forgiven me,' I said softly.

'Oh, and what may that be?' she enquired, gazing up at me with a mischievous twinkle in her eyes.

I hesitated for a moment then said, 'By letting me kiss you now. . . just a friendly kiss, to show that there's no ill-feeling,' I added hastily.

She looked at me without saying a word for a few moments, and I wondered if she was going to slap my face. But her eyes were still twinkling, then she started to chuckle . . .

'You've got a bloody nerve!' she said.

I took that for assent, put my arms round the young woman, drew her close to me and pressed my lips to hers. I kissed Lucille hard and passionately, but this time she didn't just passively let me as she had done in the train: she put her arms around me and responded with considerable ardour. Soon our tongues were exploring each other's mouths, but when I put a hand inside the cherry coat and started to fondle a satisfyingly full round breast, she pulled away.

'Come on,' she said rather breathlessly, 'we're never going to get home at this rate!'

The house where Lucille lived was right at the furthest end of the village street, about a kilometre from the station. It was a small but elegant mansion with bow windows, built just after the Revolution, with a fair sized garden in front and an even bigger one behind. The house was divided into flats: Lucille and her husband lived in the one on the first floor.

Gérard, the husband, was a dark, balding man of small stature. He spoke in soft, cultured tones and one had the impression that his quick, intelligent eyes missed very little. He greeted me politely but without overmuch enthusiasm.

Their flat was spacious and furnished with quiet good

taste. A cheerful log fire burned in the hearth, although the weather was not cold for the time of year.

I suddenly remembered that I had not made my phone call. They let me use the telephone which stood on a little table in their hall, near the front door. I explained to Madeleine, my wife, that I had run into an old university pal in Pointiers and that he'd invited me to spend the evening at his place. She sounded incredulous and I realised that we'd undoubtedly have a row about it when I eventually got home — but I'd worry about that when the time came! I cut short Madeleine's protests, replaced the receiver, then went back into the lounge to rejoin my hosts.

When I re-entered the room Lucille had disappeared. Gérard rose from the comfortable armchair in which he had been sitting. 'Lucille won't be long,' he said. 'She's just changing . . . would you like a drink?'

I said that I'd like a sherry and he went over to a well-stocked antique side-board to pour me one.

Like everything else in that apartment, the sherry was of excellent quality; I sat on an elegant Louis Quinze sofa sipping my drink appreciatively. Gérard and I chatted about books for a while, then the door opened and Lucille came in.

Gérard had said that she had gone to get changed, but imagine my surprise when I saw that she was now wearing a flimsy black negligee! In spite of her rather plain, homely features the young woman really did look extremely desirable. She was still wearing her high-heeled outdoor shoes.

'Have you put it on?' Gérard enquired blandly.

'Yes,' she murmured, walking over to where we were sitting. She had an exciting way of swinging her hips as she walked. My virility stirred. The young woman stood in front of us, cheeks flushed, eyelids demurely lowered. There was something about her attitude which made me think of a slave-girl being inspected on an auction-block. My virile member was now fully rampant and throbbing with desire.

'Well,' said Gérard, 'what are you waiting for? Let's see how it looks then.'

Lucille's slender fingers fiddled with the belt of the negligee. She looked uncomfortable.

'Come on, show us!' her husband insisted.

'I can't,' she whispered. 'I'm too embarrassed!' She blushed deeply; I thought she was going to cry.

Gérard put his glass down, got up from the armchair and went over to his wife. He put his arm round her shoulders and said affectionately, 'Don't worry, my love. It's all right.' He kissed her tenderly on the cheek, then he looked at me and said, 'I think it's time we had something to eat.'

The meal was a very good one: cold chicken salad, home-baked bread, Gruyère cheese, accompanied by a heady sparkling wine and followed by an equally heady sherry trifle. We ate seated round a low table in the lounge. I noticed that Lucille drank a lot of wine: Gérard kept replenishing her glass. He seemed more relaxed and friendlier towards me now. He was an intelligent, well-read man; his wife was charming too and interesting conversation enhanced the enjoyment of the meal.

A little later, when the table had been cleared and we were finishing our coffee, Gérard said to his wife, 'Now you really must show us this new acquisition . . .' Lucille was much more relaxed now, the wine had weakened her inhibitions; she had been contributing enthusiastically to the conversation, laughing unaffectedly but without vulgarity.

'Very well, monsieur,' she said, rising to her feet from the sofa where she had been sitting beside her husband. 'Your wish is my command.' Then the young woman unfastened the negligée, took it right off with a graceful gesture and stood before us wearing the white lace-edged camiknickers which she had so indiscreetly shown me in the train.

She made a delightfully erotic picture standing there clad in nothing but that flimsy undergarment, high-heeled shoes, and stockings which gave a pleasingly silky sheen to her long, shapely legs. She was obviously not wearing a brassiere, for the points of her breasts were clearly visible through the thin nylon.

'Turn around slowly,' Gérard commanded in a voice made unsteady by emotion. The lovely creature obeyed, giving me a stimulating view of a round, very feminine bottom which the nylon covering did little to conceal.

Gérard turned to me: 'She bought the camiknickers this afternoon,' he said, explaining what I already knew. 'She looks lovely, doesn't she?'

'Indeed, she does . . . lovely!' I said in a voice which I hoped didn't too obviously betray my true state, which was one of extremely rampant, throbbing, virile excitement near to the point of bursting!

Lucille smiled. 'Thank you, kind sir,' she said.

Gérard rose to his feet, moved across to where his wife was standing and took her in his arms.

'Darling!' he said. 'Darling!' Then he pressed his lips to hers in a deeply passionate kiss which seemed to go on for an eternity . . . I had the impression that they'd forgotten all about me! My own feelings were a mixture of desire and embarrassment in about equal proportions . . . I didn't know what to do!

Then the man's right hand moved down and he started to caress his wife's bottom through the thin silky nylon. Lucille's first reaction was to cuddle up even closer and kiss him even more passionately, but when the lecherous man inserted his fingers under the lacy hem of the knickers in order to caress her bare behind, it was too much for the young woman and she pulled away protesting,

'No, Gérard! No!'

She was breathing heavily, white breasts rising and falling rapidly.

A frown came to her husband's face; for a moment I thought he might be going to say some harsh things, but then he said, with a transparently false air of contrition, 'Forgive me, my love,' and took his wife in his arms again, once more sealing her lips with a deep kiss. Lucille sighed, relaxed then wound her slender white arms around Gérard.

76

The idea of a fully-dressed man making love to a naked or, in the present case, a nearly naked woman has always seemed to me to be a particularly erotic one. As I sat there watching Lucille being kissed and caressed by her husband, it was like seeing one of my dreams come true. Desire had now overcome any embarrassment on my part. I felt as though I should burst if I did not soon find some relief!

The couple were kissing and embracing with increasing abandon now and when Gérard insinuated his hand under the knickers and began to finger his wife's sex, she made no attempt to stop him: she just clasped him even more tightly to her.

At that point I could hold out no longer: something had to be done, so I undid my fly and, with some difficulty, drew out my stiff member, exposing it to the air. I didn't want to reach the supreme moment prematurely, so I contented myself with gently caressing my rampant virility while continuing to watch Gérard and his wife.

He was kissing her slender white throat now; her head was thrown back, eyes closed, mouth open, breath coming in short gasps as the man's rapidly moving fingers brought her ever nearer to the moment of supreme release.

She was teetering right on the edge when Gérard abruptly ceased his indecent stimulation, withdrew his hand from Lucille's femininity and said, 'Let's take this thing off so that our guest can see your breasts and bottom!' Whereupon he pulled down the shoulder straps of the silken camiknickers, revealing a pair of very white, very round breasts whose reddish-brown nipples were stiff and pointing, visible proof of how sexually aroused the young woman was!

Then this libertine of a husband pulled his wife's knickers right down until they were lying in a crumpled, fragile heap around her ankles. Lucille's generous but shapely bottom was now revealed.

She had offered not the slightest resistance while Gérard was thus baring her charms in front of a visitor, a virtual stranger. She seemed like a woman who had been drugged or hypnotized: indeed, she was under the influence of that most powerful of natural narcotics – sexual desire!

Lucille's husband murmured something in her ear and she stepped out of the crumpled cami-knickers then turned to face me. Her features may not have been beautiful, but she certainly possessed an extremely attractive body! She stood there before me naked, except for a frilly white suspender-belt, sheer nylons and high-heeled shoes. Her eyes were demurely downcast; mine were fastened on the dark tuft of hair at the base of her rounded belly. With my whole being I longed to possess that young woman. My turgid sex was almost painful, I literally ached with desire!

Gérard was now standing close behind his wife; one of his hands fondled a full ripe breast while the other stroked her belly. Lucille's face was flushed, her mouth hung open but her eyes were closed.

Gérard glanced towards where I was sitting, then, kissing his wife tenderly at the point where the neck joined the shoulder, he said:

'Open your eyes, darling. Look at our guest. The poor fellow is in a pitiable state!'

Lucille obeyed her husband and gazed at me with eyes which seemed to be drowning in sensual delirium. The hand which had been stroking her belly had moved downwards and Gérard's fingers were again titillating her sex lips.

'See how stiff he is, my love,' he murmured looking at my turgid organ. 'You can see how badly he needs you!'

As he spoke these words his hands never ceased to fondle, to tweak, to rub . . . Lucille was gasping and moaning; her legs seemed about to give way beneath her.

'Oh! Ah! Oh, fuck me, please fuck me!' she groaned.

'Come on, Paul, she's ready for you,' said Gérard.

I did not need a second invitation: I stood up, quickly slipped my jacket off, removed my trousers, underpants and shoes then moved across the room to join them, my erect member bobbing in front of me like a miniature flag pole.

Then Lucille was in my arms and I was kissing her, fondling those breasts, feeling that plump bottom, fingering the hot wet centre of her womanhood. My virility was hard against her bare belly.

Then, at Gérard's suggestion, the young woman knelt down on all fours on the thick pile carpet. I knelt behind her and introduced my fleshly staff into her love-nest . . . oh, what a wonderful sensation! I slid with such ease into that warm, slick, welcoming passage!

Gérard had also removed his trousers and underpants now, and as I began to make love to Lucille from behind, he knelt in front of her and she started to make love to him with her mouth. I could see the young woman's auburn head bobbing up and down as she sucked the rigid member. Gérard's head was thrown back, his mouth hung open, his eyes were closed, and there was an expression of ecstasy on his face; his hands rested on Lucille's smooth white shoulders.

As for me, I was in ecstasy too, savouring the exquisite sensations which that succulent passage gave me as I moved back and forth within it. The dear girl increased my pleasure greatly by wriggling her bottom responsively to my thrusts. My hands gripped her shapely hips. I was panting and gasping, perspiration dripped off my forehead.

Gérard was gasping too and he began to moan and jerk his head spasmodically from side to side as he approached the moment of supreme release. Lucille's head bobbed faster and faster; then suddenly the lecherous fellow pulled his glistening ramrod out of his wife's mouth and, uttering a great *'Ooooooh!'* sprayed her face with the pearly liquid of his lust!

Within seconds I too reached my peak: the pent-up forces of *my* lust spurted into Lucille's sweetly receptive love-sheath, inundating it with a copious tribute to her charms . . . Then we all sank down into an exhausted, panting heap upon the carpet and rested for a while.

Not long afterwards order was restored. Gérard and I put our clothes back on while Lucille disappeared into the bathroom for a few moments. When she returned she had washed all of her husband's sticky stuff off her face and was wearing the negligée again; she had combed her hair too.

Gérard poured us some drinks at the antique sideboard: Lucille and I sat side by side on the settee sipping ours, while Gérard took his over to the mantlepiece and stood close to the now dying fire.

'Well,' I said, 'that was truly marvellous! I should like to thank you both for giving me a uniquely memorable evening.'

'You too have given us considerable pleasure, monsieur,' said Gérard, 'and if you care to visit us again you will always be welcome here.'

'Thank you very much, monsieur,' I replied then, turning to Lucille, 'And thank you especially, dear lady, for the exquisite pleasure you have given me this evening.' I took her cool fingers in mine and raised them to my lips. She blushed prettily, murmuring confusedly that she had enjoyed my company.

We chatted for a little while longer but it was getting late so Gérard phoned for a taxi. Not long after that I took my leave of the extraordinary couple, kissing Lucille on her warm, full lips and shaking hands with her husband. I never saw them again.

I should have liked nothing more than to have made love to Lucille again, to caress her full breasts, to penetrate her sweet sex but Madeleine, my wife, was a very possessive woman and a fervent believer in monogamy.

As I had foreseen, the price of that glorious evening was a most terrible row when I arrived home: a row that went on for what remained of the night, followed by a week of coldness terminating in a painfully emotional reconciliation when at last I managed to persuade my wife that I had not been unfaithful to her and had no intention of being so in the future.

I was in a dilemma: I badly wanted to return to the village of P— but I loved Madeleine and did not want to hurt her. She was not such an exciting woman as Lucille, but she was a good companion and even after ten years of marriage I still loved her very much. Besides, there were our two children to consider.

So I had to resign myself to accepting the situation; and I did, eventually, after many weeks of bitter, soul-searching inner conflict, which made me feel quite ill with frustration at times. However, as the weeks went by and turned into months, my peace of mind gradually returned.

The following year my wife gave birth to our third child, a pretty little girl with shining eyes. I didn't have the cheek to suggest that we should call her Lucille, but I always feel that that was what her name should have been. However, something very strange is happening now: as she gets older our little girl is starting to bear a quite astonishing resemblance to the lady who should have been her mother, the seductive Lucille who was my mistress for one marvellous night!

What a Naughty Girl I Am!

Monique waited until they'd cleared the dinner things away before she dropped her bombshell.

'Do you know what I've been doing today, *chéri?*' she said, smiling sweetly up at her husband from the settee.

'You went shopping with Zabeth?' said Maurice, who was standing in front of the fire warming his arse.

Monique's smile deepened. 'I've been fucking,' she said.

'You've been what?' exclaimed her husband.

'I've been fucking,' the young woman repeated. 'In fact, I've spent the whole day fucking, fucking, fucking! I can quite truthfully say I'm fucked!'

Maurice looked at his wife through narrowed eyes. 'Have you been drinking?' he demanded angrily.

Monique laughed, a merry laugh. 'No, I haven't,' she said, 'at least not in the way you mean. But I have swallowed quite a lot of *spunk*!' She deliberately emphasized the word to bring out its coarseness.

Her husband looked quite shocked. 'You're talking like a vulgar tart!' he exclaimed.

'After the way I've behaved today that's exactly what I must be now,' Monique replied. She was no longer smiling.

Maurice's attitude suddenly became conciliatory. He went over and sat down beside her on the settee. He put his arm around her. 'Now tell me what I've done to upset you,' he said, 'because that's what this is all about, isn't it?'

Monique got up, shaking her husband's arm off, and went over to sit on a chair by the dining-room table, crossing one leg over the other. She looked at him pityingly.

'Poor Maurice!' she said. 'You won't believe me even when I tell you the truth, will you? I've cuckolded you at least a dozen times today, and with complete strangers: men I just picked up!'

Maurice looked bewildered rather than angry. 'But why would you do such a thing? It's not even as if you're very keen on sex,' he murmured.

The young woman gave a laugh which was anything but mirthful. 'How little you understand me, Maurice! Just because you haven't succeeded in arousing me you assume that I have no sexual feelings, no longings!'

'What longings?' her husband demanded. There was an incredulous note in his voice.

Monique looked sad. 'Do you find it so hard to believe that I have needs in that respect, *chéri*?' she said. The young woman's skirt had ridden up higher while she had been talking. Maurice could now see the tops of her black stockings. His penis stiffened into a half-hard state. He was finding this conversation quite erotic, in spite of himself.

'What sort of *needs*?' he said. 'After all, it's not as if I never make love to you!'

'No,' she mocked him, 'it's not as if you never make love to me . . . And that's just the trouble. It's all so bloody *respectable*: you get into bed beside me in the dark, you pull my nightie up and then you make love to me.' Monique laid a heavy, mocking emphasis upon the last four words.

Maurice looked hurt. 'Well, what do you want then?' he said.

Monique gave vent to a throaty, highly unladylike laugh. Maurice had the impression that it was her *cunt* laughing. His prick stiffened into full throbbing hardness: his testicles tightened.

'What I want is to escape from bourgeois respectability sometimes,' she said. 'And this afternoon, just for a while, I succeeded . . .'

'What did you do?'

'I told you before, Maurice, I went fucking.'

The young woman got up off the chair and stood in front of him. She raised her skirt to her waist, revealing that the black stockings were held up by a white suspender-belt and also that she was not wearing panties. Her mound covered with brown pubic hair was framed by the suspenders and stocking-tops.

'Why do you think I'm wearing these things?' she said, and her voice had acquired a dreamy sensual tone. Again Maurice had the impression that his wife's vagina was speaking to him. His dick was so hard now!

'I was bored, depressed and restless the whole morning,' the young wife continued.

'But we made love last night,' her husband protested.

Monique gave him a sardonic look. '*You* made love, you mean. You just stuck your thing up me when we got to bed – no preliminaries or anything like that – jerked your arse back and forth a few times, groaned, gasped and spurted; then you pulled it out, kissed me goodnight and went off to sleep. It never occurred to you that I might not be satisfied, that you could at least have used your fingers to rub my thing. You're so selfish sometimes that it's almost unbelievable!'

Maurice felt acutely embarrassed. He knew that what his wife said was true. What could he say in his own defence? For some reason her words had brought an old memory to the surface of his consciousness: his first mistress had been a girl who came to the house daily to help his mother with the domestic chores. He was about eighteen at the time and she would have been about a year younger, but she was much more experienced in the ways of sex than Maurice. It was really she who had seduced him. They did a lot of fucking in the six months that their relationship lasted, but the young woman always made him wear a sheath, into which he spurted his copious emissions whenever they performed. Her name was Élodie and she was a tall, thin girl with rather frizzy blonde hair: her breasts were very full and seemed bigger because of the thinness of her torso. They bounced as she walked and Maurice invariably got an erection whenever he laid eyes on them.

The particular memory which had come into his mind now was of one sunny afternoon when his *maman* was out visiting a friend and he and Élodie had the house to themselves. They had gone into his bedroom, taken off all their clothes, then they'd had a really satisfying fuck culminating in Maurice filling the rubber johnny with lots of thick, white stuff straight from his bollocks. But Elodie complained that she hadn't come at all. She suggested that it would be nice if the young man sucked her cunt. She was laying on her back on his bed, her rather frizzy hair spread out round her head on the pillow; she drew her knees up then opened her thighs as wide as they would go, displaying the hairy slit, pale pink in colour, which gaped slightly from where Maurice's penis had been fucking so recently.

'Come on, *chéri*,' Élodie said, 'suck me, there's a good boy!'

It was the first time that the young man had ever tasted snatch. He didn't find it disagreeable; in fact, once he'd got used to it, he found it exciting because of the effect it produced in his young mistress: she groaned, she moaned, and in the end she sobbed as her belly contracted in orgasmic spasms and she came quite violently, filling Maurice's mouth with a warm, rather bitter-tasting emission. By that time he'd acquired another hard-on and they'd had another fuck, longer and more satisfying for both of them than the first one.

Monique had dropped her skirt and now stood looking down at him, her arms folded across her shapely breasts. Maurice realised that she was waiting for him to say something, to try to justify himself. But he did not try to justify himself, instead he said, 'So you took your revenge by going out and behaving like a tart?'

His wife sat down again, facing him, her right elbow resting on the dining-room table where they had eaten not long before. 'Yes,' she said quietly. 'I told you before, I spent the afternoon fucking.'

Maurice had put his hand in his trouser pocket and started to caress his rigid stem through the cloth, his eyes fixed on Monique. She looked particularly attractive tonight, a girl with delicate pale features and dark curly hair which went well with the yellow dress with white circles she was wearing. Maurice noticed that his wife was wearing more make-up than usual.

'You're playing with yourself,' she said in a tone of amused contempt.

'Tell me about this afternoon,' said her husband, his voice constricted by his desire.

Monique crossed one elegant slender leg over the other, seeming not to notice how high her skirt had risen, and said, 'Well, to be honest, I didn't really fuck with twelve men: I was just saying that to wind you up, you bastard!'

'How many did you have then?'

'Well, three actually.'

'Tell me what you did with them then, you naughty girl!' said Maurice, who by now had taken his tool out and was making no attempt to hide his masturbatory activity. Monique could clearly see her husband's impressive blue-veined stalk surmounted by a shiny, plum-coloured knob.

'Well, to be honest, I didn't actually have sexual intercourse as such with the first man,' the young woman said, 'I met him in a little cinema in Pigalle. He came and sat beside me and hadn't been there five minutes when he started to feel my thighs. When he found that I didn't object to that, he started to caress my titties through my dress. Meanwhile, to leave him in no doubt about me, I reached across and put my hand on his crotch in order to ascertain what effect my charms were having on him. I felt a satisfactory hardness through the cloth of his trousers.

' "Take it out and rub it," he whispered urgently.

'I thought his accent was foreign, German perhaps. He was a rather stout, middle-aged man — I could see that much in the dim light of the cinema.

'Anyway, I could see no reason not to oblige the gentleman, so I undid his fly and, with a little help from him, got his dick out and started to caress it. He gave a grunt of satisfaction and put his arm round my shoulders; then with his other hand he started to caress my left breast, inside the dress this time: I was sitting to his left. We were sitting on one of those double seats, without an arm-rest between them, which made things easier for us. We were in the backrow too, so we were not too conspicuous.

' "You are very good at rubbing cocks!" my partner grunted as I continued to masturbate him.

'Then he put his free hand up under my skirt and started to feel my cunt through my panties . . .'

'Wait a minute,' Maurice interrupted his wife's narrative. 'I thought you weren't wearing panties.'

'I'm not wearing any now,' Monique smiled sweetly, 'but I was wearing a pair then. You see, they got a bit wet, what with one thing and another, so I popped them into my handbag,' she explained. 'Anyway, where was I? . . . Oh yes, my friend was feeling me up in the back row of the cinema, wasn't he? Far from resisting, I opened my thighs to make it easier for him. His fingers found their way under the elastic of my knickers and started to explore my most intimate feminine secrets. I gasped as they entered my sex-lips, but I continued to rub his cock.

'On the screen a tall, blond man wearing a lumberjack shirt was passionately kissing a petite, dark-haired girl. Her fingers, with their long scarlet nails caressed the back of his neck.

'A stubby finger, probably quite hairy, was rubbing my clitoris as I rubbed my companion's penis. Suddenly he gave a muffled cry and went rigid in his seat as he came, spurting and spurting. He stopped rubbing me, the animal! My hand was covered with his wet, sticky semen, which smelt very strongly, Then it was over. The man put his now limp dick away, fastened himself up and, giving me a rather sheepish glance, left the cinema. All I'd got to show for the encounter was a sticky, smelly hand and quite a lot of frustration, given the fact that he'd aroused my sexual feelings but in no way come near to satisfying them.'

Monique smiled maliciously at her husband. 'Strange how often that situation arises, isn't it?' she said. 'But perhaps it's not so strange, after all: all you men care about is your own satisfaction. Once you've had your come you don't want to know!'

'Oh, I don't know,' Maurice countered, 'that's a bit sweeping, isn't it?'

Monique thought how boyish he looked sitting there with his erection poking out of his trousers, in spite of his forty years and his receding hair-line. 'Anyway, what happened next?' he said.

'Well, no-one else came and sat by me and I was too restless to take any interest in the film, so I too left the cinema and went into a little café on the other side of the street. It was there that the second man of the afternoon picked me up.

'I was sitting at a table sipping my coffee when a voice said, "Would you mind if I joined you, madame?" A tall, well-dressed young man with dark curly hair and a shy smile stood looking down at me, waiting politely for me to give him permission to sit.

' "Not at all, monsieur," I said, with a friendly smile.

'He sat down, the waiter came over and the young man ordered a black coffee. Then he sat there waiting for his order to arrive and looking distinctly embarrassed. I tried to put the poor fellow at ease. "It's a lovely afternoon, isn't it?" I said. He just nodded his handsome head distractedly. He seemed to have something other than the weather on his mind!

'The waiter brought his coffee and set it down in front of my companion. He didn't attempt to drink it but just sat there staring at me. He had such nice eyes! Dark and gentle.

' "Aren't you going to drink your coffee?" I said softly.

' "Madame . . . madame . . ." he said, seeming to find it difficult to get the words out.

' "Yes, monsieur?" I said encouragingly.

'Then as if he had summoned all he courage, he said, "I was in the cinema: I saw what you did for the man who was sitting next to you!"

'I felt a hot flush of shame mingled with sensuality creep

to my cheeks. I lowered my eyes, incapable of saying anything at that moment.

' "I-I was hoping," the young man went on nervously, "I was hoping that you might be willing to do," he gulped, "to do something for me."

'I felt a warmth beginning to spread between my thighs, but still just kept looking down at the marble table-top, saying nothing.

' "I can pay you well," the young fellow went on in eager tones. "Whatever you ask," he added.

'Money! Here was an unexpected development, although it should have occurred to me that sooner or later someone would take me for a professional. Actually I didn't feel insulted: it added to the eroticism of the situation as far as I was concerned. My cunt felt warm and welcoming: it longed for something hard to fill it!

'I looked at my companion with a new brazen boldness. "It depends on what you want. I don't do rear entries, or any nasty things like that . . ."

'The anxious, nervous expression left the young man's face. "All I want to do is to act out an entirely harmless fantasy with you, madame, that's all." He was speaking with more assurance now. "All I want to do is to fuck you with you wearing a white lace-edged slip − a clean one that you have just put on after you have had a bath."

' "And that's all?" I said. "Nothing more than that?"

'He nodded his head. "That's all, madame, I give you my word."

' "Very well, monsieur," I said, getting up. "Let's go then." '

'Where did you take your "client?" said Maurice, deliberately and salaciously emphasizing the last word.

Monique shifted her position on the dining-room chair. She uncrossed then recrossed her lovely long legs, giving Maurice a flash of cunt as she did so. 'I brought my *client*, as you call him, here,' she said.

'Here? To this house?' her husband said indignantly, but he still kept caressing his prick, which was as rigid as ever, blue-veined and throbbing with its large purple knob.

'Yes,' Monique replied. 'He fucked me in our bedroom, on our bed.'

'Go on,' Maurice groaned. 'Tell me how you defiled our bedroom and our bed.' He was rubbing his cock quite vigorously now; it wouldn't be long before he ejaculated, Monique thought.

'Well,' she said, 'when we arrived, I made him wait in the dining-room, while I went upstairs, quickly got undressed then had a shower. Luckily I happen to possess a white slip with a lace edging, it's the one you gave me for my last birthday. I applied a few drops of that musky perfume, which you always say makes you think of my snatch whenever you smell it, put the slip on, as well as a pair of high-heeled shoes, which the young man had also asked me to wear, then called down to him to come up.

'As I stood there, waiting for my client to join me, I caught sight of my reflection in the long mirror on the dressing-table; I think I can say without undue modesty that I looked very attractive! At that moment I felt so happy that my breasts are so full and so white. My nipples were clearly outlined by the fragile nylon of the slip. My cunt still felt extremely warm and receptive.

'The young man appreciated me too. "You look lovely, madame!" he said as he entered the bedroom. Then he came over to me and timidly started to kiss my neck and shoulders. I sighed with pleasure. It didn't take him long to lose his timidity, however: he soon had my shoulder-straps down and we stood there in front of the dressing-table mirror with him sucking my titties while his right hand went up under the slip to finger my snatch and his other hand fondled my bottom cheeks. I could see our reflected image in the mirror: it was a most erotic sight!

'Then I could wait no longer. "Take your pants off, *chéri*," I said. "Let us fuck!"

'And we did! It was so nice: I lay back on the bed with my thighs widely parted so that he could have a good look at my snatch as he took his trousers off. You have always told me that my cunt is exciting to look at with its neat pale pink lips offset by dark pubic hair. Those lips must have been parted, ready to receive a nice stiff prick.

'When my client took his pants down I wasn't disappointed, for his cock was firmly in the erect position: long and rather tapering, but with quite a small knob. He quickly climbed on to the bed and positioned himself between my thighs. I reached down and guided his knob to my entrance with my fingers. He slid in easily, right up to the hilt. He gave a sigh of pleasure, I wrapped my arms and legs around him and our lips met in a passionate kiss as his arse started the characteristic movements of fucking.

'*Creak, creak, creak* went the bed as we performed our lascivious dance. I worked my snatch in response to his energetic thrusts. Then after a while we changed positions: I climbed on top of my client without uncoupling; then it was the turn of my bottie to bounce up and down. I could feel his hands gripping my buttocks and thought that if a third party had been observing us my asshole would be clearly visible! . . . Small, dark and puckered, and that thought set my juice flowing: I came, shuddering and gasping, and the man under me must have felt the warm gush on his cock. He certainly did for he gave a cry, went rigid and then he came too, jetting his white stuff into my clinging, contracting vagina.'

'Oh! Ah! . . . Oh!' Monique's narrative was abruptly but not unexpectedly interrupted at that point by these sounds made by Maurice as he too came. He vigorously rubbed his cock, sending spurts of semen into the air, face flushed, eyes closed, mouth hanging open. Monique watched her husband, fascinated. Then it was finished: he sank back against the cushions of the sofa, legs apart, his cock already losing its rigidity.

'You've got some of that stuff on your sweater,' Monique said.

Maurice looked down at the white blobs on his cashmere sweater and said, 'Oh damn!' He took a large handkerchief from his trouser pocket and rubbed the stuff off.

'I'll wash it for you tomorrow,' his wife said in a conciliatory tone. She stook up. 'You'd better pull your trousers up: Zabeth might call!'

'Oh damn!' Maurice repeated, but he obediently pulled his pants and trousers up and adjusted himself. Then Monique went over and sat beside her husband on the sofa. She took hold of his hand and looked at him affectionately. 'How was I tonight?' she asked.

Maurice smiled. 'You were excellent,' he said sincerely. He squeezed her hand affectionately, 'I'm very lucky to have a wife who had trained as a professional actress.' He leaned forward and kissed her tenderly on the cheek.

Monique looked at him quizzically. 'What would you do if I really was unfaithful to you?' she demanded.

Her husband was silent for a moment, then he said gravely, 'I don't think I could handle it, my love! I depend on you so much.'

Monique smiled at him tenderly; he'd said just what she liked to hear. 'Well there's no need to −' but she never finished the sentence for at that moment the doorbell of their apartment rang and she got up to go and let Zabeth in.

Sensual Liaisons

Il lui monstra sa femme toute nue . . .

He showed him his wife, who was completely naked.

Brantôme

I

Paris, 31st August, 1952.

Dear Mireille,

Forgive me for not writing sooner, but I was waiting until I had something *interesting* to write about, for I know how much you detest empty small talk. Well, my sweet, patience has been rewarded at last, so sit up and pay attention . . .

It all started a few days ago in the gardens of the Palais Royal. I often go to that delightful place when the weather is fine, for where is one more likely to get into conversation with a pretty lady? Things have not changed much there since the days of Restif de la Bretonne!

As it happened, that particular afternoon I didn't get into conversation with a pretty lady but with a rather severe-looking man who looked as if he might be an ex-army officer. I was sitting on a bench rather surreptitiously watching the antics of a couple of teenagers lying on the grass a few metres away – they were embracing and kissing and laughing – when the aforementioned gentleman, who was sitting next to me, said, 'Disgusting, isn't it?'

'That's a matter of opinion,' I replied. 'I'd prefer to describe it as "naughty but nice." '

'Ah,' he said, 'I see you're a free-thinker!' Yes, my sweet, he actually used that expression, 'a free-thinker.' Quaint, isn't it?

I didn't reply, so he continued, 'To be honest about it, I suppose I agree with you really . . .!

'Well, you're only young once,' I said, 'and they're not doing any harm, are they?'

'No indeed,' the military-looking gentleman agreed, then fell silent.

The young couple continued to kiss and fondle each other, apparently quite oblivious to the presence of other people. A scruffy-looking pigeon with its ridiculous head-jerking walk searched for tit-bits near their feet, apparently quite oblivious to their presence.

'I suppose, in a way, those youngsters are really sharing their pleasure with other people,' my companion said.

'Well, yes,' I agreed, with a laugh, 'it can be quite, er, *stimulating* to watch a good-looking young couple having some fun.'

The man gave me a charming smile, which made him look younger. 'You're absolutely right,' he said. 'In fact, I think *watching* can sometimes be more enjoyable than doing.'

'It's certainly considerably less demanding!' I replied, laughing again. The major (that's how I was beginning to think of him) looked thoughtful.

The young couple were getting up, brushing the grass off their clothes. As we watched them walk away with their arms round each other, the major said, 'Seeing those two reminds me of a very *stimulating* thing that happened to me recently . . . it happened here, in the Palais Royal garden. It was a fine afternoon, just like today, and I was sitting not far from where we are now, reading a paper and enjoying the sunshine, when a young couple came and sat next to me on the same bench. They were a few years older than the youngsters who've just left. The girl was extremely attractive, but her companion looked rather scruffy, and he needed a shave.

'Anyway, they wasted no words but got straight down to serious business, arms round each other, tongues half way

96

down each other's throats, quite unconstrained in spite of my presence! In no time at all the young fellow had his hand inside his girlfriend's blouse and was fondling what looked to me to be a very fine pair of tits.'

They major give me a diffident smile 'I'd like to be completely frank,' he said, 'but I shouldn't like to shock you.'

'I'm not very shockable,' I replied encouragingly.

'Well,' he said, 'watching those two young people carrying on like that had a powerful effect on me: in fact, to put it bluntly, it gave me a hard-on! . . . There, I've said it! . . . I hope I haven't offended you.'

'No, not at all,' I said . . . 'What happened next?'

Reassured by the absence of disapproval in my manner, the major continued:

'Well, after a few more minutes of necking, during which I pretended to be reading my paper, the young man muttered something to the girl, then got up and went off to the gentleman's toilet, which was not far away.

'Out of the corner of my eye, I saw the young woman take a comb and mirror from her handbag and start to comb her hair, peering at her pretty face in the glass as she did so.

' "It is very nice day, isn't it?" she remarked. From her accent I judged her to be German, or perhaps Austrian.

' "Yes, indeed, mademoiselle," I said, laying my paper aside and turning to look at her. She smiled at me with her mouth but not with her eyes, which were pale blue, slightly protuberant.

'The young woman put the comb and mirror back in the handbag. I could smell her perfume, and another odour — that of a young female animal ready for sex — mingled with it. My prick was still stiff!

' "I suppose you do not like what Carl and I do just now," she said. Her smile had disappeared: her face wore a serious expression.

' "I didn't mind at all," I said firmly. "It's nice to see young people enjoying themselves! . . . I may no longer be young," I added, "but I'm no prude."

' "Prude?" she said, looking puzzled. "Please, what is that?"

' "It means someone who's against sex," I explained, "and I'm certainly not against it!"

'The young woman nodded her head thoughtfully to show that she understood, but made no comment. It seemed to me that Carl was taking a long time in the gents.

'Suddenly the fraulein's voice broke in on my thoughts: "You like to *watch* people when they make love together?" she asked in a suggestively sexy tone of voice, which made me think of her dear hairy little crack nestling against her panty-crotch. My cock had never been stiffer. I nodded my head and managed to say that nothing could please me more.

'Then she came straight out with what had undoubtedly been on her mind since the beginning of the conversation and asked me if I would like to watch her doing it with Carl. The young woman had moved closer to me; her perfume, together with that other excitingly intimate odour, assailed my nostrils more strongly.

'"How much will it cost me?" I demanded bluntly.

'She flushed up a bit and I wondered if she was offended, but all she said was, "I should not like you to think that I am often doing this: I am not a bad girl!"

'I did my best to reassure the pretty fraulein, and then she went on to tell me some rigmarole about how she and Carl had had a terrible run of bad luck and were in desperate need of money, and so on. Anyway, to cut a long story short, we eventually agreed upon a price which did not seem to me to be exorbitant, then there arose the question of where the exhibition would take place. For obvious reasons I was not keen on the idea of taking them to my apartment, so we agreed that she should take me to their place.

'As we got up to leave, Carl came sauntering across the grass towards us, hands buried deeply in the pockets of his threadbare cords. He must have been watching us, waiting for an appropriate moment to appear.

'The young woman told him about our arrangement and he nodded his head in assent. I gave them half the agreed sum as an advance payment, the other half to be paid afterwards, then off we went to their place.

'It took us about ten or twelve minutes to walk there. The fair-haired fraulein trotted along on her high heels between us, arms linked in ours. She told me that they both came from Vienna and that her name was Helga. The young man said very little, only replying in monosyllabic grunts when she addressed him directly. I thought that he probably didn't speak French very well.

'They had a room on the third floor of a modest but pleasant hotel in a quiet side street. The room itself was small, but clean and furnished comfortably.

'The young couple wasted no time but undressed as soon as we arrived. Helga's body was of the kind which has always appealed to me — very plump, very white, extremely reminiscent of those nude beauties painted by Reubens or Titian, I forget which. Her tits were simply gorgeous, bouncing and wobbling every time she moved. How I should have loved to fondle them, feel the big dark nipples pressing against the palms of my hands, put my cock between them! But I was there to watch, not to take part: that was the agreement.

'Carl looked better without his shabby clothes. His body was lean, covered with dark hair, and his prick, even in repose, appeared quite formidable.

'They stood together by the bed for a few moments embracing and kissing with open mouths, then Helga looked across at me and said, "Let us show the gentleman how you make me come, darling."

'Then the young woman lay down on the bed and opened her thighs wide, displaying a cunt which was in no way inferior to her other charms. The light pubic down covering it did not conceal the delicate pink lips which pouted slightly, like a little girl's mouth.

'Carl came and stood near where her head reposed on the pillow. His cock was beginning to jut out aggressively. "Suck me a bit first," he commanded, speaking in German (a language of which, by the way, I have some knowledge).

99

'His companion obediently raised herself up on one elbow, opening her full lips to receive the penis which he fed into her mouth. My own penis, which had been in repose for a while, had now grown stiff again. How I should have loved to fuck that warm, receptive mouth! For that is what Carl was doing: he was moving his organ in and out as if he was fucking a cunt. But suddenly Helga retched and pushed her lover away.

' "You'll choke me!" she gasped in German. The young man muttered something inaudible, then she said, "Make me come now!"'

'She moved over to make room for him and he climbed on to the bed beside her. His cock had now attained an impressive size, sticking out like a lance of flesh from between his hairy thighs. It glistened with Helga's saliva.

'Kneeling beside the pretty *fraulein*, Carl bent down and started to kiss her midriff, gradually moving down to the soft warm flesh of her belly. As he was doing that he put his right hand between her thighs and began to play with her twat. (Forgive me for the crudity.) Then after a while, he began to lick Helga's belly, at the same time rubbing her clitoris. The *fraulein* twisted and writhed with pleasure.

' *"Ach! Ich commen!"* she moaned ecstatically as her belly contracted in the throes of orgasm, and Carl's fingers were inundated with hot gushes of female love-juice. Then in one fluid movement, without giving the girl time to recover, the young man lay down on his back, at the same time pulling her on top of him and impaling her on his still upstanding lance. It slid easily into the well-oiled passage, disappearing right up to the hilt.

'All this time I had been standing to one side watching but now, impelled by a sudden irresistible impulse, I quickly stripped off my clothes, letting them fall in an untidy heap on the floor. My own cock jutted out satisfactorily from the base of my belly but, I must admit, was not so impressive as Carl's.

'I moved over close to the bed, which was creaking

obscenely in time with the young people's fucking. Helga's ample bottom moved rapidly up and down, while her companion's hands grasped the soft white cheeks, holding them apart so that the secret eye of the anus was displayed for my delectation. As I gazed down at that scene, I began to masturbate vigorously, anxious to obtain relief. Helga's fair hair was dishevelled. I could hear her panting and smell her strong female odour. Carl grunted and groaned beneath the young fraulein.

'Then suddenly his hands tightened their grip on those lovely buttocks. "Oh!" he gasped as his semen spurted into that hot sweet love-hole, and at that moment I climaxed too, spraying my seed all over the lady's seductively wriggling arse . . .'

The major paused, a far-away look in his eyes. He seemed to have forgotten my presence altogether.

'Yes? . . . And then what happened?' I prompted.

He looked at me as if he was surprised to see me still sitting there beside him.

'Well what do you think happened?' he said irritably. 'We all got dressed, I paid them the rest of the money, and then I went home.'

'Have you seen them again?'

'No,' he replied shortly, then forestalled any more questions by looking at his watch and exclaiming, 'Good heavens! Is that the time? I must go!'

However, before he left he wrote his name and address down on a piece of paper and gave it to me, then he invited me to visit him the next day *at seven o'clock in the morning*, if you've ever heard of such a thing!

The major smiled at my look of astonishment; he said, 'If you enjoy seeing pretty women in *stimulating* situations, you'd be well-advised to turn up!' Then he stood up, shook hands with me and went off, leaving me to ponder the meaning of his strange words.

But I shall have to bring this letter to a close if it is to catch the post. The rest of the story will be contained in my next letter. This one has turned out to be much longer than

I had originally intended and I only hope that reading it has not unduly taxed your patience, dear girl. Please write soon,

All my love,
Victor.

II

Guildford, Surrey,
England,
3/9/52.

Dear Victor,

It's not so much my patience you have taxed with your never-ending letter, as my credulity. Our agreement was that we should seek to divert each other with our *real-life* erotic experiences, not recount our fantasies! The only elements of reality in your story are 'the major' and the Palais Royal garden. The rest is pure fantasy. However, choosing the cloistered atmosphere of such a place as the setting for such a tale contains an element of blasphemy which could hardly fail to please me.

Let me say that I have nothing against the idea of recounting our sexual fantasies and, judged purely and simply as a story, your long anecdote isn't bad, but I am cross with you for trying to pass it off as fact. You have sinned against the golden rule of friendship, that friends should always be honest with each other; you have also broken our agreement. Consider yourself admonished!

Nothing much ever does happen in this sleepy country town (or *county* town, as the English call it). After six months of marriage my relationship with Jamie is rapidly losing whatever sparkle it may have had. We do it once a week and, let me tell you, doing it with him is about as inspiring as being fucked by a steam-driven piston-rod, and about as subtle. Still, I suppose I shouldn't begrudge him his weekly spoonful of pleasure, boring as it may be for me: it is a small price to pay for freedom from the drudgery of earning a living and, besides, I do so enjoy spending Jamie's money!

But I may soon have something piquant to tell you as regards my erotic life: an interesting development is taking place, the first since my arrival in Guildford. I have made the acquaintance of a young man named John Dancie: we got into conversation yesterday over morning coffee in Ye Olde Tudor Tea Rooms. He's very handsome, dresses elegantly, is rather shy and is studying for an engineering degree at London University. He is living here with an elderly aunt at the moment, until the new term starts in a few week's time, which will give me ample time to initiate him into the pleasures of fucking, for something tells me that the poor lad is still a virgin. Anyway, I have invited him to come and take tea with me tomorrow and I shall, of course, let you know what happens.

I can't tell you how much I miss Paris! Guildford is a pleasant enough little town, and the countryside here is very pretty too; London is not far away either, but none of these places can begin to equal Paris in my estimation. I miss you too, you swine! Just thinking about that lovely long thing of yours makes me go all wet, and weak at the knees. Yet, for the moment, I have nothing but my fingers to console me.

So, my love, please don't keep me waiting so long this time before you write, even if you have nothing but fictions to recount to me!

Love and kisses,
Mireille.

III

Paris, 7th September, 1952.

Dearest Mireille,

I miss you too, darling! You are quite irreplaceable, for no woman understands the art of fucking as you do. I have never entered a deeper, wetter, more welcoming vagina, or one which wriggles more delightfully in response to my

103

thrusts; neither do I know a woman who is a more pleasing companion. If anyone could shake my resolve never to get married, it is you. Why did we allow circumstances to part us?

Forgive me for the nonsense about 'the major', I never really intended you to think of it as a true story: I thought you would laugh at the mystification and, perhaps, be just a little titillated too. Anyway, it was by no means entirely entirely fabricated: the young couple really were there necking in the Palais Royal garden, and I *did* get into conversation with a rather military-looking gentleman who I think of as 'the major.' What's more, he *did* invite me to visit him not later than seven o'clock on the morning of the next day.

His real name is Gilles Mouron and he lives in an apartment on the second floor of a rambling old house in a little street not far from the Luxembourg Gardens. It took me some time to make up my mind to visit him because I was afraid that he might make advances to *me*. But, on the other hand, nothing he'd said had given me the slightest reason to think that he might be a homosexual: quite the contrary, in fact.

So the next morning found me standing before the door of his apartment. It was a few minutes to seven by my watch. A small white oblong of cardboard affixed to the door bore the inscription, 'Monsieur et Madame Mouron.' The 'madame' allayed any lingering fears I might have had; I rang the bell.

My new friend opened the door almost immediately and smiled when he saw me standing there. 'Do come in, my dear fellow,' he said, standing back to allow me to enter. 'I'm so glad you decided to come!' He shook me warmly by the hand.

Monsieur Mouron did not look nearly as spruce as he had the previous day: he had obviously not been up long and was wearing a rather threadbare brown dressing-gown over striped pyjamas. On his bare feet he wore slippers which matched the dressing-gown, both in colour and in their worn appearance. I was too keyed-up to notice much about the room in which we found ourselves, except that it was spacious, well-furnished and had big windows from which one could see the houses on the other side of the street.

'I must ask you to be as quiet as possible, monsieur,' said Mouron, looking at me earnestly. I nodded my head in acquiescence and he said, 'Come this way, please.'

Then he led me across the spacious living-room, through a doorway and into what appeared to be a lumber-room. Boxes were piled on top of each other, a rolled-up carpet stood in one corner and there were quite large piles of books and magazines stacked up on the floor. It was very much smaller than the room we had just left.

Mouron closed the door softly behind us then went over to a picture hanging on the wall: it was a reproduction of a classic painting showing a beautiful nude woman reclining on a divan. He reached up and, gripping the gilt frame with both hands, removed the picture revealing what at first I took to be a mirror concealed there. I moved closer then realised that it was not a mirror but a small window from which one had a clear view of the adjoining room, which was in fact a bedroom, and on the large double bed a woman lay sleeping.

'This is a two-way mirror,' explained Mouron, who had put the picture down and come to stand beside me. 'We can see her, but she won't be able to see us,' he added somewhat superfluously.

'And, of course, the sleeping beauty must be Madame Mouron,' I said, keeping my voice down.

'Of course,' he replied. 'What do you think of her?'

'She's very attractive,' and I was speaking nothing but the truth.

The woman lay on her right side with her back towards us. It had been a hot night so she had thrown off the bedclothes, and she was not wearing a nightdress. I gazed with voyeuristic pleasure upon her naked charms: the smooth white back; two swelling buttocks divided by a deep furrow; legs which were long and slender, terminating in dainty little feet. (I remembered that Restif de la Bretonne believed that if a woman's feet are tiny, it is a sign that she has a big love-hole.) But why did I have such a disturbing feeling of *déjà vu* as I stood there gazing at Moron's wife through the trick mirror?

Then my attention was drawn to a particularly piquant detail: the lady's underthings were neatly folded on a chair near the bed, but an adorable little pair of pale blue panties had fallen on to the floor. The thought came to me that she had been wearing them only a few hours ago and that they would still be impregnated with the odour of her hairy treasure. How I would have loved to sniff the spot where it had nestled. My prick began to grow stiff.

'My wife always sleeps naked these hot nights,' said Mouron softly. 'She's got a lovely arse, hasn't she?' I couldn't help but agree.

Then suddenly the woman on the bed stirred, stretched and rolled over on to her back, revealing charms which had hitherto been concealed from us: breasts − slightly flattened by that supine position − crowned with reddish-brown nipples, a belly terminating in a mound of Venus covered with dark pubic hair and, below that, thighs which were smooth, white and round, and slightly parted. Madame Mouron must have been having a voluptuous dream, for a smile played upon her lips; further-more, her nipples were stiff. She had short auburn hair; the face was pretty but slightly marred by an air of vulgarity. Her outflung arms revealed tufts of hair under the armpits. Morning sunshine pouring in through the open window enhanced Madame Mouron's attractiveness, making her appear almost ethereally beautiful.

Then her lips moved: she was murmuring something inaudible to us; then her right hand moved down between those lovely thighs and she started to finger her cunt.

'What a dirty little girl!' the man standing beside me murmured. I made no reply, being much too intent upon watching the lubricious scene taking place next door. At that moment, I would have liked nothing more than to join his wife on that bed and to have given her a vigorous fucking. And I might have been tempted to try but for the presence of my host.

Madame Mouron spread her thighs wider apart as she continued to finger her hairy slit. It must have been getting very gooey and squelchy and a strong odour of cunt must have been impregnating the air in that bedroom. We stood there in complete silence — two voyeurs watching a naked female playing with herself . . . my prick was so stiff that it was beginning to ache. The woman's hand moved faster and faster: she was concentrating on the clitoris now . . .

'I think she's going to come,' breathed Mouron after a while.

He was right, for soon after he had said those words his wife reached her climax, writhing, twisting, gasping and no doubt drenching her slender fingers with hot liquid . . . goodness, what a storm of passionate release! It seemed to me as if she was about to die. But then at last it was over: she sank back on to the bed exhausted, breasts heaving, eyes closed, mouth sagging open.

I should have liked to hang around a bit longer, to spend a little more time contemplating that lovely naked body, but Mouron tugged my arm. 'Come on,' he said, 'she'll be getting up in a minute.'

Regretfully I followed him out of the little room and allowed him to usher me to the front door. He was obviously most anxious that his wife should not discover my presence. As I left he said that he went to the Palais Royal garden most afternoons, weather permitting, and he hoped to see me there before long. Then he closed the door, leaving me standing there alone in the corridor.

I was in such a state of arousal that there was only one thing for it — I should have to visit Marie! She would service me with her usual expertise. I ran lightheartedly downstairs and out into the street, where I'd parked the car.

It didn't take me long to get home, in spite of its being the rush hour, because I knew a route which enabled me to avoid the worst of the traffic. In fact I was there by eight fifteen, having left Mouron's place at about twenty to.

You don't know Marie Ruisseau do you, dear heart? She came into my life after your departure. She used to be a prostitute but is now a respectable married woman, having married one of her clients. The couple live in the apartment below mine. Well, the term 'respectable' is rather relative since I have an arrangement with the lady whereby, in return for a modest fee, she sucks me off whenever I feel the need for such a service, which is usually about once a week.

If anyone doubts that Parisian whores are the best fellatrices in the world, he should visit Marie. I have never known any woman who can drain a man dry with greater expertise.

Anyway, I knew that her husband would be at work by that time — he works in the administrative offices of the SNCF, I believe — so I went and paid her a visit. When Marie opened the door and saw me standing there at such a relatively early hour, she looked somewhat surprised but, nevertheless, smiled and asked me in. She led me into their tastefully furnished living-room.

'Sorry to barge in on you like this,' I said. 'I hope I'm not disturbing you.'

Marie smiled again: she has a particularly charming smile, both sexy and friendly, which transforms her normally rather plain features, making her appear almost beautiful. 'You want the usual, I suppose?' she said.

I nodded affirmatively.

'Alright, *chéri*,' she said. 'I'll go and get ready.' Then she disappeared through a door which I knew led to the bedroom.

While I was waiting, I took all my clothes off, for it always seems to me that it is best to be completely naked when one is about to be sucked off. I stood there in Adam's costume, in the centre of the little living-room, facing the bedroom door. My dick was not in full erection, but the knob was swollen, plum-coloured. My balls were full to bursting.

Then the door opened and Marie reappeared looking absolutely gorgeous. She had brushed her short blonde curls, applied plenty of make-up and she too was naked, except for her gold pendant earrings and extremely high-heeled shoes whose bright red colour matched her lipsticked mouth and nipples. Marie is a very conscientious whore: when she sucks a man off she likes to look the part.

My dick was now fully rampant and throbbing between my hairy thighs. Marie looked at it with professional interest.

'My, my,' she murmured in a low sexy voice, 'that's a lovely big cock you've got there for me!'

She came across to me, big breasts bobbing, hips swaying sensuously, and pressed her warm naked body against mine; her hand went down to cup my balls. I put my arms around the young woman and our lips met in a long kiss. A smell of perfume and female came to my nostrils. Marie's cool fingers began stroking my stalk.

'No!' I exclaimed, pushing her hand away. 'You'll make me come!'

'I thought that's what you wanted,' she replied, looking up at me with a mischievous twinkle in her blue eyes.

'Not like that,' I said, fondling one of her rather over-ripe tits. 'I want to come in your mouth, darling.'

'Well then, we'd better see what we can do, hadn't we, *chéri*?'

Then the ex-prostitute bent forward, took hold of my cock near the base and slipped the swollen knob into her mouth. Words are inadequate to describe the sweet sensations I experienced in that warm wet sucking grotto of delight. Years of taking cocks of all shapes and sizes into her mouth have conferred an unsurpassable expertise upon Marie in that domain: she is a first-class cocksucker.

We must have offered a stimulating spectacle, if anyone had been able to see us − a tall, hairy, naked man standing in the middle of a respectable bourgeois living-room while a whore, equally naked, bent forward from the waist sucking him off.

As I gazed down at Marie's bobbing head, I reached out and put my hand between her thighs; she opened them a bit wider to accommodate me. As my fingers came into contact with that gooey, hairy twat I thought about all the other fingers which must have played with it, all the rigid members which had reamed it and suddenly the expression 'a well-fucked whore' came into my mind.

Nothing more was needed to precipitate me into the abyss of an orgasm. Marie, realising that I was about to spurt, made use of all her perverse expertise to bring me off satisfactorily: she inserted a finger into my asshole and, at the same time, the dear little slut masturbated me vigorously with her mouth.

Then nothing could hold me back. I came and came and came, spunking furiously into that sucking mouth and Marie swallowed every drop of the viscous stuff: she drained me dry.

Such a shattering orgasm left me feeling decidedly weak at the knees and the young woman made me sit down on the settee and insisted upon making me a cup of coffee before I left. She really is a very nice person, a lot more sympathetic than many of the more 'respectable' women I know. You may be sure that I gave her more money than usual that morning in recognition of such excellent servicing.

But that is enough — more than enough! — about me, my dear. I was intrigued to learn of your meeting with John Dancie and look forward eagerly to hearing what happened at your little tea-party . . . how I envy him! He is a very lucky young man to have a woman like you to introduce him to the pleasures of sensual love. I only hope that he will make you as happy as you deserve to be, lovely creature. May you forget the tedium of life in dreary old England — at least for a time — in his arms. However, I fear that he will find other women extremely uninspiring after having been your lover. That has certainly been my experience anyway.

But the time has come for me to bid you farewell for the present, my beloved. I'm going straight out to post this letter now so that, with a bit of luck, you will receive it within twenty-four hours.

> A thousand kisses, on every part
> of your lovely body,
> Victor.

IV

> Guildford, Surrey,
> England.
> 10/9/52.

Dearest Victor,

Flattery will get you everywhere! And who could fail to be flattered by the charming compliments in your penultimate paragraph? For my part I can only say that I have never found any man with whom I have felt such a close bond of sympathy as with you. The rest seem to me to be, to quote Jaques Vaché,* 'a fine collection of marionettes!'

As for the second instalment of your 'serial', it's not bad but two things marred my enjoyment of it: the first was the coarseness of the language, the second your attitude towards poor Marie.

I'm very far from being a prude, as you know, Victor; and I'm certainly not objecting to your use of crude words for moral reasons, but rather on aesthetic grounds. In my opinion, such expressions diminish the effectiveness of erotic writing since they lack subtlety, and without subtlety there is no genuine eroticism. A woman's charms partially concealed by semi-transparent gauze are always much more tantalizing than blatant nudity. An erotic writer should use language like that gauze, to arouse the reader by making him use his imagination.

*An eccentric young man whose letters to André Breton during World War I reveal him to have been a profoundly original thinker. He committed suicide in 1919.

As for the episode with Marie, frankly I found it distressing because of the way in which you denigrate the unfortunate woman. To describe someone who is doing her level best to give you pleasure as a 'whore' and, even worse, as a 'cocksucker' reveals a nauseatingly bourgeois attitude towards a class of women who deserve our sympathy rather than our contempt. How do you reconcile such an attitude with your professed left-wing views, Victor? I know that you are not really a cruel or heartless man, but your letter has revealed a side to your character which I find deeply disturbing . . .

As regards John Dancie, he is proving to be more delightful every time I meet him. He is such a mixture of timidity, impetuousness and intense desire that just thinking about him makes the thorn in my pale pink rose grow sharper. (An unsubtle metaphor but picturesque, isn't it?)

You will no doubt recall that the Marquise de Merteuil* prided herself upon her ability to become a whole seraglio of seductively different women for her lovers. Well, my dear, that is what I intend to be with young Dancie: every time we meet he will have the impression of being with a different woman. I shall make him fall madly in love with me.

The process of seduction started on the fourth, when my aspiring lover came to tea. I played the role of a respectable yet discreetly voluptuous housewife to perfection . . . I wore a simple black dress with a plain white collar and red belt, a combination which goes well with my dark hair and rather pale complexion. I applied only a hint of perfume and very little make-up but, on the other hand, my stockings were sheer, positively arachnean in fact, and my shoes had very high heels.

As it was a fine afternoon we had our tea in the garden. I encouraged Dancie to talk, to confide in me, and listened to him with flatteringly close attention, all the while making sure that my skirt rode quite high, revealing as much of my thighs as was consistent with the role of a hitherto chaste

*The beautiful but totally unscrupulous female protagonist of Dangerous Liaisons, the famous novel by Chodleros de Laclos, first published in 1782.

wife on the verge of succumbing to a young man's irresistible charm.

John Dancie is far from being a brilliant conversationalist. He is not well-versed in literature or the arts, but nevertheless he is intelligent and sensitive and has very expressive eyes: while we talked about commonplaces, *they* spoke to me of much more intimate things: the pleasure of watching my slender white fingers, with their tapering scarlet nails, as I poured his tea, or the silky sound of my nylon-clad thighs as I crossed one leg over the other, or the sight of my tiny feet tightly encased in their high-heeled shoes.

A pretty garden on a lovely afternoon forms a setting which is ideal for the opening scene of a comedy of seduction. The sun shone, the grass couldn't have been greener or the flowers prettier, the birds were singing amorously and before he went home my young admirer was head over heels in love with me, convinced that he had found his soul-mate. Ah, the sweet illusions of youth!

But naturally I did not permit any significant physical intimacy to take place during that first *tête-à-tête*: it wouldn't have suited the role I was playing. Besides, a man never values what he obtains too easily! I allowed him to kiss me, that's all.

It happened just as he was leaving: I had walked with him as far as the front gate and I engineered things in such a way that he had the impression that he'd taken a tremendous liberty and that I had succumbed to his over-whelming charm against my better judgement. It was an extremely arousing kiss. He held me very close and I could feel his virile force pressing against my belly. Our mouths opened; for a divine moment our tongues intertwined. Then I broke away protesting, but not too vehemently, of course. He apologised profusely, red-faced with confusion and lust. Naturally I forgave him; in fact, I invited him to come to dinner the following day.

'It will give you an opportunity to meet my husband,' I said maliciously. His face fell comically, but he said he would be delighted to come.

113

After Dancie had gone, I went upstairs to wash and change: it was necessary, for my panties were quite wet with all the excitement. Furthermore, frankness compels me to admit that when I stepped out of the dainty undergarment a perverse temptation assailed me, a temptation impossible to resist. So, to my shame, I took off my dress, lay down on the bed — then did to myself what your Madame Mouron did. Wasn't I a naughty girl!

When Madame de Merteuil was expecting a lover, she would read erotic books to get herself into appropriate mood. In this respect too I follow in the footsteps of my illustrious predecessor.

I possess a little volume which I bought in Paris last year. Its title is *Rosalie et sa bonne*,* and it recounts the sexual experiences of a young woman in the service of a courtesan. This novel is not at all badly written and admirably demonstrates the point I made earlier that one can create an erotic atmosphere without resorting to the language of the gutter. That is why I am enclosing an extract with this letter. Read it, dear heart, and let me know what you think of it.

Anyway, I spent the afternoon preceding my rendezvous with Dancie comfortably ensconced in a deck-chair in the garden with my copy of *Rosalie et sa bonne*. The book not only got me into the appropriate mood (with a little help from my fingers) but it also gave me some inspiration for the second phase of my campaign of seduction.

What form that inspiration took and what happened that evening I shall tell you about in my next letter, my sweet. This one has gone on quite long enough, for I still have the extract from *Rosalie et sa bonne* to type. I hope you appreciate all the trouble I am putting myself to on your behalf.

Love and kisses,
Mireille.

*'Rosalie and Her Maid.'

Rosalie and Her Maid (Extract).
(Typed by Mireille Digby-Haines on her husband's battered Remington on the 10th September, 1952).

After she had shown the gentleman out, Brigitte returned to the bedroom. Her mistress was sitting in front of the dressing-table mirror brushing her long golden hair. The young woman's features wore a petulant expression.

'Men!' she exclaimed as Brigitte began to move about the room picking up fallen garments.

'The gentleman did not please madame?' Brigitte enquired solicitously.

'That's putting it mildly,' Rosalie sighed setting the hairbrush down and swinging round on the stool to face the maid.

'No *man* has ever been able to satisfy me properly,' she murmured looking meaningfully at Brigitte.

The latter was holding a pair of Rosalie's knickers, which she had just picked up off the floor. Now, returning her mistress's gaze, she raised the dainty silken garment and pressed it to her lips and nose, inhaling the intimate female odour which emanated from it.

'My goodness! What a dirty little girl you are!' Rosalie exclaimed, but her tone was far from severe.

She stood up and removed the flimsy black silk negligee she was wearing. Brigitte, now clutching the knickers against her bosom, gazed in admiration at the young woman's naked charms.

'Madame is so beautiful!' she sighed.

She particularly liked the small round tip-tilted breasts, the curve of the belly and the rounded smoothness of the thighs, but what she positively adored was the sex: it made her think of a little girl's sex, for it had been depilated, rendered totally devoid of pubic hair! One could clearly see the pale pink love-lips, which were slightly pouting. As she gazed at the object of her lust, Brigitte felt a sensual warmth spreading between her thighs.

But Rosalie's voice broke in upon the girl's reverie. 'Go

and put those things in the dirty-linen basket, then bring me my pot,' she commanded, but the gentle tone softened the authoritativeness of the words. Brigitte hastened to obey and returned shortly carrying a large china chamber-pot of the kind which our grandparents used to keep under their beds. It was attractively decorated with a flower pattern and inside, at the bottom of the pot, the words *Donnez-moi à boire** were inscribed. (They had a ribald sense of humour in those days!)

The girl set the receptacle on the carpet at her mistress's feet, then stood there waiting while the courtesan squatted down on it, for she had been through this ritual many times and knew how it must end.

The tinkling sound of golden liquid gushing forth filled the room. It seemed to Brigitte that there could not be a prettier sight in the world than that of her naked mistress doing tinkle bells! She felt both moved and honoured, for she knew that no-one else was ever permitted to share such intimate moments, not even the wealthiest of Rosalie's lovers.

'My goodness, that's a relief!' the young woman sighed as she got up.

Brigitte picked the pot up and went into the bathroom where she emptied its contents into the lavatory then pulled the chain. When she returned, her mistress, still nude, was reclining on the bed, thighs spread immodestly apart blatantly displaying the vertical slit of her sex.

'Take your dress off, darling,' said Rosalie, in a voice made languid by desire. 'I want you to suck me.'

The girl complied immediately, anxious to please the woman she loved. She quickly slipped out of the maid's uniform revealing herself to be naked, apart from a suspender-belt, extremely sheer black stockings and red high-heeled shoes. Brigitte's body was slender, white, almost boyish with its tiny breasts and tight buttocks, but the very prominent elongated nipples which crowned those breasts betrayed the girl's essential femininity. She was a green-eyed brunette with a bush of wiry pubic hair between her thighs.

*Give me something to drink.

'Come to me, my love,' Rosalie murmured plaintively. 'I need you!'

Obediently Brigitte climbed on to the bed, heart beating rapidly with excitement. She lowered her head between those open thighs and began by lovingly kissing the flesh on the inside of them, near the sex.

'That's lovely!' the courtesan said in a dreamy voice. 'Now kiss my pussy!'

As the girl pressed her lips to those other lips, which were so incredibly soft, she could smell a faint odour of urine mingling with a deeper feminine odour. Then using her fingers she gently separated the labia and started to lick the pale pink inner corolla: it tasted salty.

'Oh, that's wonderful!' sighed Rosalie ecstatically.

Brigitte loved these moments of intimacy; they made all the other dreary hours of servitude seem worthwhile; but she hated the men who visited Rosalie every day, defiling that lovely body with their long stiff things; yet nevertheless she realised that they stoked up the flames of the courtesan's desire, increasing her dependence upon Brigitte.

She was panting and gasping now as the maid servilely licked her gaping sex, concentrating especially on the clitoris . . . but suddenly she pushed the girl away, then rolled over on to her stomach saying, in a falsely coy voice, 'Now see to my little botty, darling!'

'Little' was not the word Brigitte would have used to describe her mistress's bottom. She thought of it rather as two large pale pink blancmanges, which quivered delightfully with every movement Rosalie made. No wonder the courtesan's lovers were all crazy about it!

Now the girl leaned forward, placing her hands upon the other woman's hips, and began to kiss the twin hillocks. She continued like that for a few moments, covering them with wet warm kisses while her mistress moaned softly with pleasure. Then a plaintive, falsely coy voice came from the prostrate form saying, 'Aren't you going to put your tongue up my button-hole, dearest?'

When she heard those words, Brigitte felt herself almost

117

overwhelmed by a delight not untinged with awe. This was the supreme privilege, to be allowed to pay homage in the sanctum of sanctums! Reverently, the maid separated the two mounds of flesh revealing the aperture, crinkled and reddish-brown, staring up at her like a tiny eye. Then she bent down and started to lick it with an agile pink tongue.

'Ooh! What a naughty little slut you are!' Rosalie's voice quavered in delirium. 'You'll make me come if you do *that*, you naughty girl!'

But she didn't come then: it was never an easy task for Brigitte to bring the young woman to a climax. After a few more moments of savouring the perverse delight of that probing tongue, Rosalie rolled over on to her back again and the girl had to suck her clitoris until, shuddering and gasping, she came and filled Brigitte's mouth with a warm, bitter-tasting liquid . . .

V

Paris,Tuesday, 16/9/52.

Dearest Lady,

Let me begin by saying that I am partially in agreement with your remarks concerning the use of obscene words in erotic writing: if such words are used unimaginatively they can indeed become boring and deadeningly monotonous. However, to maintain as you do that coarse expressions always have an anti-erotic effect is going too far and is a distinctively female prejudice. Most men would disagree with you about this, I feel sure. It seems to me that there is room for different ways of writing about sexual experience; the sole criterion should surely be how imaginatively it is done.

As to your objection regarding my 'denigration' of Marie, you of all people should know that one can no more be held accountable for what one says in moments of sexual delirium than for one's behaviour during the course of a dream.

118

There are all kinds of anti-social ideas floating around in a person's subconscious mind which are apt to surface at such moments, but they by no means necessarily represent that person's conscious attitudes. In fact, I like and respect Marie as a person; if you will look at my letter again you will see that my concluding remarks about her are quite kind. Although our relationship is a commercial one I don't think any the less of her for that, any more than if she were a florist, for example, and I bought flowers in her shop.

However, if my choice of words upset you, I am truly sorry, Mireille. Our friendship is of the greatest value to me and I would not intentionally do or say any-thing which might jeopardise it. In future I shall try to express myself more moderately and to use obscene words more sparingly.

But now, to return to Monsieur Mouron, it gives me the greatest pleasure to be able to tell you that his wife is now my mistress. Yes, dear girl, I have had her, and a delightful experience it was too. She is a woman who is truly passionate, a woman who responds with ardour to a rampant male's thrusts.

It came about like this: I returned to the Palais Royal garden that same afternoon and found Mouron sitting in the same place feeding the pigeons. They took off in a flurry of grey feathers as I approached. I sat down on the bench beside him.

'Why do you do it?' I demanded.

'What, feed the pigeons?' he replied, falsely innocent.

'No,' I said, 'Exhibit your wife to complete strangers.'

'Do I detect a note of moral disapproval?' Mouron smiled with a touch of irony.

'Nothing could be farther from my mind,' I replied. 'I'm just curious, that's all.'

He said nothing for a moment or two and then politely but firmly made it clear that he had no intention of satisfying my curiosity. Explanations were banal, disappointing things in his opinion. 'Anyway,' he said, 'you probably wouldn't understand: how could you, when I don't fully understand the situation myself?'

Mouron distributed the last of the breadcrumbs to the birds, who had returned while we were talking. 'Words are often such misleading things, don't you agree?' he added, looking at me with a hint of mockery in his eyes.

The last thing I felt like at that moment was a philosophical discussion. I hinted that I should like to visit his apartment and see the delectable Madame Mouron again, or even meet her perhaps, but my companion did not respond and left shortly afterwards, saying that he had some business to transact.

As he walked away towards the entrance, a trim slim little figure in his smart blue tweed jacket, I felt a flush of resentment towards him . . . what the hell was his game? What had his purpose been in inviting me to his place anyway? I hate unsolved mysteries, even though there is some truth in what he'd said about the banality of explanations. I'd felt certain that he would invite me to his apartment again, and that perhaps I might even get to fuck his wife! A terrible sense of disappointment rose up like a big black cloud in my mind, spoiling that lovely sunny afternoon for me. I left the little public garden feeling very sorry for myself.

When one is in that kind of mood things are bound to go wrong: a thousand petty vexations come to torment one like a swarm of piranha fish. I tried to amuse myself for the rest of the day, to distract my mind from thinking about the Mourons, but without much success. I visited a little cinema in Pigalle and saw a so-called sex film, which was about as erotic as a brick wall. Then I went to a restaurant where, if anything, the food was even more disappointing than the film. In fact that word 'disappointing' sums up the whole of the second half of the day. I returned home feeling even sorrier for myself.

It took me a long time to get to sleep that night and when sleep did eventually come it was disturbed by dreams, mostly of an erotic nature. One of them was particularly striking and I have written it down for you, but on a separate sheet of paper which I am enclosing as a kind of appendix to this letter.

120

I woke up at five o'clock the following morning with an erection like a rampant bull, the dream still vivid in my mind. I tossed and turned for ages, vainly trying to get back to sleep. The memory of Mouron's wife lying naked on her bed haunted me. My penis was so stiff that it ached.

By six o'clock I'd had enough. I got up, went downstairs and made myself some coffee. As I sat in the kitchen sipping the hot dark liquid, nibbling some toast, I made up my mind to go round to Mouron's apartment that very morning. It was not a rational decision, but what man is capable of thinking rationally under the influence of lust?

A little while later, as I climbed the stairs leading to the floor where the object of my desire lived with her husband, I had no idea what I was going to say to him, nor indeed what his reaction would be when he saw me standing there, but that did not deter me.

As I rang the doorbell I glanced at my watch: it was a few minutes past seven, almost exactly twenty-four hours since my first visit. No-one answered, so I pressed the button again. The light steps came from behind the door, then it opened and I found myself face to face with Madame Mouron! I was somewhat taken aback, for it hadn't occurred to me that *she* would answer the door. It should have; after all, the lady did live there.

'Monsieur?' she said in an interrogative tone.

'Forgive me for disturbing you, madame,' I said, quickly adapting myself to this unexpected situation. 'I'm a friend of Gilles. Is he in?'

Madame Mouron pulled her long white dressing-gown with the blue flower pattern more closely around her. 'No, he's not here,' she replied. 'He's had to go away on business for a few days.'

'When do you think he'll be back?'

'Not before Friday,' she said. 'Can I help at all?'

'Well,' I replied, moving closer, 'to be frank, madame, what I wanted to see him about really concerns you too.'

A strange, indefinable look flitted across Madame Mouron's features. 'How do you mean?' she said.

'Look,' I said, lowering my voice confidentially, 'it's rather a delicate matter . . . Would it inconvenience you if I came in for a moment?'

She looked a bit doubtful at first, then obviously decided that it would be alright, for she smiled a charming smile then stepped back, gesturing to me to enter.

I found myself in the spacious, nicely furnished living-room once again and Mouron's wife invited me to be seated. I sat down on an elegant settee while she perched on the arm of a chair facing me. The lower part of the dressing-gown fell open, revealing her knees and part of her thighs; very nice they looked too — smooth and well-rounded. There was no doubt in my mind that I had got her out of bed, for she had that unmistakable tousled look and wore no make-up but, in spite of that, the lady looked remarkably appetizing. My penis was beginning to stiffen again.

'Now,' said Madame Mouron, crossing one slender leg over the other and clasping her hands on her bare knee, 'what exactly is this delicate matter which concerns me?'

Then I told her everything — how I'd met Gilles in the Palais Royal garden, how I'd come to the flat the previous morning at his invitation and then, choosing my words with the greatest care, I told her how we'd watched her through the two-way mirror, but my tone was more passionate than indignant: it was not so much a denunciation of Mouron's conduct as a paean of praise for his wife's charms. I spoke warmly of the enchantment of seeing her lying naked in the morning sunlight and, referring discreetly to the masturbation, said how what would have seemed indecent in any other woman became delightfully erotic in her case . . . But then my tone became pathetic, almost pleading, as I spoke of the intense desire she had aroused in me. 'It's impossible for me to sleep,' I lamented. 'I just can't stop thinking about you. The vision of your lovely body has become an obsession with me . . . you are *so* desirable, madame. But you have destroyed my peace of mind!

A dramatic change had come over Mouron's wife as I had been speaking: her cheeks were flushed, her eyes sparkled, but one would have said more with excitement than anger.

'You poor boy!' she exclaimed, getting up off the arm of the chair. She came over and sat down beside me on the settee. It was quite a low settee and the angle of her body caused the dressing-gown to gape open partially revealing a bare breast. The warm odour of a woman who had not long since left her bed filled my nostrils. I felt my penis stiffen expectantly into full erection.

She saw where my gaze was directed and glanced down at herself but made no attempt to cover the exposed breast. Then, emboldened by that silent acquiescence, I put my hand inside the dressing-gown and fondled her breast: it felt incredibly soft, yet so firm. She did not try to stop me but gave a sharp intake of breath and quivered as I came into contact with her bare flesh. Then I put my other arm around the lady's shoulders, pulled her warm body to me and our lips met in a very long kiss. It was very agreeable. I was still fondling that lovely tit and could feel the nipple hardening with desire against the palm of my hand.

When at last we drew apart in order to get some air she said, 'I don't even know your name!'

'It's Victor,' I said, equally breathlessly. 'Victor Boulanger.'

'My name is Cécile.'

'I've always liked that name. It's very pretty and it suits you,' I said with sincere fervour.

She smiled at the compliment and said, 'You're a real charmer, Victor, but what are we going to do about this?' placing her hand on the bump my erection was making in my trousers. Her eyes shone. 'It seems to me that the least I can do is to let you fuck me after having caused you so much anguish,' she continued. I felt a surge of excitement; however, before I could take the sexy creature in my arms again she jumped nimbly to her feet saying, 'But first I must go and get myself ready.'

Then Cécile moved swiftly across to a door which I knew led to the bedroom, but before disappearing inside she turned to me, smiled and said, 'Don't go away, darling . . .

I shan't be long; that's a promise.' Then she went into the bedroom, closing the door softly behind her.

Five or six minutes passed while I waited, speculating about what my new ladyfriend meant by getting herself ready. Did that mean putting some perfume on, or squatting down over the bidet to freshen up her intimacy, or perhaps taking some birth-control precaution? I soon had the answer to these questions, for some disturbing sounds started to come from the bedroom: they were the soft complaining cries of a woman striving for fulfilment.

I rose to my feet and moved across to the bedroom, then opened the door quietly. Cécile lay on the bed as she had done the previous morning, her fingers playing between her parted thighs: so that was what she'd meant by getting herself ready. The naughty girl!

She looked over to where I was standing and said, 'Come and help me, darling!' Her voice sounded so sensual that I felt as if her vagina had spoken those words. Perhaps, in a way, it had!

I moved across to the bed and stood looking down at the masturbating woman, my painfully stiff erection straining against my trousers. Her soft white tits wobbled with her movements. The first rays of the morning sun streamed in through the window, lending their enchantment to the scene. The rumble of distant traffic came to my ears; a bird perched on a neighbouring television aerial.

'What's the matter, darling?' I asked in an unctuously lascivious tone, undoing my fly and taking off my trousers and underpants.

Cecile looked up at me like a woman drowning in lust and said in a coy little-girl voice, 'I need someone to play with my pussy, chéri!' She stopped masturbating and opened her thighs wider, offering her cunt to me.

'Rub it for me, my love,' she whispered, moving over to make room for me.

Who could refuse such a request from such an indecently seductive lady? I climbed on to the bed and, remembering what Helga's lover had done, I knelt beside Cecile, bent down and started to lick her belly, and at the same time my fingers explored the miraculously soft, moist centre of her being. She moaned softly and I felt her fingers cradling my dangling testicles.

'Rub me, *chéri*! Oh, rub me!' she crooned.

It didn't take long to bring her off, to reduce her to a palpitating, gasping jelly. Then it was my turn: I pulled my companion up into a kneeling position, made her part her thighs wide, then slid easily into the already well-prepared passage. The bed bumped and creaked in time with my vigorous thrusts. I gasped and sweated profusely; my balls swung to and fro; her white backside juddered and my hands gripped her hips. Then Cécile cried aloud as she came again and her flooding warmth provoked my own orgasm. I came too, ejaculating copiously into that palpitating love-hole.

After we had rested for a while, she got up, put her dressing-gown on and went to make us some coffee. Then I too got up, put my trousers back on and went into the living-room.

A little later, as we sat together on the settee, sipping our coffee and nibbling at some croissants, Cécile explained a few things to me. She told me what I had already guessed, that she had known all along about the two-way mirror, as well as Mouron's perverse practice of bringing men home to watch her. Although this excited her sometimes, she didn't really like it; but it provided a stimulus without which Gilles would no longer be able to fuck her. Then, speaking with a frankness which is rare, even in a woman who has just been shafted, Cécile explained that ever since she had been a little girl her vagina had always been extremely demanding: even now at the age of forty she needed at least three comes a day. Not only did she love Gilles, but she needed him to keep giving her frequent proofs of his affection with a nice stiff cock. (Obviously I'm paraphrasing what Cécile told me in my own crude way). That's why she went along with his perverse games, even though they were not really to her liking.

I asked if we could meet again, but the lady made it quite

125

clear that she didn't think it was a good idea, explaining that although she occasionally fucked with the men Gilles brought home, she made it a rule never to get involved in anything even remotely resembling an affair for fear of jeopardising her marriage. Cécile added, with a charming smile, that she feared there was a danger of her becoming too attached to me if we were to meet more than once. I didn't press the point then and left soon after that . . . but we shall see.

Once again I must humbly beg your pardon for being so prolix, dearest girl, but I do so love to tell you everything!

As regards the extract from *Rosalie et sa bonne*, which you were kind enough to send me, if the rest of the book is as full of piquant details as this brief sample, then it must be very good indeed. If you could find it in your heart to let me borrow your copy, I should be extremely grateful and, of course, I would take the greatest care of it.

But now I must bring this voluminous missive to an end. Please write soon.

All my love,
Victor.

Victor's Dream

She was reclining on her right side on a chaise-longue, facing away from me. Her dark hair was caught up in a loose chignon at the nape of the neck.

I stole up to her, caressed those round buttocks, then gently prised them open to expose her most intimate orifice. Then I moistened my fingers with saliva, gently inserting them, stretching the narrow passage to prepare the way. The lady did not turn her head to see who could be taking such liberties with her *derrière*: she just kept uttering little *ohs* and *oohs* and *ahs*.

Then, when I could wait no longer, so keen was my desire, I eased myself on to the chaise-longue behind the lovely creature and, holding my stalk with eager fingers, presented

126

the swollen head to the tiny but well-lubricated orifice, gently inserted it, then slid into that hot, that oily, that oh-so-tight passage! The lady cried out at this invasion of her fundament, but made no attempt to stop me.

I paused for a while, savouring that delightful sphincter gripping my swollen organ, while my hands caressed her breasts and my lips kissed her neck and smooth round shoulders. Then slowly but surely I started to move, sliding back and forth within her, gradually increasing speed until I was pounding in and out, both of us gasping and groaning, accompanied by the obscene creaking of the chaise-longue upon which we lay. And then the moment of supreme ecstasy was upon me: my more than rigid organ shot hot sticky gobs of whitish stuff into that most tender of receptacles until my testicles were drained.

That was my dream. I never saw the lady's face, nor the front portion of her body, although the full roundness of her breasts seemed very real to my touch. I've no idea who she was, but I do know where the inspiration for the dream came from. Do you remember the painting of a nude woman which concealed Mouron's trick mirror? Well, that was lady to whose charming *derrière* I paid such perverse homage in my dream. The picture is not a well-known one and the subject may never have existed except in the artist's imagination, but obviously she made a powerful impression upon my subconscious mind!

VI

Guildford, Surrey, England.
Monday, 22nd Sept., 1952.

Dear Victor,

I'm glad to see that you have taken some notice of what I said in my last letter. Your story has benefited from the use of more restrained language: not only is it pleasanter to read, but it somehow seems more convincing now as well.

The account of your dream pleased me too. Thank you for sending it to me.

Your enthusiastic reaction to the 'extract' from *Rosalie et sa bonne* is extremely flattering to me, my dear friend, because you see the book does not exist. I wrote the so-called extract myself. I have often told myself such erotic fairy-tales while indulging in the most indelicate form of self-love, but this is the first time I have committed one of them to paper. Your kind remarks tempt me to think that it might be a good idea to try to expand this fragment into a complete novel. What do you think?

Dancie arrived promptly at seven. He received the news that my husband would not be present with ill-concealed joy. Of course, I'd known all along that Jamie wouldn't be there, but I find that nothing puts a man in a better humour, or more predisposes him to be bold in love than the sudden removal of an anticipated constraint.

I was wearing a green silk creation, all frills and swirling skirts, which covered my breasts but left my arms, back and shoulders bare. My face was carefully but discreetly made-up. I had also applied just a touch of a very subtle perfume.

We had our dinner in a little room which I have annexed as my private bed-sitting room. It is on the first floor at the back of the house, and one has a charming view of a small wooded hill from the window. Dancie expressed his admiration for the view with considerable enthusiasm, but the presence of my bed disturbed him, as indeed I'd intended it should; several times I noticed his eyes straying towards it during the meal.

We had a chicken salad accompanied by a fine sparkling wine (French, of course) followed by summer pudding, a delicious English dessert, for which my mother-in-law gave me the recipe. We sat by the open window and, as we ate, were able to look out at the dusk-shrouded trees, smell the sweet evening scents and listen to the last songs of the birds. It was enchanting.

Naturally, our conversation centred upon the topic of love: love in general at first, but as the wine began to take effect, lowering our inhibitions, we passed from the general to the particular: that is to say our growing affection for each other. Dancie took hold of my hand across the table and, in a voice husky with emotion, told me how much the kiss we'd exchanged the previous day had meant to him. I expressed myself a little more reticently, leaving him in no doubt that I found him attractive but giving him to understand that doubts and scruples were preventing me from surrendering to my feelings. I'm really quite a good actress; perhaps not up to the standard of the Comédie Française, but very competent nevertheless!

By the time we had finished our coffee darkness had fallen but it was a fine night, so I suggested we might go for a stroll. Dancie said he'd like to, but I'm sure that he'd been hoping for a romp rather than a walk; however, he did not know what was going on in my mind.

'Well, I'd better change if we're going out,' I said, rising to my feet.

'But that's a lovely dress.' Dancie exclaimed.

'Yes, it is nice, but not really suitable for walking,' I said, going across to my wardrobe and opening the door.

As I stood there, pretending to be making up my mind what to wear, I unfastened my dress, then took it off. My lingerie that evening consisted of an apricot brassiere and an adorable little pair of matching panties, which tightly moulded my sex and bottom in the most provocative manner.

'Now what on earth shall I wear?' I said, admirably counterfeiting a puzzled expression. 'Come and help me choose something, John.'

Dancie rose to his feet and came across to the wardrobe. His face was flushed; his eyes gleamed hotly. Choosing something for me to wear was obviously not what he had in mind. Instead he took me in his arms and started to kiss me with the utmost ardour, pressing my body close to his. I could feel a promising virile hardness against my belly.

'What are you doing?' I gasped, when at last I managed to disengage my lips.

'Loving you, sweetest girl,' he said, his voice heavy with desire. Then I could say no more, for he was kissing me again. His hands were everywhere; all my resistance melted. My arms went around him and I started to respond to his kisses with an ardour equal to his own. In no time at all my bra and panties were lying on the floor and I was naked but for a suspender-belt, nylons and my high-heeled shoes: a combination which always seems to me to add a delightful touch of indecency to a woman's nakedness.

It didn't take long for Dancie to divest himself of his clothes either; then we were on the bed, kissing, embracing and feeling each other intimately. But when he tried to penetrate me, I held the young man back.

'Have you got a sheath?' I demanded.

The poor lad looked crestfallen. 'No, I haven't,' he said. 'Does that mean I can't make love to you?'

'Well, I certainly don't want to get pregnant,' I replied. 'However, if you look in that little drawer I think you'll find what you need, you naughty boy!' (Of course, I'd made sure earlier that one of Jamie's condoms was in the drawer of the little bedside table).

Dancie took the fragile piece of latex from the packet and I fitted it onto his cock, which was long, rather tapering and very stiff. Doing that for a man always makes me feel exquisitely lewd! Then I lay back on the bed, opened my thighs as wide as possible, the young man climbed eagerly between them and I guided his rigidity into my hairy intimacy with my fingers. He gave a loud cry of delight as he felt himself engulfed, but immediately started to piston in and out so rapidly that I had to make him slow down, for I didn't want my new lover to come too quickly. Nothing could be more frustrating for a woman.

Unbeknown to Dancie, it was possible for me to watch him fucking me, for I had left the mirrored door of the wardrobe open at such an angle that it reflected the bed and everything taking place upon it. I could clearly see his long tapering shaft glistening with my secretions as it appeared then disappeared again with each thrust. It's the nicest sensation in the world to have a man between one's thighs, to feel his tool probing one's entrails, but to be able to *see* what is happening at the same time is a rare treat. I watched fascinated as Dancie's buttocks bounced up and down, his hairy testicles swinging with his movements. Unfortunately however my pleasure was destined to be brief, for suddenly the young man gave a loud wail of lust and, with quick short jabs of his weapon, shot a copious emission into the rubber.

I don't think he was a virgin, judging from some remarks he'd made during our previous conversations, but quite obviously he lacked experience in sexual matters. My desires were far from satisfied, so I showed him how to use his mouth, tongue and fingers to bring a woman to the moment of supreme pleasure. Still, I must admit that he was more than willing to learn and he showed great aptitude. Altogether it was a very satisfying evening and he proved his admiration for my charms twice more before leaving. I didn't encourage him to stay the night for, as you know Victor, no matter how fond I am of a lover, I prefer to sleep alone.

Did I tell you that the young man possesses a motor-cycle? It's truly superb machine, all gleaming new and very powerful. His enthusiasm for it has communicated itself to me. He's promised to take me for a spin in the country tomorrow afternoon. I feel quite excited, for this will be the first time I have ever had a ride on one: the first time I have ever opened my thighs to a motor-bike. I'm sure that it will be quite an erotic experience. I wonder if I shall come?

Love and kisses,
Mireille.

Editor's Note.

The correspondence ends abruptly at this point. The following newspaper clipping will explain why. It was found with the letters from Mireille in a drawer in Victor's writing-desk. How it came into his possession is not known.

Extract from *The Surrey Herald*, Wednesday, 24th Sept. 1952.

A Tragic Accident

Yesterday afternoon a motor-cyclist and his pillion passenger were killed when they collided with a bus on the Farnham-Guildford road. The driver of the bus and his passengers were unharmed.

The motor-cyclist has been named as John Dancie, 19, a student at London University. His passenger was Mrs. Mireille Digby-Haines, 32, of 12 Highclere Close, Guildford.

Estelle

Adèle Urbain

When a woman regularly satisfies a man with her mouth she changes, she becomes different from other women: her lips become fuller and redder, her cheeks rosier, and her eyes positively glow with a worldly-wise, knowing expression. Furthermore, if the lady gets into the habit of sucking right through to the conclusion: that is to say until the man ejaculates in her mouth, then swallowing his viscous fluid, it will not be long before her breasts become whiter and begin to swell. The nipples are affected as well: they will become unusually elongated, a deeper, more provocative shade of red.

An aura of perverse sensuality emanates from such women; men are irresistibly drawn to them, like wasps to a honey pot. Such women are always surrounded by male eyes gleaming with lust: wherever they go heads turn and virile members stiffen to attention. Such women's mouths have become sexual organs: deep, wet, sucking female genitalia, ever ready, eager to drain a man of his life's essence. Impossible to look at such a mouth without immediately longing to pay a copious seminal tribute to its charms!

The trouble is that when you get a woman into the habit of sucking, you concentrate her attention on the male *member* in a quite unique way, which does not happen during normal sexual intercourse: not only do you fill the lady's mouth with it, you fill her *mind* with it too.

It was a great pity that Henri Petitcon didn't know about

these matters because, if he had, he could have saved himself a lot of unhappiness; but, unfortunately, Henri was the kind of man who acts first and thinks afterwards, if at all. A very macho bull in a shop full of delicate feminine china; a fool rushing into situations where no self-respecting angel would ever consider setting foot; in short, a man ruled tyrannically by the sceptre of flesh between his legs.

He lived in a small two-roomed apartment in an old house situated in a rather run-down Parisian suburb. Estelle, his wife, was a homely, girl-next-door type who mothered Henri and cooked him special meals on a battered, leaky little stove. They had no kids, although they had been married for five years: they couldn't afford them on Henri's meagre income as a shoe salesman. Estelle worked, of course, but didn't make much as a typist in a small office.

However, in spite of their lack of money, Henri ought to have been happy; he was young and in reasonably good health, the apartment, though modest, was cosy and, most important of all, he had a wife who loved him and did her best to make his life as enjoyable as possible. She kept their two rooms spotlessly clean, found imaginative ways to brighten them up and never complained about their impecunious circumstances.

She also did her best to keep Henri happy sexually, although in that domain the unfortunate girl had her work cut out, for as I have already said, a harsh task-master ruled the young man's life. In fact, Henri's vital organ ruled both their lives with a truly iron rod.

However, Estelle really did her best. Every night, even though tired out after a long day's work, she would dutifully spread her pale thighs to Henri's vibrant, thrusting need. She was not a very sensual girl but, even so, she tried hard to satisfy her demanding husband. When he got tired of doing it in bed she docilely sat astride him on a chair in their living-room bouncing up and down, breasts jiggling wildly, until he achieved a climax. Then when he asked her to parade in front of him wearing nothing but suspender-belt, stockings and high-heels, like a whore in some third-rate brothel, Estelle complied; as indeed she did when he told her to kneel on all fours on their somewhat threadbare carpet while, puffing, sweating and pouring forth a stream of obscene words he took her from behind.

But when Henri brought home some pornographic magazines which a colleague in the shoe-shop had lent him, then wanted to try out some of the things they showed, for the first time in their marriage their relationship became strained. The trouble was that nearly all the pictures in those magazines showed women making love to male organs by using their mouths or tongues in a variety of ways and, unfortunately, Henri became obsessed with the idea of getting Estelle to do the same for him.

The poor girl was deeply shocked. It seemed to her that no man who really loved his wife could ask her to do such dirty things, and she told him so. For the first time she refused to do as Henri asked. So began a long struggle between them.

He kept on at her every night about it. He begged and pleaded, even threatened to leave her. She tried to persuade him to be satisfied with normal intercourse, then cried softly into a dainty, lace-edged handkerchief when he remained obdurate. They spent many a sleepless night together, Henri lying on his back, quivering with resentment, staring up into the darkness, while Estelle lay with her back towards him, sniffing audibly or whimpering in short, fitful dozes.

Of course, he got his way in the end. In a rare moment of insight it suddenly occurred to Henri that one of the most characteristic features of feminine psychology is the tendency of women to copy each other — it is this tendency, one might say this instinct, which makes the wheels of the fashion industry go round. If he could persuade his wife that other women fellated their partners, she might be more willing to fulfil his fantasies. He told her that one of his colleagues had confided to him that *his* wife did it quite regularly for *him*, then a few days later he showed her a section in a translation of an American book on sexology which said some very reassuring things about the 'normal' and

135

'widespread' practice of fellatio. This book was by an eminent specialist with a string of letters after his name. Estelle was impressed in spite of herself. The young woman's resolve began to weaken; her refusals became less categorical, less vehement.

Then one Sunday morning when they were having a lie-in and Estelle was nice and relaxed, she gave in to some extent: that is to say she wouldn't actually take his member into her mouth, but consented to kiss it and lick it with her dainty pink pointed tongue. Then Henri persuaded her to kneel between his thighs and make a fuss of his hairy acorns with her lips and tongue while he vigorously rubbed himself until he achieved an extremely violent orgasm.

The young man was over the moon. The satisfaction of his desire put him into an excellent humour. As for Estelle, the experience had turned out to be much less disgusting than she'd anticipated – in fact, she wondered now why she had made such a fuss about it. The couple spent the rest of that day billing and cooing like two newly-wed turtle-doves.

Of course, now that she'd taken the initial step, Estelle found it easier and easier to take yet more steps on the slippery downward path. It was not long before Henri persuaded his wife to take his virile member into her pretty mouth and suck it. At first the young woman wouldn't let him finish in her mouth, but she soon came to accept that too. In fact, after a while he would sometimes climax all over her face – not a very considerate way of behaving – but she only feebly protested.

It became a regular routine between them: every evening after they had cleared away the remains of their meal and done the washing up, Henri would eagerly divest himself of his clothes then lie down completely naked on their double bed. At his insistence, Estelle too would take everything off, except perhaps for the rather scuffed high-heeled shoes she wore to the office every day; then she would come and kneel beside her husband on the bed – after having first made him get up for a moment so that she could pull the bedspread down, in order to avoid getting any stains on it.

136

Henri had placed the oval dressing-table mirror in such a position that during these sessions it gave him an excellent view of his wife's bare bottom, her hairy furrow and the tiny crinkled reddish-brown aperture between the buttocks.

Estelle would begin by kissing and licking her husband's genitals then, after a few moments of such preliminaries, she'd take hold of his now rigid stem near the base with the thumb and fingers of her right hand, then slip the tip of the member into her mouth.

While she was sucking him Henri liked to put his hand between his wife's thighs to finger the warm, damp sex. He could watch their reflected image in the mirror as his fingers titillated the young woman's private parts in this indecent fashion: thus he heedlessly set up an association between acute sexual arousal and sucking a virile member in his wife's mind.

It never took her long to bring Henri off. After only a few minutes he would usually ejaculate in her mouth, and then it would be all over . . . and that was just the trouble as far as Estelle was concerned, for she had been aroused by those probing, stroking fingers, but not satisfied! It never occurred to Henri that a healthy young woman needed to be sexually satisfied, and Estelle was too shy to ask him! But this state of affairs would not continue for much longer . . .

As I have said, this way of making love (if one can call it that) became a regular routine with the couple; in fact, it took the place of normal sexual intercourse in their lives. Estelle didn't really mind now that she'd become accustomed to it; furthermore, there was no chance whatsoever of her becoming pregnant, an important consideration in their very much less than affluent circumstances.

Within a few weeks the young wife had become as expert a fellatrice as the most experienced of Parisian whores. Sucking a penis became second nature to her and she would swallow the odorous white seed of life without giving it a second thought.

Unfortunately this was not the only change which took

137

place in Estelle. During those weeks dramatic transformations occurred both within and without, both physically and psychologically: the young woman's lips seemed to become fuller, redder; her eyes glowed with an obscene inner fire; her breasts grew fuller, whiter, while the nipples became much more prominent; she started to walk much more sexily too, hips swinging provocatively from side to side.

But that was not all. She, who had hitherto dressed like a provincial housewife, suddenly underwent a truly startling metamorphosis: the dull little caterpillar changed into a particularly exotic butterfly. Estelle bought herself a couple of new dresses, very different from anything she'd worn previously: one was black with the skirt slashed so that it revealed most of the young woman's left thigh as she walked; the other dress was bright red, like her lips, and not only extremely low-cut but with an almost indecently short skirt. Both of them were extremely tight-fitting too.

With these provocative outfits Estelle wore very sheer nylons (the best money could buy) which lent an enticing sheen to her slender legs, while her feet were now encased in brand new shiny red shoes with teetering high heels!

To complete this metamorphosis and make it even more striking the young woman went to a hairdresser and had her straight, rather mousy hair dyed red then attractively curled into a more trendy style. She also bought a rather penetrating, musky perfume called 'Interdit' which she liberally applied to various strategic parts of her body every day.

One can easily imagine the sort of effect that the once dowdy little wife had on men now as she teetered along the street on those high-heels. How their eyes gleamed when they saw those half-revealed white breasts! How their heads turned 'to stare lustfully at that provocatively swaying bottom! The old Estelle could not have faced those probing eyes, but the new Estelle stared back at them brazenly, her lips curved in a suggestive smile.

However, I am sure that at this point the reader will be

asking himself how on earth the young woman could *afford* all those new clothes and other luxuries, for he will not have forgotten that the couple did not earn very much money between them. One might think that Henri's suspicions would have been aroused too, but as I have already indicated, his sexual instinct ruled his head, so he just enjoyed the changes which had taken place in Estelle without unduly worrying about the whys or the wherefores.

Well, the solution to the problem is to be found in the offices of the import/export company in the Rue Garencière where the young woman worked as a typist. The managing director, Dino Tauresco, a veritable bull of a man of Italian origin, had never taken much notice of Estelle in the eighteen months she'd been working for him although, like most men with Latin blood in their veins, he was a born seducer. She had satisfied him as a typist, but not in any other way.

Then one day he suddenly became aware of the changes taking place in his typist: that lush bottom which swung so enticingly as she walked across the office to a filing cabinet, those breasts jiggling under her blouse, the full red lips, and those inviting eyes. Naturally, the new Estelle did nothing to discourage Tauresco when he began to make advances to her. Quite the contrary — it wasn't long before they became lovers and he was immediately impressed with his new mistress's sexual prowess. He realised at once that she could become a very great asset in his business affairs.

For her part, Estelle was delighted with her new lover, for Tauresco treated the young woman well, taking her out to excellent meals in good restaurants, buying her expensive clothes and, most important of all, providing a sexual satisfaction which she'd most certainly never experienced with that imbecile, Henri. For Tauresco was not only endowed with a truly magnificent virile organ, he also possessed the art (so rare in most men) of titillating a woman's clitoris until she succumbed to an overwhelmingly satisfying orgasm, leaving her breathless, shaken, weak at the knees. Soon Estelle became Tauresco's slave, subjugated by his rampant thrusting member and his magic fingers.

Another thing she liked about him was the fact that he never had her in the office but always took her to a hotel.

So there is the explanation as to how Estelle acquired those expensive new clothes, shoes and perfume. Tauresco never gave her actual money, but he paid out a small fortune in hotel bills, meals, dresses, dainty lingerie, shoes, make-up, and perfume for his young mistress. However, he didn't begrudge the money spent in this way: he looked upon it as an investment. Nor did he do what some bosses might have done in the circumstances and give her a raise in salary. Instead he came up with a way in which she could make a lot of money – a lot more than she'd been getting previously, anyway: he suggested that she should have sex with certain businessmen with whom he had dealings from time to time. He would give her a hundred and forty francs every time she did it and if, as a result of her labours, he pulled off a good deal he would give the young woman a bonus of two hundred and eighty francs as well.

Estelle was by now so much under Tauresco's spell that she readily agreed to his suggestion. Within a month she'd had relations with half a dozen different man and received quite a lot of money which, at her boss's prompting, she put into a special account under her maiden name in a different bank from the one where she and Henri had their joint account. Not one of Estelle's lovers was disappointed – far from it, for the young woman's expertise as a fellatrice, not to mention her fiery responsiveness to a stiff thrusting male. member, delighted everyone.

Did she ever have any qualms about prostituting herself in this way? Did any of the former Estelle still survive within the young wife's psyche? Certainly. But now she derived a deep masochistic satisfaction from the idea of such moral degradation and, besides, she liked having money to spend.

However, things were no longer going too well at home. Henri was beginning to realise that having a sex bombshell for a wife had some serious drawbacks: he missed the solicitude which Estelle used to have for his well-being, the special little meals which she no longer had the time or the inclination to prepare for him. He became increasingly morose, peevish, suspicious; he didn't like it when his wife arrived home late, which happened frequently nowadays. He accused her of being unfaithful to him and demanded to know how she could afford all those new clothes and perfumes, then became angry when Estelle gave him evasive answers. They had quite a lot of rows and their relationship became extremely tense.

Things finally came to a head one cold, dismal afternoon in December when Henri was sent home from work early because of a power failure.

He let himself into the apartment with his key then, as he was hanging his overcoat up in the tiny vestibule, was astonished to hear voices coming from their bedroom. At first the young man thought burglars must have got in somehow, but then he recognized Estelle's voice. She was speaking softly so he couldn't make out what she said. A man's voice replied.

His face set in a grim expression, Henri walked quietly across to the partly-opened bedroom door and stood there listening intently. Now he could clearly hear what they were saying.

'My goodness! It's so big!' Estelle gasped.

'Ooh!. . . That feels so nice!' the man said, his voice gruff and heavy with lust.

Then his wife said, 'Oh, yes. . . play with my nipples.' Her voice sounded languorous. Then a few seconds of silence ensued, followed by the rhythmic creaking of the bed.

Henri felt confused, a prey to conflicting emotions. His first impulse was to burst into the bedroom and have a violent showdown with the adulterous couple; but another part of him found the situation piquant: his virile member had already stiffened into erection. Besides, he hadn't seen his rival yet; he might be muscular, a formidable adversary. So instead of behaving impulsively, Henri chose the path of prudent voyeurism.

The young man cautiously put his head round the door

and his heart beat faster at the sight which met his eyes: Estelle, completely naked except for sheer black nylon stockings, suspender-belt and high-heeled shoes, was kneeling over the supine form of an elderly, balding man wearing nothing but a white shirt and a pair of blue socks. Henri noticed how thin the man's legs were. In the fading light of that late December afternoon the twin cheeks of the young woman's buttocks gleamed whitely as they moved up and down, quivering with the motions of intercourse. He could see the man's rigid stem glistening with vaginal secretions as it moved in and out.

As he stood there transfixed with mingled lust, rage and sadness, Henri saw the man's skinny fingers grip Estelle's buttocks then pull them obscenely apart, thus revealing the crinkled brown orifice concealed there. It seemed to leer up at him, an open invitation to perverse satisfaction. Lewd squelching noises were coming from the couple fornicating on the bed; a pungent odour of female genitalia assailed Henri's nostrils.

Then suddenly, without his being aware of exactly how it came about, Henri's fly was undone, his member was in his hand and he was vigorously masturbating, eyes fixed on Estelle's bouncing white bottom.

'Oh!' cried the man on the bed, 'I'm coming! . . .'

Then as Estelle's client shot his seed into her womb, her husband came too, panting and gasping, all over the carpet.

Henri's anger died with his lust after that truly shattering orgasm. It disappeared, leaving him feeling enervated and melancholy. He withdrew from the scene of his own ignominy, before the couple on the bed had time to notice him. He went noiselessly back to the vestibule, put his overcoat back on, then quietly let himself out of the apartment.

The young man spent the next couple of hours wandering around the streets of the city, or sitting in dimly-lit cafés brooding over a cup of strong, bitter-tasting coffee. He would like to have got drunk, but couldn't afford to. He would like to get hold of that little creep with the skinny body and kick him to pieces! Then he'd give that bitch the biggest hiding of her life and throw her out of his life for good. But even as the thought came into his mind, Henri knew it wasn't true. Estelle may have behaved like a whore, but he still loved her and, in the dim recesses of his mind, realised that he was at least partly responsible for what had happened. If he hadn't made such excessive, such perverse sexual demands, none of this would have happened.

Henri returned home in a conciliatory frame of mind, determined to make things right with his wife. But it was too late. Estelle had gone, leaving a letter explaining that as she no longer loved him she was moving out and going to live with Dino Tauresco.

The poor, foolish husband never found any words which could persuade his wife to return. It really was a most distressing business. But, as is the way in such matters, he got over it with the passing of time.

Did he marry again? I'm sure he did. Did he learn his lesson? I'm sure he did not. For, as we know, Henri was ruled by his staff of life, and that would always lead him into trouble.

Translator's Postscript

The above text comes from a little book of erotic tales called *Histoires perverses*, (*Perverse Stories*) attributed to 'Adèle Urbain', published in Paris in 1958, but without a publisher's name. But there exists another version of this story which appeared in another clandestine work called *Caresses parfumées*, (*Perfumed Caresses*) in 1960. This version is entitled *Delire sexuel* (*Sexual Delirium*) and bears no author's name. The two texts are substantially the same but *Delire Sexual* has a quite different ending. I thought it would be interesting to produce a translation of this alternative ending so that the reader can compare the two versions and decide for himself which he prefers.

The young man spent the next couple of hours wandering around the streets of the suburb where he lived, or sitting in little cafés brooding over a cup of the wishy-washy stuff that passed for coffee.

At first the dominating emotion in his mind was an overwhelming sadness that Estelle could have been unfaithful to him — and with such a skinny old creep into the bargain! For quite some time he plumbed the depths of despair.

But gradually his thoughts began to take another direction: he kept seeing Estelle's naked bottom bouncing up and down while that glistening member slid in and out of her sex! As he sat there in an overheated, dimly-lit café, a cup of coffee in front of him, a half-consumed cigarette in his fingers, Henri felt himself becoming aroused by the memory of that scene; his virility stiffened into full erection. It began to dawn on him that he found the idea of watching Estelle performing with another man acutely pleasurable. The young husband had never before realised how strongly voyeurism attracted him. This was indeed a day of revelations for Henri. He returned home feeling quite light-hearted and extremely aroused . . .

He found Estelle alone, reclining on the settee in their living-room, leafing through a magazine and looking incredibly seductive in a sheer black negligee, another recent acquisition. He was only a little later than his usual time, and the young woman's relaxed manner when she looked up and smiled as he came in showed that she was quite unaware that anything unusual had occurred.

'Hello, darling.' Her voice sounded languid; it had the tone of a woman who'd recently been fucked, he thought. 'Had a busy day?'

He didn't reply but just stood there looking down at his wife, as if he were seeing her for the first time. The lower half of the negligee had fallen open, revealing Estelle's smooth, nylon-clad thighs. Henri felt his member stiffen into erection, his breathing became heavier.

'I've got something for you,' he said hoarsely unfastening

his fly and dropping his trousers. He stepped out of them, leaving them in a crumpled heap on the floor, together with his underpants.

Estelle looked at the rubicund head of her husband's vital organ, which was only an inch from her nose, gave a loud sigh and put the magazine aside. She leaned forward, making as if to take the erect member into her mouth, but Henri stopped the young woman saying, 'No, I don't want *that* tonight.' Then, leaning forward, he made Estelle move from a reclining to a sitting position.

'Open your negligée,' he commanded.

She was surprised by this inhabitual behaviour on Henri's part but complied, unfastening the belt of the flimsy garment then pulling it back to reveal that she wore nothing underneath, save for a scarlet suspender-belt and her sheer black stockings, as well as the scarlet high-heeled shoes which encased her feet.

Henri sank to his knees in front of the young woman, an expression of mingled lust and wonder on his face.

'Your tits have got so big,' he murmured. 'They're enormous!'

He put out a hand and fondled one of them, weighing it, feeling the elongated nipple pressing into his palm. Estelle closed her eyes, sighed and leaned her head back against the settee.

Then Henri parted his wife's thighs and gazed with the same expression of wonderment at what was thus revealed.

'What a lovely twat you've got, Estelle!' he said in a voice unsteady with desire. He put his hand there and fingered her clitoris which rapidly grew stiff in response to his stimulation.

'I didn't realise your clitoris had got so big,' he said. 'It's like a little penis!'

Estelle moaned with pleasure as his fingers continued to titillate her rosebud.

'Why, you're soaking wet, you little slut!' Henri exclaimed. 'I think you're just about ready for a good shagging.'

'Oh, yes!' his wife murmured, eyes still closed. 'Fuck me! I need a good fucking!'

So Henri pushed the young woman's thighs even wider apart and, kneeling there on the floor between them, he guided the swollen head of his member into her warm wetness. Then the young husband made love properly to his wife for the first time in many months. It was a great success, for not only did Henri attain a very satisfying orgasm, but he made Estelle come too!

A little while later they dressed and went out for a meal at a pleasant, candle-lit Italian restaurant in the vicinity. During the course of the meal Henri told his wife that he had seen her making love that afternoon, but assured her that he didn't mind. Emboldened by his conciliatory attitude, Estelle then told him about her arrangement with Dino Tauresco.

Our reactions to what people tell us depend so much upon the time and place, when and where we are told, for those things influence our state of mind. Sitting there in the Italian restaurant in the soft radiance of the candles, filled with that warm afterglow which only good food and an excellent wine can give, Henri felt no anger at Estelle's revelations: in fact, as he sat there listening to his wife's sensual voice and gazing at the valley between her white breasts, he felt himself becoming aroused again rather than angry.

'So that's how you got the money to buy all those new things!' he said, pouring each of them another glass of wine.

'Yes,' she replied softly. 'Do you mind? Are you angry with me?'

Henri delicately sipped the rich red liquid in his glass. 'No, not now,' he said. Then he added, 'As a matter of fact, it's given me a hard-on, the thought of you being fucked by all those blokes!'

Estelle flushed and smiled nervously.

'Shh,' she said. 'The waiter will hear you!'

'Perhaps he'd like to fuck you too,' said Henri, but there was no malice in his words.

Not long after that the young couple went home, where they made passionate love again. Both completely naked, hot and dishevelled, they rolled around on their bed, kissing, sucking and performing the act of love. Then Estelle whispered a lewd suggestion in her husband's ear . . . She got up on all fours while Henri knelt behind her, then the young woman held her bottom-cheeks open while the young man gently pushed one, then a couple of fingers lubricated with saliva into her tight rear entrance, moving them in and out for a while. When the way had thus been thoroughly prepared, he presented the swollen tip of his member to that tiny aperture and, while Estelle groaned with mingled discomfort and pleasure, entered her without experiencing too much difficulty.

'Ooh, it's so tight!' gasped Henri.

Estelle's only reply was an incoherent moan.

Then, after savouring the feel of that hot, tightly-gripping passage for a few moments, Henri vigorously made love to his wife as he had never done before, while she played with her stiffly pointing clitoris. The only sounds in the room were the rhythmic creaking of the bed, Henri's harsh breathing and Estelle's grunts as she came, not once, not twice, but three times. Then at last, with a moan like that of a dying pig, he too came, shooting his seed high up into that slippery passage in quick, short spurts.

Afterwards they slept that long, deep sleep which only satisfied lovers achieve, locked all night in each other's arms, like a corrupt Romeo and Juliet . . .

147

Pages from a Young Man's Secret Diary

Monday 3rd September, 1951.
I'm sitting in a comfortable armchair in the local library.
The rain is bucketing down outside and it's almost as black
as night, at three o'clock in the afternoon.

The war in Korea continues to rage: they were talking
about it on the radio this morning. It's been going on for
more than a year now and, of course, there's always the risk
that it could degenerate into an all-out conflict between the
superpowers. Sometimes I hardly dare listen to the news or
read the headlines on the front pages of the newspapers. Of
course, today is the twelfth anniversary of the outbreak of
the Second World War. I wonder when the third one will
start?

22.00 hours. At home. Had a rare treat this evening. It began
when I went down to the end of our garden to empty the
coffee-pot. Darkness had already fallen, and through the
lighted window of a neighbouring house I saw a truly
arousing sight. The young man who lives there with his
grand-mother was doing something to his girlfriend which
would have given the old lady a heart-attack, if she could
have seen them.

His name is Jean-Pierre and he is quite young, only
eighteen, in fact. He's rather thickset, short with dark wavy
hair and a moustache which he has grown only recently,
undoubtedly hoping to give himself an appearance of greater
maturity.

His ladyfriend is a lot older, about thirty I should think,
with a little daughter of pre-school age; and she's a divorcee

to boot. My wife tells me that their relationship has set tongues wagging in the neighbourhood. Why can't people mind their own business! Personally I think Jean-Pierre is lucky to have an older woman to initiate him into the pleasures of sex, and what man would not have envied him this evening?

His sweetheart is a few centimetres taller than him. She always dresses nicely, but her best feature is her hair, which is abundant, very fair and which she wears in a loose chignon at the nape of the neck. I've seen them out together several times, but I never expected to have the outstanding (or should I say 'upstanding') pleasure of seeing her naked! Or almost naked anyway, for all the lady wore was a flimsy white suspender-belt, stockings and a pair of high-heeled shoes — I'm guessing about the latter because the window-frame concealed the lower part of her legs. Jean-Pierre was still fully clothed: he wore a light brown sweater.

The scene was taking place in the kitchen: the couple were standing near the uncurtained window, embracing and kissing passionately. The young woman's arms were around Jean-Pierre's neck. I saw him caress a small but well-rounded titty then, after a while, his hand moved down between her thighs and he started to finger her cunt . . .

My prick was as stiff as the young man's must have been! I set the coffee-pot down on the grass near the fence then, keeping my eyes fixed on the loving couple, I undid my flies and liberated my erotic instrument, not without some difficulty, to be sure. I could feel the cool night air playing upon it.

By now Jean-Pierre was vigorously masturbating his mistress, his mouth still glued to hers. I could see the young man's arm moving back and forth as he energetically rubbed her cunt. She clung to him for dear life, like a drowning woman grasping at a life-line. I couldn't resist the temptation to join in: I grasped my prick firmly near the tip, then started to work the foreskin back and forth over the swollen glans with a vigour equal to that which the young fellow was applying to satisfying his companion.

It wasn't really possible to see the lady's vagina at that distance, but I could clearly see her thighs, her suspenders and stocking-tops as well as Jean-Pierre's swiftly moving arm. His fingers must have been wet and beginning to ache with the sustained effort, but what labour could be more rewarding than striving hard to make a lady come? The rhythm of my flying hand matched the young man's. Oh, how I should have loved to put it between those white suspendered thighs, to rub that snatch, to feel its warm wetness! . . . Then suddenly an exquisitely sweet tingling sensation ran through my quivering tool, my balls tightened, then with a groan like that of a dying man, I shot my stuff in quick spurts into the air. It was lovely, the most satisfying come I've had for a long time!

I don't know whether Jean-Pierre succeeded in giving his partner an orgasm, but shortly after I'd attained mine the couple left the room, switching the light off as they went.

Wednesday, 5th September, 1951.
19.30 hours. At home. Many years ago when I was on a fishing trip in the country, I watched a young couple having a nice long fuck in the grass. It wasn't possible for me to see very much because they were too far away; moreover they were partially clothed: the girl was wearing a dress with the skirt up around her waist, while the young man's trousers were round his ankles. I could see her arms clasping him and his bare behind moving up and down between the young lady's thighs, but nothing more. It wasn't possible to tell whether she was pretty, yet nevertheless, the scene excited me to such an extent that in the months which followed I frequently evoked it when masturbating.

Why have I written about that this evening? Well, the business with Jean-Pierre and his girlfriend on Monday night has reminded me of it. In neither case could I really see very much, to be honest, yet I found both incidents extremely erotic. I have seen photographs that were much more explicit but which completely failed to arouse me sexually, and read descriptions in pornographic novels that left nothing whatsoever to the imagination and they bored me stiff, instead of making me stiff!

All of this seems to me to show that an element of mystery is necessary to make a situation erotic. The dancing-girl's semi-transparent veils make her appear more alluring than perhaps she would be if she were completely naked. A woman's breast partly revealed may be more tantalizing than a complete exposure. A girl's skirt raised high enough to give us a glimpse of stocking-tops, suspenders and bare thighs sets our imagination as well as our heart racing. We think we should like to see everything revealed, but when our wish comes true we are so often disappointed. Can reality ever compete with the imagination? I think not.

I don't remember which poet said *Distance lends enchantment to the view*, but whoever he was, he was right. So do veils!

Thursday, 6th September, 1951.
Bought some new jazz records in town this afternoon. One of them is particularly beautiful: it's Johnny Hodges, the great black American saxophonist, playing a piece called 'Sweet Lorraine,' a slow rather melancholy air which moved me to tears the first time I heard it. I think I shall be playing this record quite a lot from now on!

Saturday, 8th September, 1951.
We went to the pictures yesterday evening. My wife's young sister, Stephanie, babysat for us. We saw *Kind Hearts and Coronets*, an excellent film full of delightful black humour, but we were both somewhat irritated by the obtrusive French sub-titles which tended to distract one's attention from the action.

Afterwards I took Marie to a little American-style restaurant in the town centre where we had pancakes with bacon and maple-syrup, washed down with numerous cups of hot strong coffee. Quite delicious!

When we arrived home I couldn't resist the temptation to play 'Sweet Lorraine' – not too loudly though, so as not to wake the kid. Marie seems to share my liking for this record. She told me she can understand why it appeals to me so much.

It was very late when we eventually went to bed but, nevertheless, I fucked Marie long and tenderly; she had a long wet come, then we fell asleep in each other's arms. A perfect end to a very happy evening!

Sunday, 9th September, 1951.

18.00 hours. It was too good to last. I thought things were going too well. Marie is in a terrible mood, and it's entirely my fault.

The incident which put an end to my wife's good humour, and which has caused a rift between us, happened this morning not long after breakfast. We were in the kitchen. Marie was at the sink doing the washing-up. She looked very seductive in a short pink nylon dressing-gown. I knew that the naughty girl had nothing on underneath it, and the thin nylon displayed her breasts and buttocks quite provocatively.

Although we'd fucked only a few hours previously, I felt a sudden renewal of desire. I went up behind the dear girl, put my arms around her, pressed myself close to that warm body and started to kiss the nape of her neck, where the little tendrils of fair hair grow. Marie went on washing up — she's nothing if not practical. I put my hands inside the dressing-gown and fondled her tits, which are of truly generous proportions. My tool had stiffened; she must have been aware of its solidity pressing against her buttocks. Then when I put my hand between her thighs and started to caress her love-slit, Marie suddenly lost interest in washing the dishes. She murmured a feeble protest but the hot wetness of that hairy slit told me how much she wanted to be poked. So I undid my flies, got my tool out then, making my wife bend forward and open her thighs a bit more, I fucked her there standing by the sink.

It's such a pity that it ended up so badly because it was one of the most satisfying fucks I've ever had. Marie's sheath was silken smooth and she wriggled her arse excitingly in response to my vigorous shafting. I always think those spontaneous fucks which take place wherever one happens to be are the best of all and, on this occasion, the element of sordidness (fucking over the kitchen sink) greatly intensified my pleasure.

Unfortunately however it intensified it so much that I got completely carried away and, before I could stop myself, I ejaculated copiously into my wife's vagina and gave her a really good cuntfull.

When Marie realised what had happened, she was extremely upset. She pushed me away and ran straight upstairs to the bathroom to squat down over the bidet and wash away my viscous tribute to her charms. When she came back down her face was tense with anger. She didn't raise her voice — Marie never raises her voice — but she said some pretty hard things to me: according to her I was selfish, stupid and immature; I never gave a thought to anything but my own pleasure. Didn't I think it was about time I grew up and started facing up to my responsibilities, she demanded: couldn't I get it through my thick skull that we couldn't *afford* another baby, etc., etc.

Her harsh reproaches quickly aroused my anger, all the more so as I was conscious that they were justified, and I said some equally harsh things back. She told me that she would never speak to me again if she became pregnant as a result of my irresponsible behaviour; I retorted that that wouldn't be any great loss to me since she never had anything to say which was worth listening to anyway.

I don't know how much longer the row would have gone on if Estelle hadn't come into the room at that point. She asked what was the matter, and why was Daddy shouting. The poor baby looked upset, so we suspended hostilities for the moment and turned our attention to reassuring her.

Monday, 10th September, 1951.
11.10 hours. I'm writing this in the eleven o'clock train to

Paris. We're only just pulling out of the station, for the train is ten minutes late.

It's a relief to be out of the house for a few hours because the atmosphere there is quite tense. I slept in the guest room last night.

I'm going to browse in the secondhand bookshops on the Left Bank, where I'm hoping to find one or two erotic novels, for I'm becoming more and more interested in erotic literature. It's a sort of compensation for all the disappointments of real life, because it seems to me that whenever one wants to fuck a woman one almost always becomes involved in a heap of troubles, and I'm not just saying that because of what happened yesterday.

14.35 hours. At the moment I'm sitting on a bench enjoying the sunshine in the Luxembourg Gardens. It's very pleasant here. The air is full of children's happy laughter and the songs of birds in the trees. The whole place has a magical atmosphere of happiness. What a contrast to that at home!

I can remember very clearly the first time I fucked my wife. We had been going out together for several weeks and that particular evening we'd been to the cinema. Afterwards she came home with me to have some coffee.

I can no longer recall whether we had coffee but I do remember that after we'd spent some time kissing passionately with open mouths, I managed to get her dear little silken panties down, in spite of her protests, and then persuaded her to sit on my lap astride me — I was seated on one of the dining-room chairs.

When I entered her it was the most exquisite sensation I had ever experienced. Marie had already confessed to me several days previously that she was not a virgin, and I slid right in without any difficulty. Words are not really adequate to express how it felt that first time. I gripped her hips with my hands and she started to move up and down. Oh, what a sweet sensation that was as my prick slid in and out! Unfortunately, however, it didn't last very long, for after what could only have been a matter of a few seconds I ejaculated copiously inside her.

Such a brief union could hardly have been satisfying for Marie but, on that occasion, she didn't seem to be particularly concerned about the possibility of getting pregnant; on the other hand however the poor girl felt ashamed for having let me fuck her when we weren't even engaged. I was her second lover.

A little later I persuaded Marie to let me undress her completely and I was able to gaze upon my companion's naked charms for the first time. What a lovely body she had, and indeed still has if it comes to that, although the breasts are a little fuller now, after her pregnancy. I couldn't get enough of it: I didn't have eyes or hands enough to show my lustful appreciation. Marie was delightfully pink with shy embarrassment, which however soon turned to desire as I sucked the little darling's nipples and fingered her clitoris. And, of course, we ended up having another fuck, a much longer one this time, and I succeeded in making her come several times!

Tuesday, 11th September, 1951.
19.30 hours. At home. The evenings are beginning to draw in now and there is a touch of coldness in the air every morning which shows that the autumn will soon be here. There is a touch of coldness in the air in this house too, which I fear could not be dispelled even by the warmest fire.

Yet in spite of the fact that the summer is dying and that my relations with Marie are still strained, I don't feel as unhappy as I might have done for I found a book in Paris yesterday which has proved to be an antidote for melancholy, at least to some extent. Its title is *Nouvelles Récréations et joyeux devis*, (New Pastimes and Merry Tales) a collection of tales written in the early sixteenth century by Bonaventure des Périers. The old French is not too difficult to follow for there is a glossary explaining the meanings of the obsolete expressions at the back of the book.

I have read several of these tales this evening and found them all quite amusing, but one in particular impressed me: it's about an eighteen-year-old who disguises himself as a girl in order to gain access to a convent where several pretty young nuns have caught his fancy.

Everything works out extremely well for him: in the course of time he becomes the lover of several of the young ladies and his nice stiff pintle (as des Périers calls it) fills a gap in each of their lives.

But unfortunately some of the older, less attractive members of the sisterhood, jealous of their more fortunate colleagues, complain to the Abbess. However, they are much too prudent to come straight out and accuse 'Toinette' (that's the young man's adopted name), for they know he has succeeded in gaining the elderly Abbess's good graces, and she would simply attribute such an accusation to jealousy on their part. So they suggest that she should assemble all the nuns and order them all to strip naked if she wants to discover a very sinful thing which is taking place in their convent.

The old lady is puzzled, but follows their suggestion: all the sisters assemble and remove their clothes but 'Toinette', who has got wind of what is happening, has taken the precaution of tying his dick down with a piece of thread so that it looks as if he has a crack at the base of his belly, like all the other nuns. He knows the Abbess is terribly short-sighted and hopes to fool her with this stratagem.

But as an old English proverb has it, 'the best-laid plans of mice and men often go astray'. 'Toinette' is surrounded on all sides by naked women, many of them very attractive. Wherever he looks he can't avoid seeing firm thrusting titties crowned with pert nipples, voluptuously round bottoms and, of course, triangles of pubic hair of every shade nestling between exquisitely tender thighs . . . How could any young man's pintle remain unmoved by so many charms so provocatively displayed? 'Toinette's' didn't, that's for sure! Just as the Abbess bent forward in order to get a better look at what she thought was the young woman's private parts, his penis broke the slender thread restraining it, sprang up and knocked the old lady's glasses off her nose! Never has there been a ruder awakening!

'Wretched deceiver!' cried the Abbess. 'So that's how matters stand!'

But things don't turn out too badly for the young scoundrel in the end. The Abbess didn't want her sisters to be involved in a highly unsavoury public scandal, so she agreed to let him go free, without taking any action against him in return for his promise to say nothing about what had happened.

It seems to me that this story is a miniature masterpiece, worthy of comparison with some of Boccaccio's best tales. It ought to be better-known: someone should publish it in an anthology of short stories, or perhaps in a magazine.

Wednesday, 12th September, 1951.
À propòs of the story about the young man in the convent: it reminds me of something I used to do about thirteen years ago, when I would have been seventeen.

At that time I had never seen a girl's cunt and, indeed, never had any opportunities to see one. My longing to know what they looked like was so intense that I used to take all my clothes off, stand in front of the full-length wardrobe mirror in my bedroom, reach my hand back between my thighs, then pull my prick right down until it appeared to be a slit surmounted by a mound covered with brown pubic hair.

These sessions of erotic experimentation invariably ended up in the same way: the lascivious feelings engendered by what I was doing quickly resulted in a powerful hard-on, which I could not resist rubbing until an orgasm overwhelmed me with its all-too-brief ecstasy. All my handkerchiefs smelt of semen in those days.

Thursday, 13th September, 1951.
15.50 hours. I'm writing this in the 15.54 train from Vivray-des-Deux-Chemins, where I have spent the afternoon. It's been one of those days when a dreamlike haze of happiness seems to hang over everything.

The day started auspiciously when Marie announced, with

a charming smile, that her period had come on − that we were no longer threatened with parenthood and the prospect of bankruptcy after all. Of course, that led to an immediate thaw in the atmosphere. We hugged each other with sheer joy and relief. She apologised for having been so nasty to me, while I promised never to take any more silly risks. I'm so glad that things are back to normal between us. One Cold War in the world is quite enough to have to put up with!

This morning was one of the mornings when I have to teach at my uncle's school but, fortunately, I was free this afternoon and, as the weather was so lovely, I decided to take the little local train to Vivray-des-Deux-Chemins, a small market town whose narrow streets are lined with ancient houses which are really charming.

I spent some time browsing in the secondhand bookshop there − it's quite small but the atmosphere is relaxed and friendly. Then I had tea in a patisserie where they do the most delicious *mille-feuilles* in France, made on the premises. After that I went along by the river for a while and read the book I'd bought and watched the water-birds, whose antics always amuse me.

Altogether a very pleasant afternoon. I only wish Marie could have been with me, but on Thursday afternoons she has to do her stint in the library.

Tuesday, 18th September, 1951.
15.30 hours. I'm sitting in a deck-chair in the garden. The sun is quite hot and I feel sleepy. Marie is doing a bit of gardening and Estelle is playing with some of her toy animals on the grass.

After lunch I fucked my wife in a new position: I made her get down on her knees and rest her head and arms on the seat of one of the armchairs in the drawing-room. Estelle was upstairs in her cot having a siesta.

I didn't give Marie a chance to get undressed completely; I was much too impatient for that, not having had sex for quite some time. She'd simply slipped her knickers off; then I lowered my trousers, knelt down behind the dear girl, flipped her skirt up and inserted my stiffness into her sticky warmth.

'You will be careful, darling, won't you?' she said anxiously.

In a voice made tense by desire, I assured her that I would, my bottom already moving in the rhythm of intercourse.

In that position I could see my prick going in and out and the delicate pink inner lips of Marie's vagina gently gripping it, like a tiny sucking mouth. Not only did I have the pleasure of fondling the soft white rotundities of her bottom, it was also possible for me to see them, and the little puckered rosebud of her anus as well.

Poor Marie was too tense to get much enjoyment from our union. She'd have been much happier if I had been wearing a rubber but, to be frank, I just can't bear the wretched things: they completely spoil my pleasure in fucking.

Anyway, she needn't have worried, for I didn't let her down: just before the orgasm occurred I pulled my cock out of her and shot my stuff all over her bottom. There was quite a lot of it because, as I said, it was our first fuck for quite a while.

All the sex manuals say that a man should never leave his partner high and dry so, bearing that in mind, I tenderly kissed Marie's lovely bum and rubbed her cunt, concentrating especially on the clitoris, until she had a lovely long gasping squishy come.

Afterwards the dear girl was so grateful and tender towards me, both for the come and my self-control. We're so happy this afternoon that it seems difficult to believe how miserable we were only a short time ago.

Monday, 24th September. 1951.
13.13 hours. I'm writing this in the little restaurant in the town centre where I take my lunch when Marie is at the library.

The past week has been a happy one: Marie and I have been getting on well and the weather has been lovely; but my interlude of happiness came to an abrupt end during breakfast this morning when I heard the news on the radio.

It seems that a Chinese bomber attacked a US aircraft-carrier called the *Princeton* off the coast of South Korea yesterday, and succeeded in sinking it. One can imagine just about how much appetite I had left for my breakfast after hearing that.

The question is what's going to happen next? Is the Cold War going to turn into a Hot War?

17.00 hours. I'm sitting on a bench facing the Public Library, waiting for Marie to finish work. I feel very tense and depressed. The whole of the front page of the evening paper is devoted to that wretched American aircraft-carrier . . .

Tuesday, 25th September, 1951.

10.45 hours. I'm sitting in a deck-chair in our garden. It's such a lovely morning! When one looks at all these beautiful flowers, the trees, and listens to the birdsong, it's hard to understand why men would be prepared to destroy all that.

We've had a terrible night. I listened to some experts discussing the Korean situation on the radio just before we went to bed and they all seemed to think that it's pretty serious. One of them even went so far as to say that he thought we could be at war with the Chinese and Russians within a few days but, of course, it all depends on what the Americans do now.

When we got to bed I was so tense that I kept tossing and turning. That got on Marie's nerves and we ended up shouting at each other. Then Estelle woke up and started crying. It was about three this morning before we eventually managed to get some sleep.

18.50 hours. I'm seated at my little writing bureau by our bedroom window, looking out at the dusk gathering in the garden. What a contrast between this peaceful scene and what is happening in the world!

We listened to the six o'clock news and if the situation in Korea hasn't got noticeably worse, neither has it improved. There's a lot of sabre-rattling, as they call it, going on: the Chinese have issued a statement denouncing American imperialist aggression. Presumably they don't count sinking US warships as aggression! Furthermore they've warned the Americans that any attack on the Chinese mainland will be considered as an act of war calling for the most drastic retaliation. For their part the Americans have announced that they are going to call up several thousand reservists. I hope the French authorities don't do that, for I am on the army reserve list.

I talked to Jeanette Van Meering, the history teacher, in the staff-room this afternoon, and she said that she didn't truly think the Americans would risk an escalation of the conflict by doing anything really drastic. She reckoned the situation would be much more worrying if General MacArthur was still in command in Korea. She thinks the whole thing will blow over in a few days. Let's hope the young lady is right.

21.30 hours. I feel much more relaxed tonight. Talking to Jeanette has calmed me, given me a more balanced view of the situation. There's no point whatsoever in getting myself worked up over something which may never happen.

In fact, I've been feeling so much better this evening that I gave Marie a good fucking . . . and something else! It happened in the drawing-room, after she'd tucked the little girl up for the night. I helped my wife take all her clothes off, except her slip. Nothing pleases me more than giving the naughty girl a good vigorous shafting when she's wearing nothing but a slip. I find that more erotic than when she's completely naked.

We stood there in the middle of the drawing-room and kissed and cuddled for a few moments. She seemed to be in an extremely responsive mood. I put my hand up under the slip between Marie's thighs where the warm wetness of the hairy love-slit told me how ready she was for fucking.

Then I made my wife get down on all fours on the carpet and got down on my knees behind her. I pulled the slip right up to her waist and gazed with pleasure at her bare bottom.

Then I undid my fly, eased my rigid member out and inserted the swollen knob between the hairy lips of Marie's vagina. I slid in easily, savouring the sweet sensations of that hot, slippery passage.

I began to move in and out, quickly gathering momentum: gasps, moans, hairy balls swinging, her wetness gently gripping my glistening rigidity, her white arse wriggling lasciviously in response to my thrusts.

Marie didn't seem to be worried about the possibility of getting pregnant tonight; she was too overwhelmed by lust to care at that moment. It would have been so easy to finish inside her, but the memory of our recent quarrel prevented me from letting go. I didn't want to risk making my wife pregnant, yet I had an overwhelming need to possess her completely; but what could I do?

Then as I knelt there, hands gripping her soft warm hips, watching my cock slide in and out, my attention was suddenly drawn to the tiny brown puckered hole nestling between her buttocks. It seemed to leer up at me invitingly.

I withdrew my tool from Marie's vagina, then asked her to hold the cheeks of her arse open for me. The naughty girl must have been feeling exceptionally randy because she didn't hesitate, but reached back with her hands to pull the cheeks wide apart, completely exposing her most intimate aperture. What a delightfully obscene sight it was! She rested her head on the carpet.

Then I placed my swollen knob, glistening and slippery with my wife's secretions, against the tight puckered ring and started to push.

'What are you doing?' she exclaimed, but her voice was candy-soft with female lust and she continued to hold her arse-cheeks wide apart for me. I went on pushing. Surprisingly, it didn't take much: I'd never before possessed Marie in that fashion, but the sphincter suddenly yielded and I slid right up inside. Her rectum seemed to be well-lubricated already with the excitement of our love-making. Nevertheless, she gasped as she felt herself being stretched

163

and filled. Never had my cock been gripped so tightly! Yet it was an extremely enjoyable sensation — hot and tight.

I started to work my arse, partially withdrawing then pushing my tool back in, right up to the hilt. Drops of sweat ran down my face and dripped off my chin. My whole being was concentrated in my wife's arsehole!

Suddenly she said, 'What are you doing to me?' and I hardly recognized her voice, so charged was it with voluptuousness.

'I'm buggering you, my little darling,' I panted, increasing the speed of my thrusts.

'That's right,' she said, in her vicious little girl's voice. 'Bugger me! Fuck me in the arse! . . . Fill my arsehole with your lovely thick cream!'

Never before had I heard Marie use such language. It came as a delightfully unexpected surprise, but it excited me so much that it made me come: with short sharp thrusts, gasping and grunting, I jetted my semen high up into my wife's velvety rectum. It was one of the most violent orgasms I have ever experienced: it drained my bollocks dry!

A little while later, when I'd had a chance to recover somewhat, Marie lay back on the carpet and spread her thighs wide then, to show my appreciation of her complaisance, I sucked the dear girl's cunt until she spent in my mouth. Sucking my wife is no hardship, for she has a really lovely cunt. It is pleasing to look at, to feel and to taste, and she does so love to be gamahuched.

But I can write no more now: I feel so tired. It seems to me that we should sleep well tonight . . .

Wednesday 26th September, 1951.
16.00 hours. I'm sitting on a bench in the public gardens, which are not far from the town centre. Two old men are seated opposite me, deep in conversation, a toddler squeals excitedly as he chases some pigeons, a young couple stroll past, hand in hand; but the sun is hiding behind some clouds, as if it cannot bear to contemplate what may well happen soon!

I didn't listen to the news this morning and we don't have a morning paper delivered, so I was at least able to eat some breakfast, but they were talking about it in the staff-room when I got to school. Mademoiselle Van Meering was saying nothing, however: she just sat there, pale-faced and silent, looking as if she might burst into tears at any moment. Unfortunately, the reassuring assessment of the situation in Korea which she made yesterday has turned out to be wrong — the Americans *have* done something really drastic: they have bombed three Chinese airfields in Manchuria!

Ever since I heard about it I've been in a constant state of terror. My stomach is aching and so is my whole body, as if an attack of flu is coming on . . .

19.00 hours. The US Joint Chiefs have issued a communiqué officially announcing their bombing attack, which took place in the early hours of this morning (Korean time), and stating that their intention was not to escalate the conflict but to make it impossible for Chinese bombers to attack any more American targets.

The Chinese have said that the air-raids were an act of war and that this latest American imperialist provocation is a bloody deed which will have to be paid for in blood. Strong stuff! But the Russians are saying nothing, for the moment.

Thursday, 27th September 1951.
11.30 hours. I'm sitting in the reading-room of the local library writing these lines. I couldn't face teaching this morning, so phoned them up and said I wasn't well, which is not far from the truth anyway.

I haven't had the courage to listen to the news or read a paper so far today, but the crisis is even invading my sleep — such sleep as I can get. Last night I dreamed that I was in my bedroom changing into my reserve officer's uniform while another officer, whose face I didn't recognize, waited for me downstairs.

What amazes me is Marie's attitude. I asked her this morning if the situation didn't worry her and she just gave an eloquently dismissive shrug of her lovely shoulders and simply said she'd got more important things to worry about. It's in the best tradition of graveyard humour, isn't it?

'Excuse me, madame, but what is your reaction to the prospect of being vaporized by an atom bomb very shortly?'

'Oh, dear me, I've got much more important things to worry about than *that*.'

13.30 hours. I'm in the train on my way to Vivray-des-Deux-Chemins again. The day is overcast and it's a lot less warm now, but at least it's not raining, and I'm hoping that the tranquil atmosphere of the little town might help to restore some of my shattered peace of mind. I'm feeling a bit calmer already, but that's probably because I still haven't read today's paper or listened to the radio, so I don't know yet whether there have been any further developments in Korea.

15.05 hours. It's very beautiful here by the river. There is a touch of autumn in the air, the leaves are beginning to change colour and the ducks seem to have a sad expression on their faces, probably because the summer is over. How lucky they are not to know that it is probably over for good, that there may never be another summer.

I've just had a *mille-feuilles* and some coffee at the patisserie, but somehow it didn't taste anywhere near as nice as a fortnight ago.

There's a big swarm of birds milling around in the sky on the other side of the river: swallows getting ready to migrate? An irresistible feeling comes into my mind that they're going to fly to some safer place, feathered refugees fleeing from war. How fear distorts one's perception!

15.50 hours. In the train going home.

They say that a drowning man clutches at straws. Well I, who am drowning in a sea of terror and despair, am clutching at erotic straws: I am hoping that by evoking stimulating scenes from my past life I may be able to divert my mind away from the growing horror of the present situation. It has always been my experience that a stiff prick seems to dispel gloomy and frightening thoughts, or to transform them into pleasant ones. Let's hope it will now.

The first scene which springs to my mind dates from the early days of my relationship with Marie, some time before our marriage. We were sitting on the settee in the drawing-room of my parents' house, where I was still living at that time.

We were resting after having had a long, satisfying fuck: we had in fact been lovers for only a few weeks. Marie was naked, except for a frilly blue suspender-belt, nylons and a pair of dark blue shoes with high heels. All I had on was my shirt and a pair of socks.

Suddenly, seized by a lewd impulse, I asked Marie to spread her thighs and show me her twat: I actually used that word too, but she must have been feeling randy that evening for she didn't seem at all shocked by it. In fact, she did as I asked without hesitation and opened her lovely thighs wide, displaying her vagina for my inspection. I could clearly see the vertical, pale pink slit with the little clitoris peeping out at the top and, above that, the mound with its forest of short, light brown hair.

I was sitting at the other end of the settee, not touching her, but just looking. My cock was already beginning to show signs of interest again, in spite of its recent orgasm.

'Now be a good girl and open your cunt-lips for me,' I said.

Once more Marie complied without protest, using her slender fingers to separate her sex-lips and display the gaping orifice to me. What a delightfully obscene spectacle it was: a slim, naked girl with short curly fair hair displaying her open love-hole to her young man.

'What does that do for you?' she asked me curiously.

I replied by showing her my penis, which was fully erect again.

The human memory is very strange: I can remember all that quite vividly but can't recall what we did next. Anyway we'll be arriving at the station in a few moments, so I'll have to leave it there for now.

21.30 hours. I've listened to the news this evening: nothing irrevocable has happened yet and I'm beginning to hope that it might yet all blow over, as Mademoiselle Van Meering said it would.

Unfortunately, however, another conflict has flared up, a domestic one this time between Marie and myself. Some bitch at the library told her about me being there this morning, and it all came out about me having the morning off. She wouldn't accept my excuse about not feeling well because of the crisis and she said we'd have a worse crisis here if I lost my job. Anyway, the row culminated in my giving Marie a slap across the mouth, a pretty hard one I'm afraid, which made the poor love cry. I've never known any woman who can cry as heartrendingly as my wife and I was instantly stricken with remorse. I apologised, cuddled her, kissed her tenderly and shed a few tears myself; then we made up. But I can do without such emotional upsets right now.

Friday, 28th September 1951.
I'm in the reading-room at the public library again, but not playing truant this time, for I don't have to work Friday mornings.

It's a grey, damp, miserable morning, not at all cold, but depressing.

Haven't listened to the radio or read the paper yet today, so don't know what's happening. Nothing much, I hope.

I've just seen the woman who told Marie about my being here yesterday, and she had the effrontery to wish me good morning. I know what I should like to have said to her, the interfering busybody! But I don't want another row with Marie.

Another particularly piquant erotic memory which comes to my mind dates from the time when Estelle was only a few months old. It was a hot night in July; I entered our bedroom and found Marie sitting on a chair near the bed, breast-feeding the baby. What a delightfully erotic vision.

Because of the heat my wife wore nothing but a flimsy white nylon slip which somehow made her look more

168

provocatively indecent than if she had been completely naked. She had pulled a shoulder-strap down, exposing her right breast which the baby sucked avidly, occasionally pausing to smack her lips or make funny noises. The breast was swollen with milk; a delicate tracery of faint blue veins increased its appearance of fragility, and the redness of the elongated nipple stood out in contrast to its whiteness.

I went over to my wife and daughter, bent down and tenderly kissed both of them, then I pulled Marie's other shoulder-strap down and caressed the exposed breast. It felt incredibly soft and warm. I could feel the nipple stiffen in response to my touch. My cock was stiffening too.

Shortly afterwards, when Marie had finished feeding the baby and had put her in the cot, we lay down on the bed together, I pulled the hem of the silken slip up to her waist, climbed over between her thighs, then slid right up into my wife's warm wet welcoming snatch. It was a truly delightful fuck, leisurely, loving and very tender. Just thinking about it now, all these years afterwards, has given me an erection!

Sunday, 30th September, 1951.
The situation in Korea so far: the Americans are sending twenty thousand additional soldiers to the war zone as reinforcements and are to call up yet more reservists. There is much speculation that a big UN offensive is imminent. There has been a lot of activity in the air too, with considerable losses on both sides but, so far, no more American attacks on China, thank goodness.

Some angry exchanges have taken place at the United Nations between the Russians and the Americans, the former accusing the latter of being willing to risk all-out global war in the ruthless pursuit of their policies of imperialist expansion. The editors of both the Sunday papers I have read today take the most pessimistic view of the situation: both of them obviously think that there is an imminent danger of the war in Korea turning into something much bigger.

Tuesday, 2nd October, 1951.

9.55 hours. There is no doubt about it, the Yanks are preparing for a big showdown with the Chinese in Korea, and perhaps with the Russians here in Europe too. They have air-lifted ten thousand Chinese Nationalist troops in from Formosa and are sending another aircraft carrier and two more battleships to the war zone. The British are also sending several thousand more troops to South Korea.

Even more disturbing is the fact that both the Russians and Americans are massing troops and tanks in Germany. Both sides have announced that they are going to hold manoeuvres, and perhaps they are just flexing their muscles, as it were, but nevertheless it is very disturbing.

Yesterday in a speech to Congress, the US president expressed the resolve of the American people not to rest until Communism is destroyed, no matter what sacrifices this may entail.

Anyway, I'm going to try to forget all this doom and gloom for a few hours: Marie and I are off to Boulogne for the day – I'm actually writing this in the train. My wife is going to see her younger sister, Pauline, and her baby son, and I shall spend some time browsing in the secondhand bookshops.

I'm supposed to teach today but managed to persuade uncle to let me have the afternoon off, although he wasn't too pleased about it. There's no problem for Marie because she doesn't work on Tuesdays anyway.

The day is overcast and rather chilly, but at least it's not raining.

20.30 hours. We're in the train going home now. It's been quite a pleasant day really. The clouds cleared away and the sun was shining when we arrived in Boulogne. We had an excellent lunch in a little restaurant in the city centre, then Marie went off with Pauline and the baby; I spent the afternoon strolling around and browsing in various bookshops.

I only found one book which interested me, an erotic novel entitled *La Double Vie d'Edmonda*, (Edmonda's

170

Double Life) by Germaine Hartmann, published in 1936. I have already read several chapters. As erotic novels go it isn't at all bad. It is an extremely voluptuous tale about a pretty, petite, dark-haired creature called, of course, Edmonda who is married to a businessman whose work often takes him away from home for quite long periods. Bored with her life of suburban respectability, neglected by her husband, Edmonda starts to lead a secret life as a prostitute, picking men up in cafés or bars and going with them to hotel rooms.

The author avoids using obscene expressions, but she writes well and succeeds in evoking a suggestively voluptuous atmosphere when describing her heroine's sexual encounters.

In the following extract she has just been fucked by a middle-aged businessman called Henri who picked her up in the lounge-bar of a hotel near the Gare Saint-Lazare in Paris. It is only the second time she has been with a client. The scene takes place in Henri's room at the hotel.

Edmonda lay on her back in Henri's bed, staring up at the ceiling which looked yellow in the soft radiance cast by the lamp. Her partner had left her for a few moments, expressing a need to visit the bathroom.

When he returned he was accompanied by another man who, like Henri, was completely naked. Edmonda gave a cry of panic and quickly covered her nudity with a sheet.

'My dear,' said Henri, 'allow me to introduce my friend, Robert. As you can see, he's very much in need of a lady's services, and is quite willing to be generous.'

Instinctively Edmonda's eyes went to the base of the stranger's belly and saw that he was in a state of virile arousal. She shuddered and quickly closed her eyes.

'I think you'd better leave,' she said in a faint voice.

'Oh come on, darling,' Henri remonstrated, padding across to the bed, his own virility swinging limply between fat hairy thighs. He knelt down beside Edmonda, who was clutching the sheet to her chin.

'You've done it with me; what difference will it make if you do it with Robert too? Except that you'll get twice as much money,' he said with a vulgar laugh.

'Please go away!' she said, looking up at him imploringly with the enormous blue eyes which had always been her greatest asset.

Henri's only response was to bend forward and kiss Edmonda on her full red lips. His hand found its way under the sheet and gently stroked one of her breasts: he felt the nipple harden responsively. Edmonda sighed and opened her mouth to the man's probing tongue. He seemed to know instinctively just how to get a woman going. His own virility began to stiffen.

'Even if you don't want to do it with Robert, at least let him see how lovely you are, sweetheart,' he murmured in her delicate little ear, and again he tried to pull the sheet down, but the lady resisted, clutching at it with her small fists.

'No,' she said. 'I don't want to!'

'Oh come on, honey; what harm can it do?' Henri pleaded, still trying gently to prise the sheet from Edmonda's grasp.

'I promise I won't touch you, if you do not wish it, madame,' Henri's friend intervened. 'You are such a beautiful woman that it would be an honour just to look at your unadorned form.' He spoke excellent French, but his stilted manner of expressing himself suggested a foreign origin, German perhaps.

Edmonda looked uncertain, her resolution weakened. She looked at Robert: he appeared younger than Henri, with abundant brown hair and a moustache.

'You just want to look? Nothing else?' she said.

'If that is all you will permit, madame,' he said respectfully.

'Henri, realising that now was the moment, gently tugged the sheet out of Edmonda's hands and pulled it down as far as her ankles, exposing her slim white body to his friend. The latter gazed in admiration at the small breasts with their pink pointing nipples, the flat belly, the slender arms and legs, and at the very centre of her femininity, marked by the tuft of hair between her thighs. The man's virility seemed to become even more rampant as he feasted his eyes on Edmonda's naked charms.

Then Henri put his arms around the young woman and pressed his lips to hers in a long, tongue-probing kiss while his hand went back to fondle her breasts again. She lay inert for a while, just submitting to his kissing and his fondling but, as her senses began to respond to the irresistible stimulation, she relaxed and put her soft white arms around his neck.

Soon Edmonda became aware of another mouth kissing her belly and a finger stroking her most intimate femininity and knew then that Robert had not been able to keep his promise, but by now she was much too sensually aroused to mind. Henri started to suck the points of the young woman's breasts while Robert kissed and sucked the very heart of her being — that other secret mouth. Between them, with their sucking mouths and probing fingers, they reduced Edmonda to a palpitating jelly of female lust.

'Take me! . . . oh, take me now!' she gasped suddenly, cheeks flushed, thighs sprawling apart in an invitation which was anything but ladylike.

Then the pretty creature gasped again as she felt the hard bone of Robert's manhood entering her. Henri drew back for a while and contemplated the lascivious scene as his friend vigorously possessed the woman on the bed. Then when Robert had satisfied his need, he immediately took his place and soon paid his second tribute to the young lady's charms . . .

A little later, as the two men were dressing and Edmonda was sitting on the edge of the bed in her slip, adjusting her suspenders and putting her shoes on,

Henri suddenly took it into his head to tell her a particularly crude joke about a prostitute. Edmonda's response was to burst into tears.

Henri looked taken aback. 'Why, whatever's the matter, love?' he demanded, nonplussed.

Robert understood, however. Wearing a shirt and trousers now, he went over and sat down beside the weeping girl, putting his arm around her shoulders. She buried her face in his bosom and wept softly, her slender body shaking.

'There, there, do not cry, young lady . . . please do not distress yourself.' He pulled a spotless white handkerchief from his pocket and offered it to her.

'My friend is thoughtless, but I assure you that he meant no disrespect to you, did you Henri?' he frowned meaningfully at the other man.

The latter, suddenly aware of his *faux pas*, apologized profusely, for although Henri was a bit brash and vulgar, he was not unkind and felt genuinely sorry to think that he had caused distress to Edmonda.

The young woman gave him a tearful smile and dabbed at her eyes with Robert's handkerchief. Then the latter suggested that she should have dinner with them, an invitation which she accepted with alacrity since, in her present mood, the last thing she felt like was spending the rest of the evening on her own.

So shortly afterwards the three of them went downstairs to the hotel restaurant where they had a very satisfactory meal. Both men went out of their way to be agreeable to Edmonda, especially Henri who was anxious to make up for his earlier tactlessness and, needless to say, he didn't attempt to tell any more risqué stories!

This episode particularly pleases me for two reasons:

Firstly, because I find the idea of two men possessing the same woman extremely exciting, and secondly, I like the kindness the two men show to Edmonda at the end. The contempt which so many men express for ladies of pleasure has always been incomprehensible to me. It is also one of the most odious manifestations of human hypocrisy.

Thursday, 4th October 1951.
20.00 hours. The big offensive has started in Korea. The Americans and their UN allies launched a massive attack against the North at dawn this morning (Korean time). Apparently the UN forces have succeeded in breaching the Communists' defences at several points and are spearheading deep into enemy territory. The US Joint Chiefs have issued a communiqué in which they speak of 'a speedy and inevitable victory', but a victory for whom? Not for the thousands of people who are going to be killed, that's for sure.

   I read this latest horror tale in a copy of today's paper which someone left in the staff-room this morning, and have been feeling scared and miserable ever since.

Saturday, 6th October 1951
Yesterday the Russians sealed off West Berlin for six hours: nothing whatsoever was allowed in or out from ten in the morning until four in the afternoon, and I really thought the balloon was going to go up here in Europe. NATO troops went on alert and American and Russian tanks were facing each other with just a few hundred yards between them, their guns trained on each other.

   It's impossible to describe the relief I felt when the news finally came through that the Soviets had called off their blockade.

Sunday, 7th October 1951.
19.30 hours. The UN advance has been halted in North Korea. Apparently the Chinese have sent tens of thousands of additional 'volunteers' to reinforce their hard-pressed allies in the field. Even as I write these lines, heavy fighting is continuing and thousands of men are being maimed or killed.

My terror has died away to be replaced by a feeling of calm resignation. Such strong emotions soon burn themselves out. If all our days are numbered now, as seems very likely if the editorials of the Sunday papers are to be believed, I am determined to try to get at least some enjoyment out of whatever time I have left.

Monday, 8th October 1951
Sheer superiority of numbers is beginning to tell: the massive Chinese reinforcements have changed the balance of terror in the slaughterhouse known as Korea. The Americans and their allies are being slowly but relentlessly driven back, in spite of continual sorties by the US airforce against enemy positions and supply lines. When will this senseless killing come to an end?

Tuesday, 9th October 1951.
I myself was the victim of an air attack this morning: I went into our garden to empty the coffee-pot when something wet and warm suddenly splattered against my forehead, like a miniature bomb exploding: it was, of course, birdshit! The culprit was almost certainly a Communist pigeon! Well, in these sad, bad times one has to try and laugh. Anyway, they say that it's good luck to be the recipient of such a present.

Wednesday, 10th October 1951.
14.30 hours. I'm at home at the moment, sitting at my writing-bureau, looking out at the grey sky and the rain-soaked garden. It is as if the world is weeping over mankind's murderous stupidity.

The situation in Korea grows worse by the hour. I read in the paper this morning that in the wreckage of a Chinese bomber forced down in the South by US fighters, an atom-bomb has been found. The Americans say that it was obviously intended for a target in the South. This is a new and terrifying development; the possible ramifications are too nightmarish to contemplate.

Thursday, 11th October 1951

14.30 hours. The bad weather is continuing: the sky is grey and it's been raining quite heavily this morning, so I'm writing this in the local library, in the reading-room. Marie is not far away — she's working downstairs in the lending department, stamping incoming and outgoing books, charging fines for late returns and all the other boring duties which fall to a librarian's lot.

I'm feeling reasonably calm at the moment, in spite of everything: we didn't listen to the news this morning and I've managed to avoid seeing any newspaper headlines so far today. I woke up at five-thirty this morning in a cold sweat of terror, but my fear just seemed to melt away once we'd got up and started having our breakfast.

However, one positive thing the crisis appears to have done is to intensify my sex life. I've fucked my wife practically every night this week. Every evening I have a rock-hard erection and we make love until we are both sweating and quivering with a pleasure which is not far removed from pain. Marie says I'm wearing her out!

But undoubtedly *La Double Vie d'Edmonda* has also played a part in making me feel so sexually aroused, for I have been reading it during the past week and it contains some extremely piquant scenes. In fact, one of these scenes has given me an idea for something to try with Marie this evening; but first I'll have to do some shopping.

20.00 hours. Marie is upstairs in bed fast asleep, utterly exhausted after a vigorous and very satisfying fuck. Earlier this evening she enacted a scene from *La Double Vie d'Edmonda* with me.

When she'd tucked Estelle in for the night, we went into our bedroom and both got undressed. I persuaded her to put plenty of make-up on and comb her pretty fair hair, then I gave her the purchases I'd made this afternoon and asked her to put them on: they consisted of a pair of very sheer black nylons, self-supporting ones, plus some red shoes with stiletto heels; oh, and a pair of blue pendant earrings.

Then, while Marie was thus adorning herself, I sat down

177

on a chair in front of the long dressing-table mirror and contemplated my reflection with a certain degree of narcissistic satisfaction for a few moments: not a handsome face, but intelligent; brown hair beginning to recede a bit, unfortunately; a reasonably well-proportioned body; a hairy chest and a satisfactorily virile column of flesh sticking up from between my thighs.

'Come and see what I've got for you, my dear,' I said, reproducing the novel's dialogue to the best of my ability.

Marie teetered across the room on her high heels and stood beside me, gazing down at my erection. She really did look very desirable. At my request she had put lipstick on her nipples and their deep redness formed a pleasing contrast with the soft swelling whiteness of the tits themselves.

'That's a lovely stiff, er, *thing* you've got there for me, monsieur,' she said softly, blushing prettily: in the story the man pays Edmonda handsomely to say such indelicate things and also for the privilege of saying even more indelicate things back to her.

I squeezed Marie's bare bottom with one hand while the other went between her thighs and fingered her damp hairy slit. Still doing my best to stick to the dialogue in the book, I leered up at the young 'prostitute; and said, 'Why don't you climb on to it, my dear? I'll give you a lovely ride-a-cock-horse!'

Obediently she came and stood astride my legs, I parted her sex-lips with the fingers of one hand and with the other guided my engorged, plum-coloured knob to the entrance, then the she slowly sat down and my rigidity disappeared inside her. She sank down until it was buried right up to the hilt in her hot snatch. It felt lovely. I never feel more manly than at these moments.

Then in the indecently insinuating tone which Edmonda's client must have used I said, 'Tell me, my dear, how many men have you had this week?'

My partner lowered her long eyelashes and said softly, 'Six, or it may be seven, monsieur, I-I'm not sure.'

I feigned shocked surprise. 'My, my, what a dirty little

girl you are, to be sure! Aren't you ashamed of yourself?'
I demanded.

Edmonda/Marie did not reply but simply hung her head
in a reasonably convincing simulacrum of shame and
continued to sit astride me, her client/husband, my rigid
weapon buried deep inside her.

'Did they all put their stiff things up you?' I said.

'Yes, monsieur,' she replied in a barely audible voice, still
keeping her eyelids demurely lowered.

'Then you must be getting very good at fucking,' I said.
'You'd better give me a demonstration of your expertise.'
Whereupon my wife started to rise and fall upon my stalk.
Looking over her shoulder, I could see our copulating bodies
in the mirror. The scene we presented would have made an
admirable illustration for the novel. I could see Marie's
slender white back, my hands grasping her plump buttocks
and my glistening stalk sliding in and out of her cunthole.
Her full tits bounced and quivered with her exertions.

'Do you like being a naught girl?' I panted.

'Ooh, yes, *chéri*!' Marie gasped as she bounced up and
down.

'And do you like being fucked by lots of men?'

'Ooh, yes, *chéri*!' she exclaimed in a voice whose uncertain
timbre betrayed the approaching orgasm. 'I love the feel of
their stiff things up me!' As she uttered those words, my
scrotum tightened, my penis tingled with inexpressible
pleasure and I shot my wad high up into my wife's hot, wet,
clinging vagina.

Friday, 12th October 1951
01.20 hours. I can't sleep so, rather than lay in bed tossing
and turning and getting the wind up thinking about the
Korean crisis, it seemed better to come down here to the
drawing-room and distract myself with a bit of writing.

My account of what happened with my wife earlier is a
good example of poetic licence — or perhaps I should say
poetic licentiousness! It is in fact a pretty accurate account
of what happened in the novel, except that my version is

much less restrained than the author's, but the truth is that my pleasure was considerably diminished by Marie's less-than-enthusiastic attitude. Oh, I fucked her alright; she wore the black stockings and everything, but she wouldn't pick up her cues in the dialogue property nor really enter into the spirit of the fantasy, so that what could have been wildly exciting ended up in fact by being a rather routine fuck . . .

It's what always happens whenever I try to introduce a bit of imagination into our lovemaking. Marie seems to resent it. It's such a pity because, even after nearly five years of marriage, I still find her more sexually attractive than any woman I have ever met. Other men find her attractive too and it always seems strange to me that a woman who generates such a strong feeling of sensuality should be so uninterested in sex. I wouldn't go so far as to say that she doesn't like fucking, but it certainly comes quite low on her list of priorities. Yet I know deep within me that, for all her faults, there will never be any other woman for me.

14.30 hours. This morning a thirteen-year-old girl, a pupil in my second-year English class, put her hand up in the middle of the lesson and said, 'Please, monsieur, is there going to be a war?' Her pale, drawn features were a faithful reflection of my own anguish; however, I tried to reassure the poor child, but fear my words lacked conviction.

Unfortunately, her question was only too relevant in view of the latest development in the Korean situation: the Americans have carried out massive air-attacks on what they describe as 'military objectives' in China, and the US fleet is blockading Chinese ports, presumably with the intention of stopping Soviet supply ships from entering. The Russians will have to react, and war seems inevitable now.

In the next classroom to mine at school this morning, the music teacher was playing a gramophone record of 'Mars, the Bringer of War,' from *The Planets Suite* by the English composer Gustav Holst, as part of his music appreciation course. However appropriate such music might have seemed at such a time, I found it intolerable and would have liked nothing so much as to go in there and smash the record over his stupid head!

Saturday, 13th October 1951
13.45 hours. The Soviets sealed off West Berlin again at six o'clock this morning: they have issued a statement saying that their blockade will not be lifted until the United States ceases its aggressive action against the Chinese People's republic. There's no way in which the US is going to give in over this, so it looks like we'll be at war within the next twenty-four hours. The President of the Republic is to address the French people on radio and television at nine o'clock this evening.

I'm sitting at my writing-bureau in my room, looking out at the garden. The weather has changed again and it's an absolutely beautiful afternoon, marred only by the frequent whine of military aircraft passing overhead.

I didn't go to school this morning: there didn't really seem much point in doing so yet, incredibly, Marie has gone into the library as usual. Presumably, she'll still be there stamping books when the bomb drops.

I feel sick inside: sick with fear, it is true, but also sick with disgust that our leaders could have let things degenerate to such a point.

I can't bear to sit still any longer: I'm going for a walk.

Saturday, 13th October, 1956.
10.30 hours. Something very strange, something quite extraordinary has happened to me. I'm trying to understand it but am not succeeding and fear that I never shall succeed in solving this enigma. How can one simply mislay five years of one's life? Amnesia? Perhaps, but that doesn't really explain what has happened to me.

The last thing that I can recall about what I am already beginning to think of as my former existence is the few moments when I'd left the house and was walking along the street in a cold sweat of terror about the coming war then, after that, nothing – a complete blank until I woke up here in the general hospital yesterday afternoon with such a frightful headache that it seemed as if my skull would explode at any minute.

Marie was sitting by my bedside and she gave a cry of joy and relief when she saw that I had regained consciousness. She hugged me, smothered me with kisses; her hot tears splashed down on to my face. Never before had I known my wife to be so emotional, or so demonstrative! Her emotion communicated itself to me and I wept a little too.

When we had both calmed down a bit, she told me that I had been knocked down by an army lorry from a nearby military base when I was crossing a street not far from our house, that an ambulance had brought me here to the General District Hospital, and that I had been unconscious for several hours. No bones were broken, but my head had struck the road when I fell causing quite a nasty abrasion.

After we had been talking for a while, a nurse came and insisted that my wife should leave, saying that I mustn't get overexcited, that I needed to rest. I protested but Marie said she was sure the nurse was right and that she would come back and see me in the evening. She gave me a tender kiss, smiled at me, squeezed my hand then departed, promising to come back later.

The nurse, a pretty young woman, but with rather severe features, took my pulse, enquired as to how I was feeling, then made me swallow a couple of capsules washed down with a glass of water, saying that they would relieve my headache.

As she was about to leave the room I said, 'What's happening about the war, nurse?' The fear must have been apparent in my voice.

The young woman looked at me in surprise and replied, 'What war would that be, monsieur?'

'The war in Korea, of course,' I said impatiently.

She looked somewhat puzzled, as if she couldn't really understand my interest and said, 'It finished three years ago: they signed a peace treaty I believe.'

'But that's impossible!' I exclaimed, struggling up into a sitting position. 'Only a few hours ago we were poised on the very brink of war. The Superpowers couldn't possibly have changed their minds and signed a peace-treaty in such a short time. Things just don't happen that way!

The nurse looked somewhat alarmed by my loud vehemence. She said, 'I'll fetch Doctor Martin.'

Well, I had a talk, quite a long talk, with Doctor Martin, a young man with dark brylcreemed hair and sympathetic features. He asked me quite a lot of searching questions about the Korean War and also some others concerning my memory of things in my own life. What eventually emerged from all this was the extraordinary fact that it is now the year 1956! But whatever happened to 1952, 1953, 1954 and 1955, not to mention the last three months of 1951?

However, Doctor Martin was extremely reassuring: he assured me that there was nothing to be too concerned about by my inability to recall these missing years. Obviously, he said, I was suffering from a form of partial amnesia; an unusual form it is true, but X-ray photos had revealed no serious damage to my skull or brain and he felt certain that the trouble would right itself in time.

I wish I could say that his words reassured me, but they didn't. Something very strange has happened to me, and I'm not sure what, but I do feel sure that it's nothing to do with amnesia.

Monday, 15th October 1956.
19.30 hours. Back home again. I was discharged from the hospital yesterday afternoon.

I've spent a lot of time today looking through old newspapers and magazines, researching the Korean War. I could find no trace of an American aircraft-carrier called the *Princeton*, nor any references to American attacks against China. Apparently General MacArthur, the supreme commander in Korea, wanted to bomb Chinese airfields in

Manchuria, but he was relieved of his command early in 1951 by President Truman.

It seems that the dreadful international crisis of that year, which brought the world to the brink of nuclear war, never actually happened! One might be tempted to think that I dreamed it during my unconscious state after the incident but, in that case, how can one account for the fact that all of these events are recorded in my diary? (I actually had it on my person, in my jacket pocket when the accident occurred, which will explain how it was possible for me to make entries in it while in hospital).

Tuesday, 16th October, 1956.
10.30 hours. I'm sitting in a comfortable armchair in our living-room writing this. The weather is quite wintry outside, with strong winds whining around the house and dark clouds scudding across the sky.

But, in spite of the bad weather, this world of 1956 is a much pleasanter place to be than that of 1951, that's for sure! People seem to be friendlier and more relaxed. Marie is different too: although she is now thirty-eight years old, she appears slimmer, younger-looking than the Marie I knew in 1951. She seems more cultivated as well, much more interesting to talk to, and less inhibited as regards sexual matters.

But, of course, the most dramatic change is in our daughter, Estelle: she is no longer a toddler, but a little girl, eight years old now. She is very pretty and affectionate, and intelligent too. Apparently she is doing extremely well at school and I am delighted with her.

It seems that I am no longer a teacher: apparently I resigned from my post at my uncle's school in 1953 and have since become quite a successful writer of books for very young children. It's impossible to get bored in this world, it is so full of surprises.

However, Marie still has her part-time job at the local library.

Wednesday, 17th October 1956.

12.55 hours. I'm seated at my writing-bureau looking out on the garden, a stormy windswept garden at the moment. It seems odd to think that the last time I sat here, or can remember sitting here, was five years ago! It's all so vivid in my mind, that lovely afternoon, spoilt by the lowering storm-clouds of war. Now the storm-clouds are real, not metaphorical, but infinitely less threatening. The world is at peace, more or less.

Marie is at the library all day today. Estelle is with her grandparents (Marie's mother and father), so I have the place all to myself.

Last night something happened which showed me just how different my present wife is from the Marie I knew in 1951. It must have been about seven-thirty. I was sitting on the settee near the fire, reading the evening paper. Marie had gone upstairs to make sure that Estelle had settled down for the night. She didn't come straight back down: I could hear her moving about overhead in our bedroom.

When the dear girl eventually reappeared she had changed into a seductive, figure-hugging dress which I had never seen before.

'Do you like it?' she demanded, pirouetting before me.

It was a scarlet dress with a white collar, a darker red belt at the waist, and decorated with a motif of white dots. The skirt was almost indecently short. An impression of *déjà vu* began to assail me.

'I like it very much,' I said. 'Is it new?'

'Yes,' she replied. 'I bought it today.'

I noticed that Marie was wearing much more make-up than usual. The deep red of her lipsticked mouth matched the flamboyant colour of the dress. Her fair hair, which she wears longer now, was caught up by a scarlet ribbon into the currently very fashionable 'pony-tail' style.

'Do you mind if I sit with you, monsieur?' my wife said.

'Er, of course not,' I replied, somewhat surprised by her tone of mingled deference and suggestiveness.

She came and snuggled up beside me on the settee, linking

185

her arm through mine. A powerful musky perfume assailed my nostrils, reminding me irresistibly of the hairy treasure nestling between her thighs. My penis began to stiffen, for the first time since my accident.

We sat in companiable silence for a few moments, then suddenly Marie stretched one of her legs out, used her free hand to hitch her skirt up so high that her suspender was visible, and said, 'Do you think I have nice legs?'

Well, Marie's legs really are very nice, very slender and shapely, and they looked even nicer in the extremely sheer black stockings she was wearing. Her small feet were encased in scarlet leather shoes with stiletto heels. My sense of *déjà vu* grew stronger. My penis throbbed between my thighs.

'They're very nice,' I said, my voice heavy with desire. I put my hand on one of her nylon-clad thighs: it felt incredibly smooth and softly elastic to the touch. Marie sighed and lowered her leg but made no attempt to pull her skirt down; in fact, as my hand explored higher, the naughty girl opened her thighs wider to make it easier for me . . . When my fingers slipped under the elastic of her panties and started to part her sex-lips, she murmured, 'Take me upstairs, *chéri*: I want to feel your lovely big thing inside me!' And as she said that, her dear little hand was feeling me through my trousers.

So we went up to our bedroom with our arms round each other. As we climbed the stairs Marie still had her hand on my cock and she murmured, 'You will not be sorry you chose me, monsieur: everyone who comes here says what a good fuck I am!'

When we were in the bedroom we undressed quickly, but Marie retained her high-heeled shoes, stockings and suspender-belt. Her tits seemed fuller, whiter than I remembered them, and she had applied lipstick to the nipples, which stuck out aggressively.

She looked at my erection with professional appreciation and said, 'My, my, what a fine upstanding cock!' Then she lay down on the bed, opened her thighs wide, displaying her hairy slit, held out her slender arms to me and said, 'Come

186

and fuck your little whore, *chéri*: she needs a big stiff cock up her!'

I didn't need a second invitation. I got between those widely spread thighs and felt the young 'prostitute's' cool fingers guiding my knob into her incredibly wet warmness. Oh, how lovely it felt as I slid right up into that velvet softness! Soon the bed was creaking rhythmically as I energetically fucked my wife, my own honey-sweet little whore. But she didn't just lie there submitting passively to me, far from it. She was responsive in a way which would have been inconceivable with the Marie of my former life, moving her ass lasciviously and using her hands imaginatively to increase my pleasure. She was much more vocal than the old Marie too.

'Oh! You're so big, *chéri*!' she moaned. 'Oh, yes, that's right, darling, fuck me hard! Don't stop! Ooooh! You're making me all squelchy! . . .'

The bed squeaked obscenely, I grunted, Marie whimpered and I felt her fingers stroking my sperm-laden bollocks. 'Oh, monsieur, you shaft me so much better than any of the other gentlemen who come here,' she sighed. And again that powerful impression of *déjà vu*, of having enacted this scene before, assailed me.

Then suddenly she cried, 'Spurt your stuff into me, darling! Make me pregnant! . . . I want to have your child!' And as the young 'prostitute' uttered those words, she fingered my asshole!

Nothing more was needed to bring me to a climax: I came and came and came, inundating my beloved girl's open love-hole with a copious emission of sperm, the first orgasm I had experienced for five years or, at least, the first I had any knowledge of . . .

It was a little while later, as we lay side by side on the bed, recuperating after our exertions, that I realised that the *déjà vu* sensation which had persisted throughout our lovemaking came from the fact that we had just enacted one of the closing scenes from the novel *La Double Vie d'Edmonda*, which had given me so much pleasure when I read it back in 1951. There could only be one possible explanation for this: Marie had read the book and gone to considerable trouble to recreate a scene which she knew I found particularly exciting, even buying a dress just like the heroine's and reproducing as exactly as possible what she said and did. Needless to say, I was deeply touched by such evidence of her love for me and lost no time in telling the dear girl so.

As we lay there in the soft light cast by the bedside lamp, Marie told me that while I lay unconscious in hospital she had come to realise how much I meant to her. That without me life would have no meaning for her. She remembered all the times she had disappointed me over sex and had made a solemn promise to herself that, if I recovered, she would strive to make me happy in future.

I held the dear love close and, my eyes prickling with tears, said that I knew that I too must often have disappointed her in the past with my self-centred behaviour, that life without her would be nothing but a dreary wasteland, and I swore that in future I would try my hardest to be more considerate.

Then we both wept a little, exchanged some more tender words and eventually fell asleep in each other's arms.

Thursday, 18th October, 1956.
But the question still remains, how did I make that extraordinary transition from the world of 1951 to this present time of 1956? What happened to the years between? And what about the Korean Crisis, which apparently never happened?

Well, I have given quite a lot of thought to these matters since I left hospital and have come up with a possible explanation. It seems to me that the amnesia thesis must be discounted because of the evidence contained in my diary.

What could perhaps have happened is this: on an afternoon in October, 1951, distracted and worried by the threat of imminent war, I walked in front of an oncoming

188

vehicle, was knocked unconscious and, at the same time, was precipitated not only into the future, but into what science-fiction writers call 'an alternative reality' or 'space-time continuum'. Far-fetched? Maybe, but it seems to me to be a more satisfactory explanation than the amnesia idea. It provides a solution to the problem of how I was able to write so convincingly in my diary about a series of historical events which apparently never actually took place: they did happen, but in another space-time continuum.

Of course, if my theory is correct this raises a host of disturbing questions: for example, what happened to us in that other world in 1951? Were we all killed in A-bomb attacks? And how many alternative realities are there? Are there dozens or even thousands of alternative Maries and Estelles and versions of myself?

But, of course, all of this is just speculation. It seems very unlikely that I shall ever be able to find out exactly what happened or how it happened; but it is already beginning to seem less important. What is important is the fact that I have an attractive and intelligent wife, a little girl who resembles her and that we all love each other very much. When one has so much to be happy about who needs explanations?

Letters from *Sex-Erotica*

When the first number of *Sex-Erotica*, which was an English language magazine, appeared in Paris towards the end of 1959, it was by no means a new phenomenon in the history of erotic literature. Magazines specializing in sexual matters had appeared as early as the eighteenth century, and in the nineteenth century productions such as *The Boudoir* and *The Pearl* were destined to become classics of the genre.

Nevertheless, *Sex-Erotica* broke new ground in the field of twentieth-century publishing. In fact, it was quite daringly innovative for its time and became the prototype of present-day erotic magazines such as *Forum* and its French counterpart, *Union*. It contained short stories, articles on a variety of subjects such as fellatio, prostitution, venereal diseases and sodomy, an advice-column and, of course, several pages of readers' letters. These recounted the writers' sexual experiences in language which left nothing to the imagination. The editor made no attempt to tone them down, undoubtedly believing that since they were written in English the authorities would feel no need to take action. In this he proved to be wrong, unfortunately: after only three issues had appeared the police raided the publishing offices and warehouse in the Rue Garencière, copies of the magazine were seized and it was officially banned in April, 1960.

The selection of letters which follows is taken from the second issue, which was dated October, 1959.

191

Dear Editor,

I am a thirty-year-old housewife and I live with my
husband, Alain, on the outskirts of Marseilles where we have
a pleasant apartment in a residential area. I am fair-haired,
slightly below average height and my husband says my most
attractive feature is my legs, which are long and slender; my
feet are very small and dainty too. I hope you will not think
me vain if I say that I agree with Alain: I am very proud
to have such nice legs and I lavish a great deal of care on
them. I make sure that they are always smooth and soft and
never wear anything but the sheerest nylons. I always buy
good quality shoes with quite high heels and the expressive
glances of the men I meet are the proof that my time and
money have not been wasted.

Alain has a secure position as the manager of a small
insurance company and earns enough for us to live
comfortably if not luxuriously. We've been married for six
years now but as yet have no children, although that is not
because we haven't been trying. It was Alain's dark good
looks, his blue eyes and his kindness which first attracted
me to him and, on the whole, my life with him has been
a happy one.

I have always been a very sensual woman. Alain says that
I am as sensual as a pussycat on heat, and he's right. I love
the feel of a stiff male member stretching me and filling me.
Nothing pleases me more than a pair of strong masculine
hands fondling my breasts, gently tweaking my nipples and
making them become turgid with desire. My husband is a
virile man and he possesses me several times a week, which
suits me fine.

Over the years we have, of course, varied our ways of
making love: we graduated from the conventional 'mamma
and papa' position, sometimes I believe, called 'the
missionary position', to me being on top, and sometimes
I sit astride Alain on a chair in the living-room, or even in
the kitchen, both of us being completely naked — he is

especially fond of this way of doing it because it allows him to see my titties jiggling and quivering with my movements as I slide up and down on his erect member. Sometimes too we have tongued and sucked each other's sexual parts. The first time my husband sucked me it nearly sent me crazy and I filled his mouth with my love liquid! However, he didn't seem to mind. At first I didn't like taking his organ into my mouth, but I persevered because I didn't want to disappoint him, and have now become accustomed to it. To be honest, it is not really a great hardship for me to take Alain's penis into my mouth for although it gets very stiff indeed when he is aroused, it is not a very big one (he has no complexes about this, by the way) and I can take the whole erect member in quite easily.

So you see, dear editor, we are not totally unsophisticated in the matter of eroticism; however, quite recently a new and more perverse element has crept into our rapports. My husband's assistant manager is a young man called Bertrand: he is a fair-haired lad, intelligent, good-looking and quite charming when he can overcome his painful shyness. It is his shyness which has prevented him from ever having much to do with the opposite sex, although he is twenty-three. From the beginning he impressed Alain with the quality of his work: he should do well in the world of insurance. Then he befriended him, taking pity on the young fellow's lonely bachelor existence: he has a small apartment in the suburbs.

My husband has brought him home for a meal several times in the evening after work and nothing untoward happened on those occasions, but the last time he came to dinner something occurred which made me realise that Alain has a perverse side to his character which I knew nothing about.

It was just after dinner: we were sitting around drinking our coffee and I should mention that we had had quite a lot of wine with the meal, so our inhibitions had been lowered, I suppose. Anyway, Alain began chaffing Bertrand upon the fact that he never seemed to have a young lady.

The young man looked depressed. 'It is true,' he said

193

sadly. 'I should love to have a girlfriend, but my shyness prevents me from getting one.'

'When you say *have*,' Alain leered, 'do you mean it in the sense of *possess*?'

Bertrand coloured up. 'If you must know,' he said in a tone of despair, 'I've never *had* a woman in the sense you mean, or in any other sense!'

This sudden, unexpected confession made with such a melancholy expression on such a handsome face, moved me to pity. My eyes filled with tears.

'You poor boy!' I said. He gave me a sad smile.

'Then you're a virgin,' said Alain, who can always be relied on to state the obvious.

Bertrand nodded his head. 'I've never even seen a woman's naked body,' he said, 'let alone made love to one!'

Alain considered this statement gravely for a moment or two; then he turned to me and murmured, 'We must do something to help this poor young chap, Adèle.'

I nodded, intuitively realising what my husband had in mind. My cheeks flushed with sudden excitement.

'What can we do?' I asked.

Alain's face was flushed too. He said, 'Well, darling, you could begin by taking your blouse and bra off and letting Bertrand see your titties.'

I felt myself blushing furiously, but a damp warmth was beginning to spread between my thighs. I wriggled uneasily on the sofa where we were seated. 'I don't know if I should. . .' I said.

'Oh, please do, Adèle!' the young man pleaded. 'You're so lovely and I should consider it the greatest privilege!'

Well, as I have said, the wine had lowered my inhibitions; otherwise I don't think I would ever have considered doing such a thing. Both men looked at me expectantly as I rose slowly to my feet. Alain's right hand had disappeared into his trouser pocket; his mouth hung open slightly, as it always does when his penis has turned into a bayonet.

I undid the pearly buttons of my pretty white blouse with tantalizing slowness, exposing the deep cleavage between the white slopes of my breasts, whose whiteness was accentuated by the fact that I wore a black brassière. Then I took it right off and put in on an arm of the sofa. Bertrand gazed at me with an expression of mingled admiration and lust. Then I reached behind me, unclipped my bra and took it off. I put it with the blouse on the sofa, then turned to face the young man. There was no need for him to speak: the expression on his face was an eloquent testimony to the fact that my titties are pleasing to look at. Alain says that my nipples are 'provocative,' whatever that means.

'Well,' my husband demanded. 'Do you like them?'

'They're gorgeous!' the young fellow replied with a fervour which was obviously sincere.

Alain got to his feet and came and stood behind me. His hands came round me and cupped each breast, weighing them, fondling them and gently tweaking the prominent red nipples. I closed my eyes and leaned back against him. I felt my husband's warm mouth nuzzling my neck at the point where it joined the shoulder.

'Now we must show him your twat,' he murmured and he started to undo the short black skirt I was wearing. The skirt slid down to my ankles, then I was standing there clad in nothing but a tiny pair of white panties, stockings and my high-heeled shoes. Bertrand's eyes were fixed on the place between my thighs where only a fragile covering of nylon protected my most intimate femininity. I felt my cheeks flushing hotly — but not just with shame.

'Now we must take your knickers off, darling, I heard my husband say in my ear, his hot breath tickled my neck. Then the perverse man hooked his thumbs into the elastic and I felt him pulling the tiny garment right down until it lay in a crumpled heap around my slender ankles.

'Step out of them, sweetheart,' he commanded, but in gentle tones. His voice seemed to come from far off, and feeling as if I were in a dream, I stepped daintily out of the skirt and panties. Alain picked them up and put them on the sofa with my bra and blouse.

Instinctively my right hand had gone to cover the secret

spot between my thighs, while I had brought my left arm up to cover my titties. This was the first time since my marriage that another man had seen me naked. I felt both shame and a delightful sense of voluptuous intoxication. The little bud at the top of my love-cleft was quite rigid with desire.

'This won't do at all, darling,' Alain murmured reprovingly. He gently removed my arm from my breasts and my hand from my pubis, exposing them to our young guest's avid gaze.

'We're supposed to be completing this young fellow's sexual education, and we can't do that if you cover up your cunt and tits!'

So there I stood, naked but for a flimsy white suspender-belt, very sheer stockings and my black high-heeled shoes. Bertrand's eyes were fixed with a burning intensity on the hairy nest between my thighs. Oh, I knew that it was not right to let a man who was not my husband gaze at my naked breasts and my sex like that, but I found it terribly exciting: it was making me feel all funny and wet down there.

'Now, young fellow,' said my husband, 'pay attention. These are my wife's titties,' he pointed at my gently curving white breasts. 'As you can see, she's got a nice pair.' He fondled them, but took care to stand to one side of me so as not to obstruct Bertrand's view. 'There's nothing like feeling a good pair of tits to give you a solid hard-on,' Alain continued.

Our young guest gazed at the lascivious scene, totally fascinated. He wriggled rather uncomfortably on the armchair where he sat.

'Have you got an erection?' my husband asked him with shocking directness.

Bertrand nodded, flushing up with embarrassment.

Alain smiled. 'So have I,' he said. 'There's nothing to be ashamed of in getting a hard-on in the presence of a pretty woman: it's a compliment to her charms, you know. Isn't that right, Adèle?'

I flushed too, but made myself smile and nod at the young man. He timidly returned my smile.

My husband resumed his demonstration lecture: 'These are her nipples,' he said, pointing at the tips of my breasts. He gently manipulated them with his finger and thumb. 'As you can see, they're bigger than we men have, and they grow elongated and stiff when a lady needs a good fucking.' The young man looked longingly at my nipples. I noticed that his right hand was in his pocket, obviously caressing his dick. Oh, how I should like to have sucked it for him and to feel his lovely thick, viscous sperm filling my mouth or, better still, my twat. (Please forgive my crude language, which is hardly ladylike, I know, but I'm always like that when I'm sexually aroused).

My husband made me turn round then bend over and grip my ankles with my hands so that my ass was pointing towards Bertrand. 'Now, young fellow,' I heard him say, 'as you can see, Adèle has a lovely arse and this position gives you a clear view of her holes.' I felt his hands separating my arse cheeks and he continued, 'This, of course, is her arsehole and I think you will agree that it's a pretty little orifice. Then a little lower down is her cunt.' I could almost feel the young man's eyes burning into my most intimate feminine secrets. My clitoris was a rigid little projecting finger of lust.

'Adèle,' I heard my husband say, 'why don't you use your fingers to hold your twat-lips open so that our guest can see inside?' With an increasing feeling of unreality, I complied and used my fingers to separate my sex-lips, revealing the rosy wet interior of my love-hole to Bertrand.

'As you can observe for yourself,' Alain said, 'a lady's snatch gets very wet when she's aroused.' He pointed to my clitoris: 'Do you know what this is?' he demanded.

'I-I think it's called "the clitoris," ' Bertrand replied hesitantly.

'That's right,' said Alain. He began to titillate the stiff little protrusion with a skilful finger, which made me breathe heavily and wriggle my botty. 'As you can see,' he

197

continued, 'it makes a woman very excited when you stimulate it, and prepares her to receive your cock. Talking of which . . .' The lewd man undid his fly, dropped his trousers and pants, which fell in a crumpled heap around his ankles, and he inserted his stiff member into my most intimate recess. I gasped as I felt him enter me and slide right up into my vagina.

I know that I shouldn't have let things go so far, but my husband had got me into such a state of sexual excitement . . . All I knew or cared about at that moment was the lovely feel of Alain's stiff thing inside me. Furthermore, the knowledge that Bertrand was watching increased my excitement to fever pitch.

I could feel my husband's hands gripping my hips as he started to thrust in and out.

'The advantage of this position is that you get really deep penetration,' he gasped as he pumped away. I could feel my titties swinging beneath me with our movements as we fucked. The only sound that came from Bertrand was an eloquent groan.

At that moment my whole world was in my cunt and that hard bone of lust pistoning away inside it. Gone was all sense of decorum or dignity. I was just a naked female being fucked in public. And as that idea came into my head my lewd feelings overwhelmed me and I came, flooding my husband's organ with my orgasmic spending – and that set *him* off:

'Oooooh!' he wailed, and with vigorous strokes shot his stuff high up into my writhing vagina.

'Oh! Oh! Aaah!' Bertrand cried, and I realised that he had come too. In fact, he'd sprayed semen all over his trousers and I had to get him a damp cloth to sponge it off.

The poor boy seemed very embarrassed and I too felt ashamed of my wanton behaviour. He left not long after that, but before he went he kissed me tenderly on both cheeks and told me that I was the loveliest of women. What a sweet boy he is!

But now I am wondering what is going to happen the next

time he visits us. In a way I already feel as if he is my lover. Will Alain encourage me to give myself to the young man? Is that what he really wants? Is that what I really want? Oh, it would be just too perverse for words! But I keep thinking about Bertrand's penis, which I saw after Alain had withdrawn from me: it is bigger than my husband's and I keep imagining what it would be like to feel it inside me. Oh dear, I don't think I shall be able to resist if they both want to fuck me next time!

Yours sincerely,
Adèle C . . .

*

Toulon,
16th October 1959

Dear Editor,

Let me begin by telling you a few details about myself. I am a bookseller, forty-five years of age, and I have been married to my wife, Édith, for twelve years. She is a slender, dark-haired little woman with a quiet voice, and is a few years younger than me. On the whole our marriage has been a happy one; Édith is a very submissive woman who does her best to make me happy, and I am reasonably satisfied with her performance as a sexual partner.

My problem arises from the fact that I am an extremely complex personality. My desires are apparently quite contradictory: I want Édith to give herself to other men, but at the same time I want her to be a faithful wife: I want her to be a lady of easy virtue *and* a respectable woman.

In recent weeks my desire to see her being possessed by another man has been particularly strong. I told my wife about this and, after several long arguments, she agreed to accept another sexual partner, but on the condition that the encounter would not take place in our own home. I readily agreed to that and one evening a couple of days later we checked into a little hotel in a none-too-respectable quarter of the city.

When we got to our room, at my request my wife undressed and lay down on the bed, completely naked. She has a lovely slender body and her skin is very delicate and soft to the touch. I kissed her breasts, sucked her nipples and stroked the tender pink petals of flesh between her thighs to get Édith into a receptive mood, then I produced a large pocket-handkerchief and told her that it would be best for her to be blindfolded, explaining that it would make it easier for her if she didn't actually see the man who I was about to fetch.

'You can pretend that it's me who's taking you,' I said.

The dear girl agreed that it would be best to be blindfolded and I tied the handkerchief in place; then I kissed her gently and told her to lie there quietly while I went downstairs and fetched our 'guest', if that is the correct word.

She quivered and said, 'I feel so nervous! Will it be alright, *chéri*?'

I did my best to reassure her, then left the room, closing the door quietly behind me. I quickly went to the bathroom at the end of the corridor, locked myself in and proceeded to prepare myself: I smoked a cigarette for a few minutes in order to make my breath smell of tobacco — I am, of course, normally a non-smoker — put some aftershave of a kind that I never use at home on my cheeks and generally tried to get myself into the frame of mind of another man. Obviously, I was going to play the part of the strange lover and these preparations were simply to convince Édith that, in Rimbaud's famous words, Je' *est un autre* ('I' is someone else). This was my way of assuaging my desire to give my wife to another man and yet preserve her virtue.

As I walked back along the corridor to our room, I really felt myself changing, being transformed in a Jekyll and Hyde fashion from a rather pale, thin intellectual into a rather earthy, squat, vulgar bloke with formidable virile equipment between his fat hairy thighs. Indeed, as I inserted my key in the lock and let myself into the room, I was so stiff down there that I had the impression that my erect penis was considerably bigger than usual.

Édith still lay on the bed, her naked body now covered by a sheet. 'Who's that?' she said nervously, raising her head and automatically turning her head in my direction, although the blindfold prevented her from seeing anything.

'It's all right, love,' I replied in an assumed voice, deeper and coarser than my normal tone. 'Your 'ubby said it'd be all right for me to come and see you. I'm going to give you a good shagging!' Then I gave a vulgar laugh. Édith shuddered and pulled the sheet right up to her chin.

I quickly divested myself of my clothes then moved across to the bed, my erection jutting proudly from the base of my now fat, hairy belly. My testicles felt heavy and swollen with seed.

I took hold of the sheet with my 'short', 'stubby', 'nicotine-stained' fingers and said, 'Come on, lady, don't let's be bashful. We both know why I'm 'ere.' Then I gently but firmly pulled the sheet down until Édith's pale nudity was completely exposed.

'Now don't do that, baby, I remonstrated, pushing away the hands with which she tried to cover her dark pubic bush and her white, pink-tipped breasts.

'Oh, please, please!' Édith murmured.

Her gentle, pleading tone only served to intensify my excitement. I fondled those soft breasts and found, to my surprise, that the tips were rigid little darts of female desire. I put my hand between her thighs and found confirmation of that desire in the warm wetness between the hairy sex-lips. Obviously Édith was finding the situation as exciting as I did.

I wasted no more time on preliminaries but climbed on to the bed, pushed the little lady's thighs apart and got myself between them, but imagine my surprise when I felt a small soft hand guiding my organ into the right place! Édith is usually so reticent when we perform the sex act.

But at that moment I was in no mood to reflect upon my wife's changed attitude: all my attention was centred in my virility and the sensation of being inside my partner's vagina which gripped it yet yielded at the same time. As I put my arms around her warm body, she wrapped her arms and her legs around me: I could feel her heels resting on the top part of my buttocks.

'That's right, *chéri*,' she sighed as I started to move my bottom, 'give me a good fucking! Oh yes, fuck me!'

Never before that night had I heard Édith use such language and never had I known her to respond so ardently to my shafting: she gasped, moaned and raised her pretty bottom to meet my jabbing penis. Her hands stroked my body and cradled my hairy testicles.

'Am I a good fuck?' she panted at one stage.

'You are, lady,' I grunted. 'A real hot little slut!'

'Oh, yes!' she cried, to the discordant accompaniment of the bed springs. 'That's what I am: a hot little slut!' Then she came, flooding us both with her warm secretions and at the same moment she put a finger into my rectum and cried, 'Fill me with your juice, darling!' And, of course I did . . . I ejaculated violently inside my wife in one of the most satisfyingly lovely comes I have ever experienced.

Very shortly afterwards I left, saying that I would send her husband back to her. I went back along the corridor to the bathroom, where I cleaned my teeth and washed my face to get rid of those unfamiliar odours of tobacco and after-shave. Then I went back to our room and we left the hotel soon after that. Later that same night, in our bed at home, I made passionate love to Édith again, but this time she responded in her usual rather restrained way.

Ever since then my state of mind has been one of utter confusion. On the one hand I feel betrayed, as if Édith really had cuckolded me with a stranger but, on the other hand, the memory of her abandoned response is driving me nearly crazy with lust. I feel that she has been hiding an essential part of herself from me, and this hurts me deeply. I'm also afraid that I may have awakened a desire in her to give herself to other men. I couldn't bear it if she left me, yet part of me would love to repeat the experiment. What can I do to restore my peace of mind?

Yours truly,
Robert C . . .

Editor's response: It seems to me that you could begin by treating your wife with more consideration. Do you realise that your attitude towards her is an extremely selfish one? You say that you feel as if she's betrayed you, concealed part of herself from you, but what about the way in which you have deceived her? If you want to assure yourself of a place in her heart why not begin by becoming a loving rather than just a lustful husband? Start by trying to find out what *her* desires are and by being honest with her about your own needs. It seems to me that you already have the answer to your problem: you could satisfy both your sexual needs and your wife's by acting out fantasies which are agreeable to both of you, but in future please refrain from deceiving her. If you really love Édith take her into your confidence: treat her as you would a trusted and valued friend.

*

Poitiers,
3rd October, 1959.

Dear Editor,

I think I must be a unique phenomenon, or at least a most unusual one, for I am a cuckolded husband whose ignominy has brought him nothing but pleasure, the most exquisite pleasure!

It happened this way: I was sitting in our living-room one evening a couple of weeks ago watching the television when the doorbell rang. I went to answer it and found that Madeleine was my caller: Madeleine is a sophisticated blonde with mischievous blue eyes who lives with her husband, Charles, in the flat above ours. We had always been on good terms with the couple and had spent quite a number of pleasant evenings together.

That particular evening the young woman's face wore a serious expression which made her appear older. I asked her in and offered her a drink, which she refused.

'Do you know where Émilienne is?' she demanded, abruptly silencing my attempts at small talk.

I replied that my wife was visiting her mother, who lives on the other side of the city, as she usually did most Wednesday evenings. At this Madeleine gave a short derisive laugh which was anything but humorous and said, 'Wrong, my dear Gustave! You are quite wrong, you poor boy!'

I felt perplexed both by my visitor's words and her almost aggressive attitude. 'Where is she then?' I said.

Madeleine got up from the sofa where she had been sitting. 'Come on,' she said, making for the front door. 'I'll show you . . .' She preceded me up the rather narrow stairs leading to the next floor, her bottom was but a few centimetres from my nose. Madeleine's bottom is quite big but well-proportioned and the tight blue skirt she was wearing set my imagination going. My penis began to stiffen.

When we reached her front door she told me to be as quiet as possible, then she inserted her key in the keyhole and we entered the flat. When we were in the living-room she indicated a door which I knew led to hers and Charles's bedroom.

'They're in there,' she said in a voice which was almost a whisper.

My heart beat faster. I had the feeling that this must be a dream and that I would wake up in a moment or two. I stood there as if paralysed, not knowing quite how to react.

Madeleine solved the problem for me: she went and got one of her elegant dining-room chairs and placed it close to the door, but not right up against it: in fact it was about a body's width away from it − this is an important detail, as you will see.

'Get on the chair and you'll be able to see for yourself what your wife gets up to when she's supposed to be visiting mummy,' she hissed.

I should explain that there was a glass skylight over the

door and when I stood on the chair I could easily see what was going on in the bedroom beyond. But the sight which met my eyes filled me more with surprise than anger. Émilienne was there with Charles and they were both stark naked, except that the lady was wearing a white suspender-belt, sheer nylon stockings and white shoes with high heels. My wife is not beautiful but she has a sympathetic face framed by fluffy brown hair, which she wears quite long and, considering she's turned forty, her body isn't at all bad, especially her tits which are voluminous but well-shaped.

I felt surprised because I'd never before realised that Émilienne felt attracted to Charles and, besides, he really isn't much to look at with his bald head and middle-aged spread; however, as I could see, he had a weapon of formidable dimensions jutting out from the base of his hairy belly.

At that moment the couple were standing in front of the long dressing-table mirror, contemplating the lewd tableau which their reflection presented: he stood behind Émilienne, pawing her gently swelling udders, nuzzling her shoulder and saying something which, of course, I couldn't hear, while she caressed his tool with her long slender fingers. A languid post-coital, post-orgasmic smile played upon her lips. There was no doubt in my mind that the lady had just been fucked!

I was suddenly aware of Madeleine standing below me, between my legs and the door.

'What are you doing?' I whispered.

The young woman smiled up at me and said in low sensual tones, 'Don't worry about me, Gustave. Just enjoy the show.'

In the bedroom the scene had changed: Émilienne was now lying on her back on the bed, thighs apart, and using her fingers to spread her cunt-lips open so that her lover could see inside. I noticed her pink slip together with her dear little pink knickers draped on a chair.

Meanwhile Madeleine had undone my zipper and got my cock out, then I felt an exquisitely pleasurable sensation as the naughty girl took my engorged knob into her mouth and started to tongue and suck it. It was so lovely that my legs almost gave way beneath me!

The couple on the bed were now performing 'sixty-nine': Charles lay on his back on the big double bed while Émilienne straddled his face. He was sucking and tonguing my wife's juicy twat while her head bobbed up and down, her mouth filled to capacity by the man's stiff, blue-veined cock.

My partner continued to suck me with the greatest artistry, although her position must have been anything but comfortable. In fact, never before had I been sucked off with such expertise. Within a very few minutes she brought me to the verge of orgasm, for no-one could have resisted that artfully sucking mouth. Then she deftly inserted a finger into my anus and I came, inundating her tongue and palate with my spurting, sticky semen. Madeleine went on sucking me until I was finished: she drained my testicles of every drop of vital fluid.

What my wife and Charles did after that I cannot say, for there is no longer any pleasure to be derived from watching someone copulating when one has just come. I got down from the chair feeling extremely enervated and sat down on it to recuperate for a few minutes while Madeleine disappeared into the kitchen, presumably to rinse the taste of my spunk from her mouth, for I could hear a tap running.

When she returned she told me that she and her husband liked to make love to other couples: they had seduced my wife some weeks previously and since she, Madeleine, found me very attractive she had chosen this way of introducing me to their activities and hoped that I would have no objection to becoming her lover. Needless to say, I hastened to assure the young woman that nothing could please me more and that I felt extremely flattered.

Not long after that we were joined by Émilienne and Charles. He wore a dressing-gown and she was wearing one of Madeleine's negligées, the thin silk of which did little to conceal the sharp-tipped thrust of her splendid tits. Our hostess served coffee and some delicious gâteau and we sat around and discussed the situation in the most friendly manner. I had never seen my wife looking lovelier: her eyes sparkled, her cheeks were flushed and she spoke with animation.

Later Madeleine came back with me to my flat and we spent a marvellous night together, sucking and fucking and generally getting to know each other's bodies. She is a wonderful mistress who not only knows how to suck a man off expertly but also how to use her arse when fucking. Émilienne stayed with Charles, of course, and I can only hope that she found as much satisfaction in his arms as I did in Madeleine's.

Since that night we have spent a number of happy evenings with Charles and Madeleine. Far from posing a threat to our marriage, this new relationship seems to have given a new zest to our sex life, and our affection for each other is in no way diminished.

Yours sincerely,
Gustave R . . .

Euphémie and Her Lovers

Thérèse d'Ambley

Translator's Note

During the ten years following the end of the Second World War, the historical adventure novel enjoyed a tremendous vogue in France.

It started in 1946 with the publication of the French translation of the American best-seller *Forever Amber*, by Kathleen Winsor. It had an immediate success and it wasn't long before French writers began to explore the possibilities of the new genre. But was it really a new genre? Perhaps it would be more correct to call it the renaissance of an old genre, for in the previous century writers like Alexandre Dumas had already produced such classics of the historical adventure novel as *The Three Musketeers* and *The Count of Monte Cristo*.

At all events, the successor to *Forever Amber* in the best-seller lists was *Caroline chérie*, by a French historian, Jacques Laurent, writing under the pseudonym of 'Cécil Saint-Laurent.' This novel, which recounts the adventures of a young woman during the Revolution and the Napoleonic wars, appeared in 1947 and proved to be immensely popular both at home and, in translation, abroad. In fact it was such a success that it was made into a film, and the author wrote several more novels recounting the adventures of Caroline and her son.

After this the floodgates were open and a constant stream of such works appeared in the bookshops: works such as *Tender is Perrine*, by 'Philip O'Creach,' *Emerald*, by 'Erik J. Certon', and the now famous *Angélique* series by Anne and Serge Golon, which recounts the adventures of a young lady in the 17th century.

Unlike their nineteenth century predecessors, these new novels contained quite a lot of nearly-explicit erotic episodes and, as the titles indicate, most of them narrated the exploits of a heroine rather than a hero. In fact, these young ladies were all so bold, brave and resourceful that one could almost consider the books in which they appeared as early feminist manifestoes!

The heroine of *Les amours d'Euphémie* (1958) from which the following extract was taken, is a good example of this new emancipated type of female character. However, the novel itself differs from the others I have mentioned in the fact that the erotic episodes contained in it are more explicit, and there are more of them. For this reason the book could only be published and sold clandestinely. Obviously, the author's name is a pseudonym and it seems unlikely now that his (or her) real identity will ever come to light.

The story is set in the late eighteenth century.

A Midnight Adventure

When at length I left Milord Southall's residence and started to make my way back to my lodgings, Phoebus (to express myself in the language of our modern romance-writers) had long quit the firmament, leaving to chaste Diana and her starry train the task of illuminating the earth with their pale radiance: in other words, it was a moonlit night.

As I walked along the deserted street, I heard a nearby church bell start to chime the hour of midnight. Considering the amount of money I had lost at the gaming table that evening, my mood was astonishingly light-hearted. In fact, as I approached the Palais Royal I was whistling Grétry's celebrated air, 'Où peut-on être mieux qu'au sein de sa famille?' (Where can one be happier then in the bosom of one's family?) A rather fruity-voiced contralto had been singing it during the course of the evening at Lord Southall's house.

I like the tune but, in view of my extremely acrimonious relationship with my father, could hardly appreciate the words, except perhaps in an ironical sense. When that august gentleman got to hear of the present state of my finances, as inevitably he must, his wrath would know no bounds: I owed money to my tailor, my boot-maker, my grocer, my landlord and now, to make bad matters worse, I had lost nearly twenty thousand francs at Milord Southall's. So why were my spirits not downcast? My father, no doubt, would have said that it was because I'm an irresponsible jackanapes and, truth to tell, perhaps he may have some right on his side, but I prefer to think that the real reason for my light-hearted humour that night was because some obscure part of me, some strange sixth sense perhaps, foresaw that which was about to happen next.

As I was walking down a street bordering the Palais Royal garden, a woman stepped from the shadows and accosted me in these terms: 'Good evening, *monsieur*. Would you care for a little female company?'

Her voice was soft and refined, not at all what one would normally associate with a woman of the streets. In the combined light cast by the moon and a flickering street-lamp I saw standing before me a girl rather above average height clad in a long dark cloak and wearing a mask which effectively concealed the upper part of her face. Everything about her, her dress, her bearing suggested a young lady of good family rather than a harlot.

'Well,' says I, 'have you a place where we may go, my dear?'

'Can you not take me to your house, *monsieur*?' she countered.

And in the end we agreed that she should accompany me

211

to my lodgings, since they were at no great distance from where we stood.

As we walked, the young woman took my arm in the most familiar way, pressing herself against me as we went along the street. I could feel the soft swelling contour of a breast against my arm and her sweet perfume assailed my nostrils in the cool night air. My affair stood up and strained against the forefront of my breeches. It felt most uncomfortable in that tight constraint.

Fortunately we soon arrived at my rooms. No indiscreet eyes saw me take the young woman into the house, not even those of my servant for I had told the fellow not to wait up. However, knowing how much I hate to enter a darkened room, he had had the good sense to leave some candles burning in my bedchamber.

When we were safely in my bedchamber and I had locked the door behind us, I helped my companion to take off her cloak and then asked her if I might be allowed to see her face. She made no bones about it but complied at once with my request, removing the mask and placing it with her cloak, which I had draped in my usual untidy fashion over the back of a chair. Then she stood there in the soft light shed by the candles and I gazed at her more with astonishment than desire, wondering how on earth such a lovely creature could have sunk to such base prostitution.

Oh, it would need the pen of a Richardson or the deft brush of a Greuze to do justice to such charms! Her delicate pale face was framed in luxuriant dark hair which she wore unpowdered, thus giving an air of naturalness which only served to enhance her beauty. A rather proud chin gave an impression of wilfulness but which was tempered by a pair of the loveliest, most expressive eyes I had ever seen. When I add that the young woman's velvet habit and white muslin skirt were of the finest quality you will understand my astonishment.

'Well, sir,' she demanded, 'do you like me? Do you think me worthy of sharing your bed?' Her eyes flashed boldly as she spoke.

Such brazen words spoken in such refined tones had a powerfully aphrodisiac effect upon me. The girl's eyes fixed themselves upon the flagrantly obvious swelling in the front of my breeches and a wanton smile overspread her sensual mouth. She came across to me, hips swaying provocatively, and laid her slender fingers on the cloth of my breeches at the point where my proud charger strained against it. The shameless hussy (who was yet so unlike a hussy in most respects) looked up at me boldly and murmured, 'You really do like me, *monsieur*, don't you?' and her hand caressed me in that place where a man is most responsive to caresses.

I needed no further encouragement to take the lovely creature in my arms and to kiss her passionately upon those cherry-ripe lips. Her arms went round me and she responded to my kissing with the most unrestrained ardour, opening her mouth at once to my exploring tongue. Nor did the girl protest when my indiscreet fingers ventured under the gauze which covered her bosom and felt a sweet swelling globe, so firm yet so incredibly soft! She simply gave a deep sigh and I felt her fingers caressing the nape of my neck.

When at last we paused in our kissing for want of breath I said, 'Dear lady, I do not even know your name!'

The lovely girl's cheeks were flushed, her eyes were languid, her white breasts rose and fell precipately, an eloquent testimony to her troubled state.

'My name is Euphemia, *monsieur*,' she replied breathlessly.

I told her what a pretty name I thought it was, then went to kiss her again, but she gently pushed me away and asked me if I would assist her in taking off her dress. It was a task which I performed with the greatest enthusiasm, for it has always seemed to me that helping a lady to take her clothes off is one of the most delightful preliminaries to making love. It was not the first time that I had played the role of lady's maid: I undid bows, unfastened hooks from eyes and unlaced stays with great dexterity and in next to no time I had disrobed Euphemia.

When the lovely creature was all but naked, protected only

213

by the most diaphanous of shifts, we embraced again and I pressed hot kisses to her eyes and cheeks, and lips. My hands resumed their exploration of her soft warm curves and when one of them ventured up under the hem of the shift she did not try to stop me.

Oh, the gentle heat that radiated from that region! My fingers entered into contact with the incredibly soft flesh of thighs and a curving belly at the base of which they discovered a fleece softer to the touch than lamb's wool.

'Oh, yes, darling! Yes!' Euphemia gasped as I explored the deep wet crevice of her most intimate femininity. She clasped me convulsively to her and pressed her lips to mine as if striving to become one with me. At that moment a positive uterine madness seemed to take possession of the girl, sweeping aside any last vestiges of female modesty.

'Oh, take me, *chéri*! Take me!' she pleaded. 'I want to feel you inside me!' Then her knees gave way and she seemed to fall into a kind of voluptuous swoon, leaning with all her weight against me, whereupon I carried the wanton creature across to my bed and laid her down upon it. I hastily tore my velvet jacket off and flung it aside, then undid the flap of my breeches permitting my stiff yard to stick forth his bald rubicund head.

Being far too consumed with lust to waste more time in undressing further, I flung myself upon the bed, positioned myself between the fair Euphemia's thighs, which she had opened wide to welcome me, and immediately felt myself engulfed in sweet, warm, liquid bliss.

But what words exist which could adequately describe my sensations at that moment? The Goddess of Love had never before condescended to grant me such ecstasy, although I had always been one of her most devoted followers. I am not exaggerating when I say that I myself was near to swooning with delight.

And oh what a partner Euphemia was in the lascivious dance of lust. She responded to my rampant thrusting with a total abandonment which must be uncommon even among the most sensual of women. Like some new Messalina, she

214

made love to me with all her being: her delightfully agile bottom, her lips, her probing tongue and, above all, with her hands: they positively took possession of me. They were everywhere — and I do mean everywhere! — stroking, caressing, exploring, poking, weighing; and all the while that refined voice was whispering such unladylike words in my ear, goading me on until at last I could contain myself no longer but, sweating profusely, grunting like some animal, I spilled my manly seed into her womb: I gave her the very essence of my being.

Then 'Oh, damnation!' she exclaims, pushing me away and jumping out of bed as if her pretty bottom had been burned. 'I meant to ask you to withdraw, but got quite carried away! It would never do for me to get pregnant now. Can you give me some water? I ought to wash myself immediately.'

With some effort I hauled myself to my feet, went over to the wash-stand, poured some water from the jug into the bowl, then set it down at the lady's feet. Whereupon she hitched her shift up round her slender waist, squatted down and washed away my generous tribute to her charms. To watch her doing that gave me inexpressible pleasure, for I think that a woman performing such intimate ablutions is one of the most charming sights in the world.

When she'd finished and dried herself with the towel I handed to her, I persuaded her to lie down with me on the bed again for, although my desires were appeased, I like to cuddle a pretty woman after making love. In fact I'm not sure but that such moments of post-coital, tranquil tenderness are not the best part of intercourse between the sexes.

'I'll pay you extra money for your time, of course, my dear,' I said as we got back on the bed.

Euphemia gave me a disdainful smile and shook her pretty head dismissively. 'I want no money,' she said. 'In spite of appearances I am not a whore, chevalier.'

'You know me then, *mademoiselle*?' I exclaimed, raising myself up on one elbow.

My companion looked up at me, amused by the expression of astonishment upon my face. She raised her hand and tenderly caressed my cheek with her long sensitive fingers.

'Yes, I know you, Charles,' she replied. 'In fact, it is because I know you and because my father has wickedly abused your trust that I am here with you tonight.'

Then the lovely creature revealed that she was none other than Milord Southall's daughter, his only child; that she knew the 'noble' lord had won all my money by the wholly ignoble practice of cheating at cards and that she had chosen this way to compensate me.

But one thing puzzled me: 'How is it that I have never met you at your father's house?' I asked. 'I've been there two or three times before this evening.'

'I've been in England for the past few weeks, and I only arrived back yesterday,' she said. 'Besides, I don't much care for my father's parties, nor for the so-called gentlemen who attend them . . . present company excepted, of course,' Euphemia added, giving me a reassuring smile and stroking my cheek again.

'But why should your father cheat his guests?' I asked. 'I thought that he was one of the richest men in England.'

'So he was, at one time,' Euphemia replied, a bitter note creeping into her voice, 'but he squandered his whole fortune on his pleasures, and what I can't forgive him for is the fact that he squandered all my mother's money too, and broke her poor dear heart with his ill-usage of her.' The lovely girl's eyes grew moist and a tear coursed down her cheek. She brushed it away with the back of her hand and said, 'That's enough about my father! What I should like to know now is whether you consider that I have acquitted my family's debt of dishonour towards you, my dear chevalier? Would you say that my caresses are worth twenty thousand francs?'

I gallantly replied that in my opinion the possession of her person would be cheap at twenty times twenty thousand francs and that a lifetime would not be long enough to pay sufficient homage to such charms as she possessed, and I expressed my astonishment that one so young should be so skilled in the erotic arts.

'Oh, as to that,' Euphemia laughed, 'my father has an excellent library and from my tenderest years I have always had the freest access to it, including certain works which I have since learnt are considered to be extremely dangerous for young girls to read. By the time I was sixteen I was familiar with most of the great works which deal with erotic matters: I had read Ovid's *Art of Love*, Brantôme's *Lives of Gallant Ladies*, Boccaccio's *Decameron*, as well as more recent publications, such as *Memoirs of a Woman of Pleasure* and *The Sopha*.*

My fair companion fell silent for a moment. She looked so lovely lying there all but naked beside me that I could not resist the temptation to put forth my hand and caress one of her snowy swelling breasts. I felt the rosy point react to my touch immediately.

Euphemia closed her eyes and smiled. 'You have a very gentle touch, chevalier,' she sighed 'just like Thomas.'

'Who is Thomas?' I said, my curiosity awakened.

She opened her eyes. 'He is one of my father's footmen, and he was my first lover,' she replied, looking at me with an expression almost of defiance.

'A footman?' I laughed.

'Yes,' she said, looking somewhat annoyed. 'And what of it? Haven't you ever tumbled any of your mother's maids?'

'Of course I have,' I said, and added somewhat sententiously, 'Nature's imperious desires abolish all class distinctions.'

'Well then, why should I not make love with a footman if I so desire, sir?'

'Of course, you're right, dear girl,' I said in a conciliatory tone, for the last thing I wanted at that moment was to quarrel with Euphemia, although privately I thought it

*Published in 1741, this was one of the most widely-read erotic novels in the eighteenth century. The author was Crébillon the younger. An English translation exists but it has been out of print for many years.

wrong of her to demean herself in such a way. 'It is neither my right nor my desire to sit in judgement on you, believe me, dear lady,' and I kissed her tenderly upon the lips. She responded to me with an enthusiasm which showed she bore me no grudge and I could easily have taken the seductive creature again then and there if my curiosity at that moment had not been stronger than my desire.

'This Thomas must be quite an exceptional fellow,' I remarked when we drew apart.

'Oh, indeed he is,' replied Euphemia, her lovely eyes bright with the remembrance of him. 'It was he who completed my education in the art of love, who gave me my first practical — as distinct from theoretical — experience of sexual intercourse. He taught me a great deal and gave me much pleasure while doing so.'

'How did you come to make love with him then,' I asked, 'if that is not too indiscreet a question?' Meanwhile my impudent hand had somehow found its way up under Euphemia's shift and was caressing the sweet softness of her inner thigh, not far from the hairy centre of all joy.

'It happened last year,' she said, 'when I was residing at my father's house in Lincolnshire. I had gone to the kitchen to see our cook about some matter concerning dinner that evening. As I approached the door leading to that region, I could hear some strange noises coming from beyond it: cries and grunts and moans. The door was not completely closed but stood somewhat ajar, so I applied my eye to the narrow space and saw a sight for which, in spite of all my readings, I was completely unprepared, and which both shocked and fascinated me.

'Thomas was there with Sally, our cook, and he was doing something to her which was very rude indeed — something which reminded me of the way a stallion on heat behaves with a mare.

'I should tell you that Thomas is a very tall man of sturdy build. In spite of his English name, there is something in his dark handsome features which makes me feel that he must have some Spanish or perhaps Italian blood in him.

'As for Sally, she's a fine figure of a woman, as we say in England, a buxom country-bred wench with an impudently pretty face, bold dark eyes and a saucy tongue.

'At that moment she was in what our modern novelists would call a compromising position: that is to say bending over and supporting herself with her hands on the back of a kitchen chair, petticoats up to her waist, exposing a bare white bottom of truly generous proportions while Thomas, clad only in shirt tails, serviced the shameless hussy from behind with vigorous thrusts: I could see his buttocks clenching and unclenching with his efforts. His hands grasped her ample hips and I could hear him panting.

'But suddenly, for no apparent reason, he stopped and then withdrew from Sally and so, for the first time in my young life, I was able to see what a rampant male member looked like. Oh I'd seen plenty of illustrations in Papa's books, of course, but at that moment I realised that they had given me only a feeble idea of the real thing. What they had failed to convey to me was the sheer *beauty* of the virile organ, and Thomas's was particularly fine, not over-large but pleasing to the female eye with its upward-curving blue-veined stalk culminating in a swollen tip which made me think of a nice juicy plum by its shape and colour. I gazed at it in fascination and a longing such as I had never known before took possession of me.'

As she was speaking, I took my companion's hand and placed it upon my own member and she instinctively began to caress it with her slender elegant fingers.

'For a moment,' she continued, 'Thomas just stood there gazing down at Sally's bare posterior, then she turned her head and asked him why he'd stopped. "I want to see your pretty flower, sweetheart," he replied. "Pray, be a love and show it to me." Whereupon the shameless baggage put her hands back behind her and used her fingers to open up the petals of her fleshy rose. I could clearly see the pink glistening interior set in a mossy nest of brown pubic hair.

'I was shocked that any woman could be prevailed upon to display her most intimate secrets to a man so brazenly but, nevertheless, to see her behaving with such indecency increased my excitement to fever pitch and filled me with a wanton desire to imitate her . . . oh, that's lovely, Charles!'

Euphemia gasped out those last words because my fingers had found their way into her moist flower and were caressing the rigid little stamen, which is the female equivalent of a penis.

'Ooh, that's *so* nice darling!' she moaned in a languishing voice as my caresses became faster and more insistent.

I love to stimulate a woman with my fingers, to feel her female wetness and see her convulsed with tumultuous uncontrollable passion. Neither was it long before I got Euphemia to that state: her belly contracted, she writhed and wriggled her pretty behind, she uttered little cries and gasps, and the dew of love rained down upon my flying fingers . . . then a little later, when she had had a chance to recover, I begged my fair companion to go on with her story. 'Very well, chevalier,' she smiled tiredly, 'but you must promise to be good or I shall never get to the end of it.'

I promised to keep my fingers to myself and Euphemia continued: 'Thomas gazed at Sally's blatantly displayed charms as though he could not feast his eyes enough upon them, then he stretched forth his hands and lasciviously fondled her buttocks and fingered her love-grotto, and all the while his virility jutted out with unfaltering vigour from the base of his hairy belly. But then Sally pleaded impatiently, "Oh, don't torment me so, Tom! Pray, put it in, there's a good dear lad!"'

'Whereupon the footman guided the engorged rubicund tip of his instrument into the place Nature intended for it, while his partner continued to hold herself obscenely open to facilitate his entry. Then, gripping Sally's ample hips with both hands, he began to service her with robust stallion thrusts which were so vigorous that they made the cheeks of her derrière shake and quiver. She'd placed her hands on the back of the chair again in order to support herself.

"Oh, Tom, my dearest love,' cried Sally, "how I do love to feel your great big thing inside me! Oh, how good you make a woman feel!" The languishing tone in which she uttered these words left no doubt of her sincerity in my mind and, oh, how I should have loved to change places with the fortunate wench at that moment. Oh, how I longed to fall a sacrificial victim to that dear weapon!' And, as she said those words, Euphemia's hand went of its own accord to my virile member and once more took possession of it, to my inexpressible delight.

'The couple were now nearing the end of their furious gallop through the countryside of lust,' my companion continued, her artful fingers performing marvels at my groin. 'Panting, gasping and muttering incoherently, Thomas rode his docile mount without mercy: I could see the hairy purse containing his generative acorns swinging back and forth. Then suddenly Sally cried out, "Oh, ooh, ah!" she wailed, 'Oh, I'm coming, my beloved!" "And I'm not far behind, dear lass,' her rider panted. Then, as before, he abruptly withdrew but this time he took his weapon in his hand and rubbed it vigorously until many drops of milky fluid spurted out and splashed down on to his partner's back and bottom.'

Euphemia withdrew her hand, to my great regret, and regarded me with solemn eyes. 'In doing that,' she said, 'Tom proved himself to be a perfect gentleman, in spite of his humble condition: much more so than many so-called 'gentleman' who have no scruples about making a poor girl pregnant, then leaving her in the lurch.' Her dark eyes flashed with indignation. 'Oh, what a shameful thing it is when a woman finds her love repaid by such betrayal and base ingratitude!' she exclaimed.

'I quite agree,' I said. 'Such scoundrels hardly deserve the name of "gentleman". But tell me,' I went on, anxious to divert her from this moralising digression, which I found displeasing, 'in what circumstances did Thomas become your lover?'

'Oh,' she yawned then stretched like a sleepy cat, 'it would

221

take too long to tell you now, chevalier. I'm tired out, and so must you be. It's very late and we should try to get some sleep, otherwise we'll be no use for anything tomorrow.'

'Well, I do not know how I can sleep,' I replied. 'Just look at the state your story has put me in!' and I showed my pretty bedmate my fine upstanding member, which quivered expectantly in my hand.

Euphemia raised herself up on one elbow, gazed thoughtfully at what I was showing her then said, 'Well, my dear Thomas taught me many aspects of the erotic arts and among them were methods of giving satisfaction to a man when I didn't really feel in a humour to lend myself to the full possession of my person . . .'

'What methods were those then?' I demanded eagerly, my curiosity equalling my desire.

'Methods such as this one,' the lovely girl replied, sitting up in the bed; then, bending forward, she grasped my stem with her fingers near the base and took its engorged tip into her mouth and, with artful movements of her head and tongue, began to suck it. Oh, what words are there which could describe the celestial bliss I experienced as that charming head moved up and down? O Euphemia, supreme mistress of the voluptuous arts, if you had lived in a less prudish age you would have been crowned with laurels in recognition of your skills.

She only stopped once for a brief moment in order to remove a hair from her mouth. As she did so, the wanton lass looked at me with a smile and said, 'You men are all such hairy beasts!' Then she resumed her task.

It took her but a few minutes to give me complete satisfaction, for who could have long held out against the flicking tongue, those lips, that deep wet mouth? And when finally the shameless hussy put a finger into my most intimate recess, I could resist no longer but discharged copiously, profaning that lovely mouth with my jetting lust, and she went on sucking until she'd milked me dry.

When at last I'd finished and sank back into the pillows with a contented sigh, Euphemia rose up from the bed and went across to the wash-basin where she spat out what I'd given her then rinsed her mouth out with a glass of water, and for that I couldn't blame her because one cannot expect a lady of quality to swallow such stuff: if one wants that one should go to a professional lady of pleasure.

When she came back into bed I was already half asleep. She cuddled up close to me, whispered 'Night night, chevalier. Sleep tight!' Then we drifted off into the Land of Nod clasped in each other's arms.